Upper Peculiar

UPPER PECULIAR

Tales from Above the Bridge

JOSEPH HEYWOOD

LYONS PRESS

Guilford, Connecticut

An imprint of The Rowman & Littlefield Publishing Group, Inc.
4501 Forbes Blvd., Ste. 200
Lanham, MD 20706
www.rowman.com

Distributed by NATIONAL BOOK NETWORK

British Library Cataloguing in Publication Information available

Library of Congress Cataloging-in-Publication Data:

Names: Heywood, Joseph.
Title: Upper peculiar : tales from above the bridge / Joseph Heywood.
Description: Guilford, Connecticut : Lyons Press, 2019.
Identifiers: LCCN 2019022089 | ISBN 9781493039562 (hardcover)
ISBN 9781493039579 (ebook)
Subjects: LCSH: Upper Peninsula (Mich.)—Fiction. | GSAFD: Mystery fiction.
Classification: LCC PS3558.E92 U66 2019 | DDC 813/.54—dc23
LC record available at https://lccn.loc.gov/2019022089

∞™ The paper used in this publication meets the minimum requirements of American National Standard for Information Sciences—Permanence of Paper for Printed Library Materials, ANSI/NISO Z39.48-1992.

For Dave and Diana Stimac: A shot and a beer—and a book!

Contents

Think of What's His Face, Shakespeare

THE STRANGER HAD ONE EYE THAT TILTED UP LIKE ITS GYROSCOPIC track had been installed off-kilter, and napalm-red eyebrows like something from cut-rate costume shop clearance. He sat like a fat kid in trouble, his back pushed straight against the chair back. *Who the hell is he?* Stewbart Montana wondered.

Red Brow asked, "You know how long I've been waiting to *meet* you?" The voice was sandpaper scraped over burnt toast.

"Is that rhetorical?"

The man smirked and made a faint whistling sound that, once heard, made it difficult to focus on subsequent words.

Montana said, "Listen, I've never seen you before, met you, or heard of you, whoever you are—so how could I even *begin* to know?"

"Good, good, exactly, exactly, how *could* you know?" Red Brow said with a raspy chuckle.

This was the day Montana turned fifty-five and got an early retirement buyout from his corporate mama. If not exactly a golden parachute, it was definitely something better than a base metal. The timing of his departure had been chosen by Stew to coincide with May Day, a nebulous symbol and statement that few of his soon-to-be former suit colleagues would appreciate. The currency here had been two things: money and power, one mirroring the other.

Stewbart Montana's plan was to move to his camp in the Upper Peninsula to fish for trout and hunt for the rest of his life, but on his way out of Human Resources with his retirement paperwork neatly packed into in a fat manila envelope, Glendella Stone, deputy administrative assistant to the first deputy administrative assistant (DAAFDAA) to the CEO stopped him. "Might George have a moment of your time?" No titles in this corporate culture, ranks treated as invisible cloaks, everything collegial and on a first-name basis in the chumdom.

Stew and George Barclay had traveled the world together, and the CEO invariably snuck smokes from his subordinate, even here at home in his HQ corner office in a building where all smoking was banned. Stew smiled. Maybe George needed a smoke before Elvis left the building forever.

Stew Montana had grown up in Baraga County in Michigan's western Upper Peninsula and could not wait to get back. All the work and exhausting travel he'd done for thirty years had been toward only one end: to get home to the woods, *his* woods. It had been a hard three decades of shit-bird tasks and assignments over which he had little or no choice, and often loathed. But the nightmare was finally over and he was feeling a mixture of relief and magnanimity. Stew told Glendella. "Sure, you bet. Why the heck not?"

The woman led him through the CEO's rugby pitch of an office into his so-called private inner sanctum office, where there was no sign of George Barclay, just the strange, roly-poly man with the bright red eyebrows in a wrinkled short-sleeve seersucker shirt and a wide black tie sprinkled with what looked to be spaghetti stains. The man had Coke-bottle-thick eyeglasses with military black frames, appeared to be about fifty pounds overweight and was perspiring like a coronary was in progress.

Stewbart looked at the strange man who keened at him, "Boy oh boy, oh BOY, and holy COW!" Brow said, enthusiastically reaching out with his hand. "I've been waiting a long damn time, Mister. *Looong* damn time."

Thirty years of talking to reporters from all around the world, most of them out to break or snip off the corporation's unfeeling (largely nonexistent) nuts, had taught Montana the tactical value of prolonged silence. Montana let the man's hand hover in the air, unshook.

Red Brow said, "Mather AFB, Sacramento, state of Caliphony, back in nineteen and sixty-five and nineteen and sixty-six. Oh yeah, by the way, I'm Connerly. Sorry about that. Got so excited I plumb forgot my dang manners. Exchange names first, that's accepted social convention in this dad-blamed world you've been in, son. I've got to keep telling myself to take this one step at a time. I am, as I said, Connerly and you are Stewbart Montana, formerly USAF Captain Stew Montana, instructor navigator, combat support veteran, holder of a dozen Air Medals and one Distinguished Flying Cross recommendation quietly quashed by political potlickers. Let's be clear. Fuck-job is what that was, SAC and TAC not seeing eye-to-eye on risking aircrews or aircraft, especially to help another command's assets. The DFC should have been yours, but wasn't." The man set a small dark blue box on the desk. "Go ahead . . . *look*."

Montana opened the box, found a Distinguished Flying Cross, and had no idea what to say.

"It's yours, Captain. Should have been yours way back, but now we've fixed that. We like to *fix* things. Too many people don't realize how important it is . . . for morale, and all that good stuff," the man said, and sighed to punctuate the sentence.

"Okay then, that concludes the preliminaries. Let's us get on back out to the West Coast. You were then a student attending undergraduate navigator training, and you and all your classmates were ordered to report to base theater one on a Saturday morning. You had no idea what it was about, not then, not since, and having reported as ordered, you were all seated in the theater and given a test that lasted eight grueling damn hours. Test done, you never heard about it again. You ever wonder what all that was about, Captain?"

He remembered, but had never really thought about it. The Air Force had its new brown bars doing all sorts of silly things that went unexplained. You already knew from your AFROTC days that when you put on your country's uniform, you tacitly agreed to endure a level of imposed ignorance and ambiguity. Montana remembered and said, "Would you rather fuck a leprous woman or a red sheep, French kiss a homosexual, or cut Hitler's throat with a fruit knife? *That* test?"

"Exactly, bingo, that's the one, son. Ever wonder what that was all about?"

"We were not in those days encouraged to wonder much about top-down stuff. We were at the bottom of all chain-of-command downdrafts.

4

Our orders were simple: do what you're told, and don't fuck up." The corporation had been only marginally looser in such matters.

Connerly cackled. "Those were in some elemental ways very much the good old days. And like old Vick Hugo the giant black frog once scribbled, they were simultaneously the best and worst dang days too."

Stew Montana flinched. Hugo wasn't black and had not written the cited lines, which belonged to the Englishman Charles Dickens. *Three Musketeers* author Alexander Dumas had been black.

"That test you took measured certain . . . uh, shall we say, attitudes and aptitudes, and you were among the first of many thousands of uniformed officers to have taken that same dad-blamed test. Since the fall of 1965, tens of thousands of men and women have taken it."

Connerly paused. "Here's the neat thing, really neat. Your score— yours alone—remains the pinnacle—the highest *ever* achieved."

Stew wondered where this was going.

"I sure as heck argued up the line for you, and all but got my butt canned, but because you had the highest score so early in the process, it was decided way above my pay grade to pass on inviting you into the program. As a result, we brought in people who had scored close to you but not as high. But see, I never stopped believing your exclusion early on was a major bureaucratic up-fuck and thus I never stopped monitoring and watching you. I came to think of you as a kind of pure control in a secret, undeclared double-blind clinical trial test thing. Result: I know more about you than you know about yourself, Captain."

"Program?"

Connerly sighed. "Now, here's the thing, and it's a real biggie. I've been green-lighted to invite you in, thirty-five dang years late, but that's runway behind us, Captain. So let's us look ahead together. The way this deal works is that *if* I provide the major program details to you, such exposition in and of itself commits you to joining. *Any* interest from you in hearing details is adjudged tacit acceptance, and mind you, this has been tested in court and upheld by several covert legal cases at the highest levels of our government. Put another way, Captain, this means there's no backing the heck out. You're in for a nickel, and like that, capisce?

Montana tried to reason his way through the moment. "You're telling me I need to refuse this program *before* I know what it is?"

Connerly nodded. "Yessir."

"Okay, I refuse. I don't want to know."

"Wait," Connerly whimpered. "Hold your damn horses, son."

"I thought you couldn't explain it."

"Well, I *can't*, but nothing in the regs or rules precludes me from talking about the bennies—all that good stuff that will accrue to you when you join up."

Stew Montana said, "With all due respect, I'm *not* interested. I've got my *own* plans." Stew was certain he heard the man with the red brows say "when," not "if," such language manipulation an unsubtle sign of genetically programmed sales reps and highly skilled product floggers.

Like the finely tuned and trained used-car salesman Connerly appeared to be, he blithely pressed on. "One, the lump sum you just took out of your thirty years with this outfit? No taxes on it, *ever*. And the salary and retainers you'll draw from the government? No taxes ever. No federal, no state, county, local, nothing, nada, zip and zilch, not one fucking centavo."

Connerly sailed on, barely pausing for breath. "All your work expenses will be covered one hundred percent when you are working, whenever you're working, with no preset limits. You will, of course, have total control over your means of travel, lodging, food, hookers, whatever and everything, cost to the government never being a consideration. There's also a retainer for the times when you are not working in the field, as when you're in various forms of training to keep you current in your field and skills."

Montana kept his head still and warned himself to remain quiet.

"Here's the thing, Captain. We know *everything* about you."

"We?"

"Technically it's me who knows all, but because I also represent our mutual employer, I guess that means they also know, me being them, or of them, syllogistically speaking. Are you with me so far?"

Connerly was more than a little difficult to follow. "Can I go now?"

"Okay, Captain, you're hardheaded and hard-nosed, yes indeed. And I already know this from your test results, which showed that you have absolutely no faith in pure faith, and that's fundamentally okay. So how about this: When you leave here this morning, you will be meeting one Jannavanna Holroyd, the lovely third wife of your local mayor and one very torrid little tamale, if I may be so bold. You meet her this same day every week in the park outside town and repair to the Parkside Motor Hotel where you copulate with great enthusiasm and energy for two, sometimes three hours. This has been going on for six years. I have photos. Care to see?"

Montana felt his throat go dry and he stood up. *What the fuck?* "I'm leaving."

Connerly said, "See, the bottom line with this deal is that we don't give a second shit if you hump Mother Teresa during one of her fund-raising swings through the U.S. of A. Your personal business and affairs are truly *yours*. Course your wife bailed on you years ago because she found out about one of Holroyd's predecessors, one Rinna Howles MacField, now chief corporate counsel for Balator Drugs in Manhattan. Talk about torrid! Yahoo, youch, and sheer sheesh! The truth is, I don't think Rinna's had a decent fuck since she broke things off with you." Connerly lowered his head and dropped his voice. "And I'm not making that up. We have recordings of her declaring that very thing to her lady friends."

Stewbart looked at his watch. Jannavanna would go apeshit if he was late. "I no longer work here, Connerly. I'm retired, and now I really have to go."

Red Brow stood up. "Hold your dang horses, Stew. You don't have to hurry, you really don't. I called Jannavanna for you and told her you'd be running a tad late."

"You *what*?"

"I called the girl, and she didn't ask any questions, not a one. Discretion is one very fine damn trait in side-candy, not to mention über-rare."

Stew moved toward the door, but Connerly moved with astonishing alacrity and blocked his way.

"Okay, so there's the thing with Jannavanna, and good for you, well done, lucky fella, hubba-hubba, and all that. But then there's the little matter of the Moscow cop you killed in nineteen and eighty-five. I think it was eighty-five," Connerly said, thumbing through a folder. "Yep, there it is, nineteen and eighty-five. Got it written right there." He snapped the page with his forefinger.

"He died?" Montana asked, shaking.

"I only *look* the fool," Connerly said. "And look at you right this minute. A normal fella would be shaking in his boots, prolly thinkin' about horse-pissin his Levi's, but not *you*. You stand there cool as a polar bear surfing an ice floe. You are one very cool cucumber, Captain Montana. You twisted the knife up under that Soviet asshole's rib cage and gave it the old side-to-side kill-shizzle. Just the way you were taught to do in military training."

"*He* pulled the knife on me." Stew Montana said. He had hoped that whole sorry mess was buried and lost in Russia's murky post-commie morass.

"Hell, we know *that*, Cap'n. That sumbitch Russky thug was going to take your wallet and maybe cap your ass, but you were calm, took control, and changed the outcome in your favor, just as your test results predicted. You dealt with the threat, hurried back to your hotel, packed, and next morning scooted straight to the airport and got the hell out of Dodge. Never said a word to anyone, also as predicted."

"I was sick, I don't remember," Stew tried to argue.

The man with red brows said, "That's bullroar. Yeah, I saw that you seem sickened by what happened and that bothered the dickens out of me for quite some time, you're being as shaky as some Nancy's first trip to the neighborhood queer club. You got the major pukes after you put the guy on the ground and he started bleeding out. I wondered then if maybe there was a flaw in the test, which overwhelmingly showed you to be the perfect and complete sociopath. I wondered if there was something we had missed, or if something had changed that we didn't know about. The assumption remains that sociopaths never change. They can't. Once imprinted, or more to the point, failing to be imprinted, if you prefer, a true sociopath remains forever so. Your kind can modify behaviors, in fact all y'all're terrific at that, real maestros of most things, but you can't feel or act on values you don't or can't feel. You gettin' what I'm saying, Cap'n?"

Stew Montana found himself frozen in place. This could *not* be happening. Not now, not to *him*. He was *retired*, dammit.

Connerly did not let up. "Despite my reservations and concerns, your hasty planning and execution of emergency egress were dadgum impressive. By the way, that dead Russky cop's name was Gregorevich, a very naughty boy with a long record of shakedowns, assaults, and more than a few casual homicides. He was dead when he hit the sidewalk, was the comrade. And I assure you nobody mourned his demise."

Stew said, "I do not have to stand here and listen to this . . . bull."

"Never said you did, Captain Montana, but as stated earlier, I know you and right now I know you want to know everything we have on you. The answer is we know everything there is to know, probably more than you can even admit to. We really do, son. Your government knows more about you and your life than you know."

Montana stared dead ahead. This had to be a dream! All those years ago. Sure, there was that test at the Mather AFB theater near Sacramento, and it *had* lasted eight interminable hours and nobody knew what the hell it was for. "I'm not interested," the former captain told the man with red brows.

Connerly frowned. "Then there was that *muchacho* you choked to death in San Juan. You dumped his body over the wall into *La Perla*. That time was no accident. He caught you with *your* pecker in *wifey's lovely* mouth, and who wouldn't flip out over shit like *that?*"

Stew put up his hands, trying to stop his words, but couldn't. "He jumped me."

"Well, of course that greaser sumbitch jumped you. It was a *scam*. His wife volunteered to play Paganini on your skin flute and the husband just happens to walk in and is outraged. It's a script and I suspect if the tables were turned, you'd've reacted the same way he tried to. Are you seeing the threads here, Captain? I can go on for hours."

"There are *no* threads."

"Son, your IQ's an angel's hair short of two hundred. *Sure* you get it. You know there're threads, oodles of them. So what do you think we're here to talk about, Captain?"

"I'm not here to talk about *anything*."

"See, I admire your ability to just shut things down: That's what makes you what you are. Repression has real practical implications for good mental health."

Montana said. "I'm leaving. I don't want anything to do with killing."

Connerly slapped the desk almost gleefully. "Damn Sam, son, why'd you have to go say *that* dag-nab word? Now that you've said it, I have to lay out the full offer, which, as I explained earlier, means you have just accepted our offer. By law, when you get to the point where you hear the full offer, you've already accepted it. There's no turning back from here, Captain. Point of no return, Bingo fuel and all that crap. Your course is now set and locked in."

"This is abject bullshit," Stew Montana said.

"It's our *government*, son. What the heck do you expect? Welcome aboard! I know it's thirty-five years late, but hell, I am one pleased hombre," Connerly added. "There's a whole heap of data I need to download-dump to you," the man said and looked at his watch. "But you might as well run along and get to your pump-and-hump with Ms. Jannavanna. You will not be around this town much longer, so enjoy."

Connerly stared earnestly at the new recruit. "Where in her past you think that gal learned to scream 'Shoot me the Napalm!' Just before she gets off? That girl is *something*."

Stew had often wondered the same thing, but now all he could do was shrug.

Connerly held out a piece of notebook paper, a business card, and an envelope. There was a telephone number, handwritten. "Emergencies only, blood on the decks and all that. I've got all your numbers." Connerly chuckled. "Sorry about the pun. You know much about the great British Bard?"

"I thought you already knew everything about me. If so, you know what I know and what I don't know."

Connerly nodded. "Damn straight. Think of what's his face . . . Shakespeare? Here you had this hayseed playwright, greatest writer of his time, greatest of *any* time, greatest in all freaking history, yet nobody knows diddly-squat about the man. You think that's a tad odd? I mean *how* can it be that he's the greatest writer in human history but a blivet to historians?"

"I don't know," Stewbart Montana said. *Or care.*

Connerly continued. "Because the writer's Queen Liziebit the First and HRM's government wanted it that way is why. The powers-that-were wanted his background left sub-rosa, under the radar, put it how you will. Then and now, when any great government wants something squelched, squelched it must be and shall be. So what I'm telling you, Captain Montana, is don't have you no freaking wig-out stroke over this. Your identity and security are in the best hands and are the highest possible national security priority."

This was supposed to reassure him? Stew wanted to vomit. He had no idea what to do about any of this.

The government man added, "I'll be in touch, we'll get together, do lunch, get you rolling with your new career." The man scribbled on another piece of notepaper and handed it to Montana.

Connerly had written "150K" with an account number from the Great Wolverine Bank of Detroit (a Delaware company). "Them's just peanuts," Connerly said. "Consider it walking-around money from your deep-pocketed, filthy rich Uncle Sam—just to get you into the right frame of mind. So enjoy."

Stewbart was scared, and excited. That day Jannavanna got two injections of napalm and went home humming happily. She said not a word about Connerly's call to her or the delay. It was very strange. Montana went home and had a night of what his kids used to call the "fast-moving" poop. So much for tests. Sociopath?

He was retired. Life was changing. He had worked hard and diligently to make this happen, but now more change was being introduced and the change felt heavier than anything that had come before. He was scared shitless, virtually petrified over an unknown he didn't want and had inadvertently stumbled into.

Why had he not told that fool Connerly what had really happened that day? He had taken the whole thing as a joke and picked his answers arbitrarily and randomly. And this led to the highest score ever? Holy crap! Of course the test was fucked. He was proof of it. Typical government boondoggle. He wasn't who Connerly thought he was. All from a test he answered randomly?

This was going to ruin his trout fishing.

Hearts of Wolves

ALL THROUGH LATE SUMMER AND INTO EARLY FALL, WILLIBALD "Muley" Fish had a peculiar feeling when he was in his woodshop or close to it. The feeling was mildly irritating, and it wasn't there all the time, but now that the snow was beginning to spit, as winter was looking to assert itself, the uneasy feeling was becoming more regular. Even so, he only noted it and didn't investigate what it meant or might be. There was nothing specific he could point to. Here and there, now and then, some tool or shop item was not where he remembered leaving it. *Can't Remember Shit Disease*, his older friends called it.

His wife Micarla laughed about it. "It's just the old timer's, Muley. We all got her, hey." Having spent a lifetime in the woods, Fish knew how the mind could play tricks, so why give in? Eventually it would go away.

Muley worked about as hard as one man could work, seven days a week. He had two physically exhausting part-time jobs and his own custom woodshop, where he made decorative furniture of exotic native woods, in which he inset unpolished local stones and copper-silver half-breeds.

Micarla worked just as hard. She was a high school teacher and a volunteer at the local district library, as well as taking care of the household chores, and sometimes helping Muley in the woodworking shop. Thank god, both agreed, they had no kids to weigh them down. Dogs, sure. How could you have a home without dogs? They'd wanted kids, but when none came, they stopped thinking about it and recalibrated their expectations.

Muley suspected that Micarla still harbored a dream of kids, but she never mentioned it. Neither did he, although he did think about it from time to time.

One thing Muley was especially good at was organization, always exerting spring-tight order in and on his little worlds—the only good thing he'd ever gotten from his old man, who had been a legendary drunk and logger. The old man was no good at inside jobs, or with most people, but he'd run logging jobs like he was born to the work. Muley admired his father's organizational skills and nothing else. The old man had beaten him, his brothers, and their mother. Asshole.

In Muley's world there was a place for every tool, and his own rule was to put a thing back when he was done, no exceptions. Recently he had been looking all over for his Swedish-made Gränsfors forest axe, which he used to knock bark off logs, and found it, but not where he was certain he'd left it. "Who the hell moved you, Swede?" he asked out loud and laughed at himself. He thought of all of his tools and machines as persons and gave each its own name.

Maybe Micarla was right. Last night she'd said, "Youse're getting paranoid." He was a good sport and grinned, but deep down something was telling him something *was* screwy. It was like hearing a new and unexpected sound in his truck. Once you knew what the source of a new sound was, you were fine. Until then it could drive you batty trying to pinpoint the damn source. But that was a sound, which was real, and even measurable at some fraction of decibels. This other thing, whatever it was, left an uncomfortable feeling, something swimming in his gut and on the edge of his mind.

Last month he was trying to fashion a joint of quilted maple, but he couldn't make the bloody thing fit. After several tries, he cursed, turned off the shop lights, and stalked home in disgust. Next night he went back to the shop and found the joint where he'd left it, only now it fit perfectly. What the hell? CRS?

Another night the paranoia got so real that he sprinkled fresh sawdust on all of his tools and machines, all over the floors, and the next day made a fast lap around the building looking for tracks in a new dusting of snow.

Next afternoon he saw that the tools had gone untouched, but the floor had been swept clean. Dammit, I *know* I put the dust down on everything, including the floor. I *know* I did and I know I didn't sweep the floor, but look at it now, clean as a rock in rain. Muley was creeped out, left the woodshop for home, and spent the night pouting in front of the TV by the woodstove.

Later that week he looked into his sawdust bin, which he expected to be almost full, and it was ... yet it wasn't arranged quite how it should be. Most dust in the shop was inhaled by his vacuum system and sent to the sawdust bin outdoors, the dust tending to land in a certain and predictable pattern that never varied. This time it didn't look quite right. He couldn't say precisely how, just that it wasn't right. Almost, but not quite. He decided to work this out in his own way and said nothing to Micarla.

One night Lucky "Goofer" Novis lumbered into the woodshop to drink Diet Pepsi and regale him with tales of his Navy days in Vietnam, the same stories Goofer always hauled out. This time, Goofer had surprised him with a new story.

"We had this baby captain, a brown bar El-Tee Jay-Gee, fresh out of Annapolis and fast-boat school. He tried to take charge like John-Fucking-Wayne and it got so annoying that our pharmacist's mate, Dick Doc Doe, slipped a drug into the skipper's tomato juice and within hours the skipper was pissing blood-orange streams, and this got him to thinking that maybe this it was internal bleeding, and maybe he was dying from a kidney crash, as had his old man and his grandpap before him. The crew took the El-Tee over to the base dispensary, and when he come back a week later, it was like he'd had a personality transplant. Turned out to be a real fine man and a great skipper," Goofer said, "After we set his course straight for him."

Muley thought, blood-orange urine? "The drug didn't hurt him?"

"Negative, just turned his piss red and deadened his dick a tad."

"You bullshitting me again, Novis?"

They'd known each other since high school. It had been Goofer, in fact, who had called him long distance from his R&R in Australia and yelled through the phone, "The pro pussy's world class over here, but this war sucks." Then, in a conspiratorial voice, Goofer told him, "If you can get out of this shit, Fish, do it. Go queer if youse got to."

Muley never seriously considered changing his sexual orientation. No need to. He loved to party, was heavy into drinking beer and booze, homemade wines, popping pills, taking acid trips, and smoking dope. Anything new that came along, Muley would be one of the first to step up and try it.

The coppers pinched him three times in one year for drunk and impaired driving, and the court took away his license. Though he never heard for sure, he figured Uncle Sam had enough problem children in uniform, because he was never drafted and eventually his drinking and drug habit got so bad he had to quit, which he did cold turkey. He hadn't had a drink in all the decades since.

The lottery came along later and his number was never under 350, and after that, the war was over and eventually Congress dumped the whole draft.

"What's that red piss drug called?" Muley asked his old chum.

"Never knew no official name and probably they don't even make it no more. Dick Doc called it the P-Bomb."

"For real?" Goofer was renowned for stretching truth.

"Course."

"Liquid or pill?"

"Was pills Doc mashed into a powder he dumped into the skipper's morning 'matey juice.'"

"How long did it take to work? You said hours. Was it really hours?"

Goofer stared at him. "What's turning your crank? That shit was a long time ago in a place far, far away, Muley. I hated that whole gig. I mebbe think it took a day or two, but my mind, she ain't all that clear on some of the fine points from them times no more."

Muley said. "Your mind's always been cloudy, man."

Goofer let loose with the laugh that had earned him the name Goofer.

Henrietta "Henny" Hannarkola had been Muley's high school senior class president, their resident brain. She had gone off to college, become a pharmacist, and moved back to the area. She and husband Lucien owned eight pharmacies in the western Upper Peninsula. She had not changed her name to her husband's Brogonoli. Their son Lars now ran the chain's business while Henrietta still managed the pharmacy in L'Anse, where she filled prescriptions and still hung with lifelong friends. Retired Lucien spent his time fishing Keweenaw and Huron Bays.

Muley saw the woman light up when he walked in. He'd never hit on her when they'd been in high school, and he'd always had a vague feeling that this had somehow disappointed her. "Henny," he said, "gorgeous as ever."

"Belay the sugar-talk, Fish. Folks might get the wrong idea."

Muley saw two pharmacy techs grinning and nodding. Henny held her hand out to him and wiggled her fingers, always right to business. "Got a scrip needs filling?"

"A what?"

"A scrip, a prescription."

"No I ain't got one of them, just a question."

"Ask."

"There's a drug the Vietnam guys usta call P-bomb or something like that?"

"Phenazopyridine," she said. "You got man-plumbing problems?"

Man-plumbing? "Me? No, geez, I'm just askin'. The Vietnam guys say it can turn a fella's pee red as blood."

"They're right," she said. "You been hanging at Wingey Wednesdays out to the Cousington VFW again? I swear, the things you vets talk about."

"I'm thinking about a prank is all. How long's this peanut stuff been around?"

"Phen-azo-pyr-i-dine, not peanut stuff. It's really old, been around for many decades."

"Can it hurt people?"

"Every drug can hurt someone, Fish. Given your background in recreational chemical sports, you ought to know that, hey."

"Got to have a scrip for P-stuff?"

"Do indeed."

"It cause permanent problems?"

"Like most drugs, the effect tends to be dose-dependent, meaning the more you ingest, the greater the effect."

"How long's the red last?"

"Not long. When do you plan to use this?" Henny asked.

"Not sure. Could be this week, but I dunno for sure."

"You know you're going to use it soon, but not on whom?"

Muley nodded.

"Man or woman?"

"Not sure yet. All I know is it ain't Micarla."

The pharmacist chuckled. "*Knew* that. She'd skin you." The woman's eyes turned squinty. "You sure you don't have a little dose of the pipe-burn?"

He felt himself blush. "I ain't never cheated on Micarla."

"Most commendable," Henny said as she walked away. She came back ten minutes later with a small orange plastic pill container.

"I need to see a doc for the scrip, yah?"

"No, I just called Dr. Linsemann for you." She explained how to use the drug and added, "But no refills, okay? This is it, all you get."

"What do I owe?" he asked, reaching for his wallet.

"Get out of here," she said with a smile. "Let me know how the prank turns out," she added, and winked.

———

Micarla said at dinner, "Youse're up to something, you. I can tell."

"Am not," he said.

"That cinches it. Day before yesterday you asked me to get chocolate milk for the woodshop fridge. You *hate* chocolate milk."

"You get it?"

"Two quarts, cartons."

"Good, thanks."

"You're welcome, Mr. Sneaky."

"Don't be so nosey, maybe it'll be a surprise."

His wife laughed. "Jesus, Muley, we've been married thirty years and I guess I know when youse got something cooking."

———

Their dog, Brillo, was a mixmaster-retriever mix and hell on wounded birds and anything else that moved—except wolves. Brillo was not stupid, and she was the best dog he'd ever had. He'd once read how a salmon could smell two parts per billion in water molecules from its birth river and find its way home with no more clue than that. With two wolf packs, one on either side of the village, and their house on the western tree line, Brillo never got to run loose and came a time when she was getting old that she hacked and coughed from dust whenever she hung with him in the workshop. When she was young, she'd be with him every night and pinch six or seven mice and carry them around like small prizes, dangling them out of her mouth like Christmas ornaments.

At the moment the workshop was as dust-free as it ever was and he took Brillo with him. She was beside herself as soon as they got inside. This could signal only one thing: He gave her a treat and whispered, "Find."

The dog looked at him like he was demented, but dutifully hove into the command, her nose going like a weed-whacker. The only thing that scored any interest: his fridge. As Brillo had no further interest inside the shop, Muley leashed her, and they toured the exterior. On the southwest side she showed interest in the dumpster, which was emptied once a week and served as the neighborhood trash and garbage bin. Recycling in Baraga County was thought to be a liberal notion and therefore dangerous. It had not dusted snow in a couple of days, and there were no tracks to indicate anything in the crusty old snow. Why the hell was Brillo interested in the fridge and the dumpster?

The next night Muley sat on a stool in the shop, with Judas Priest's "Dreamer Deceiver" assaulting his eardrums through the Devilet Gold-Phantom speaker system, which could deafen the Roman Coliseum with Christians and lions on the fight card. He nursed a Diet Pepsi, and let a mind-map take shape, again noting those points the dog had signaled or showed interest in. Outside dumpster and inside fridge? A link? Dumpster alone could be animal alone. But both the outside dumpster *and* inside fridge had to mean an intrusion, possibly an animal, but more likely a human.

He didn't really care about the dumpster, but someone coming into his workshop was a different deal and, if true, could not be allowed to stand. There was too much expensive and complex equipment in this place, several hundreds of thousands of dollars' worth, and inadequate insurance, a potentially large liability risk. Micarla was forever flogging him about calling their insurance guy, but her complaining never rose high enough to warrant action. Remember the microwave, his wife reminded him, the story of a new oven which carried a warning for consumers to not dry their pets or small children in it. Jesus what a world. The shit greedy lawyers did to people. Were there people *that* bloody stupid?

Winter was getting more and more serious, nights cooling, a little snow falling now and then as temps continued to drop and frost kept reaching deeper underground. Winter soon for sure, no humidity, and no hunting right now, and lousy fishing unless you put your boat into Keweenaw Bay and knocked your way through skiff ice all the way to open water.

Right now he had fists-full of custom orders for Christmas gifts, but the mystery juice in his gut was flowing again, and this state of not knowing something he loathed above all others. It made it difficult to concentrate on his work, and finally he gave into trying to solve the mystery.

By fall the western wolf pack had moved away from the beaver ponds on lower Plumbago Creek, where they spent the summer teaching their pups to hunt and kill beaver. The wolves rarely let themselves get in sight of the village, but tonight when he stepped outside the shop around ten, there was a pale-colored wolf not ten feet away. It was looking not at him, but back at the tree line, toward the dumpster. Was the wolf smelling his dog? Had Brillo smelled the wolf? The former, he decided. Brillo was scared shitless of wolves and the slightest whiff sent her whimpering and scurrying into the house and toward her hidey-box in the floor of the bedroom. Brillo hadn't sniffed a wolf or she'd have run. So what's Mister Wolfie so interested in?

"Hey," Muley said in a soft, sharp tone, and the wolf vanished. Darn things were invisible when they wanted to be, which was most of the time. No wonder people believed in vampires, werewolves, Easter bunnies, tooth fairies, and all that stuff.

Back at the house he got a Sharpie, and a hairpin from Micarla's sewing kit, took the cartons of brown milk out of the fridge, and did some altering. He poured a tiny amount of liquid from each into the sink and set aside the jugs. He mashed the pills into powder, divided the powder into two piles, dumped one batch into each jug, recapped each jug, shook it vigorously to let it settle and put them back in the fridge while he sponged the counter clean.

Next morning he spent two hours in the workshop sprinkling fresh sawdust in places where Brillo had shown interest. His last task was to transfer the doctored milk to the shop fridge before he took off for a job thirty miles away.

—⁓—

Two days after the wolf sighting, Muley worked late on a job in Bergland, where he was helping a crew paint an old church basement. His first inclination on the drive home was to wake Micarla and propose a little middle-of-the-night hookeyboo, but the wife liked her sleep and now he was too wired on adrenaline to sleep. Excess energy had been a curse and gift his whole life. Industrial strength A.D.D., the wife called it.

Only a couple of hours before dawn, so he drove around the shop's circle drive and checked where he had sprinkled sawdust. His thin beam light picked up a line of red against the sawdust around the dumpster. This startled him and made him smile as he parked and went into the shop, then came right back out and headed for the dumpster.

Dark, but it amazed him how the whole dumpster seemed to glow at this hour. A retired Northern Michigan art professor had once painted the dumpster virgin white and proclaimed. "It won't stink so much." Total bullshit. Still, it did sort of glow at night.

Muley was reaching for the dumpster top when he thought he heard a faint scrambling. He took a deep breath, flung open the heavy plastic lid, and found his nose nearly touching a gleaming arrowpoint. "I hope youse're handin' that thing out to me to hold so's youse can get out," Muley said.

"Could drop you where you stand," a voice said, a kid's voice, wavering with fear or hormones, probably both, definitely excited and jacked up.

"Go easy now. You kill me and cops will be all over this place, but you go on and do what it is you think you got to do."

"Cops don't make no matter to me."

"Kill somebody and see how fast that changes."

"What are you doing out here *this* time of night?" the boy asked indignantly.

"Could ask youse the same. This is *my* shop. What you think this bin is, White Castle?"

"Move. . . . I'm not warning you again," the boy said.

"You ain't warned me but the once. I don't get three strikes in this game?"

"You crazy?" the boy asked.

"Me. Youse're the one inside a dumpster brandishing a bow and arrow."

"There ain't no private sign on it and the top ain't chained."

"Kind of difficult for folks to use a dumpster with the top chained."

"You read the laws on dumpsters?" the boy asked.

"There's *laws* on dumpsters?"

"I read 'em all."

"Good for you. That must make you one of the world's leading experts. What is this, like a hobby for you, diving for treasures or something along that line?"

"I guess I ain't thought of eating as a hobby."

Muley said, "If youse need food, youse coulda asked for it."

"Ask, and people make you out to be dirt," the boy said. "I *ain't* dirt."

"You done eatin in there?" Muley asked.

The boy countered, "I ain't said that's what I was doing in here, have I?"

Muley grunted. "Point made, you said eatin' ain't no hobby. If not for food, what *are* youse doin' in there?"

"Scratching my curiosity itch."

The kid was weasel lean with pale blue eyes and short blond hair. Muley chuckled. "I got one of them same itches, had it my whole life. You got X-ray vision?" Fish asked.

"Don't joke on me."

"It's dark and with that damn lid down you'd need either a flashlight or X-ray vision."

"I guess I got me a light."

"Bullshit. There're holes in the dumpster. I would've seen a light."

"I got bat's ears," the boy said. "I go dark whenever I hear you."

Until tonight. "You get a lot of practice in dumpsters, do you?"

"Enough."

"It's easier to ask for help than steal," Muley said.

"I ain't no thief."

"Youse claim."

"What I am is a gleaner."

"That a job takes a lot of training?"

"Gleaning takes know-how," the boy said, "and knowing the law."

"Makings of a veritable profession," Muley said. "You gleaners got you a union like electricians and carmakers?"

"You're making fun of me and I have the draw on you."

"You'd better let fly if that's what the gleaner manual calls for."

"There ain't no manual."

"Could be if you wrote one."

"Why would I do that?"

"Share what you know, pass it to up-and-coming gleaners, help them make an easier go of it."

"Nobody *chooses* to glean. You do it because you've got no other choice."

"Sounds like a tune from *Annie*."

"I don't know an Annie," the boy said.

"You ought to. You and that freckled redhead got a lot in common. You wouldn't be an orphan, would you?"

"What's that matter?"

"I suppose it doesn't. You want some help crawling out of there?"

"Who says I'm comin' out?"

"It's in your voice."

"You're nuts, old man."

Muley said, "You may have you a point there."

"You callin' the cops?"

"You want me to let them handle this?"

"I guess I've handled my share of cops."

"How about we settle this business man to man, just you and me?" Muley pushed the arrow aside and held out his hand, "Grab hold, Robin Hood."

"I read about him," the boy said, "only I'm just me, without no merry men."

"It's the philosophy that matters, not the head count."

"I don't get you," the boy whined, taking Muley's hand and popping up to the lip of the dumpster, easily dropping over the rim to the ground. He landed soundlessly as a cat.

"You ain't the only one don't get the likes of me," Muley said. "I've been called crazy and worse my whole life. You need to see a doctor, kid?"

"Why I want do that?"

"Thought you might have a thing or two on your mind, like bleeding to death."

"I ain't afraid to die."

"Good, we'll take your word on that. Most of the rest of us are."

"It mean anything, I got red pee?" the boy asked sheepishly.

Muley didn't answer right away. "Depends on the cause. If its pecker cancer, it'll kill your ass."

"I thought just old people got the pecker cancer," the boy said.

"God made it available to all ages, all races, all religions. Pecker cancer's an equal opportunity death sentence."

"I don't want me no pecker cancer."

"Nobody does. You recently eat or drink anything you shouldn't have?"

"Might've had some chocolate milk out of your fridge."

"Fresh chocolate milk on your regular diet?"

"I ain't got no regular diet."

"Sure you do. It's the whatever-you-can-steal-to-eat diet. That one's been around long time before you. Times I've been on it myself."

"I don't steal."

"You just said youse were in *my* fridge."

"And you think that's me?"

"You just *said* it was you."

The boy looked confused. "Oh yeah."

"Lousy liar, kid. I know it's you. How old are you?"

"Sixteen."

"Why you on the run?"

"I ain't on no run. I been here since late July."

Muley felt light-headed. How did he miss *this*? *Had* he missed it? "*Here*?"

"Hereabouts, anyways."

"You goin' to school?"

"Tenth grade, L'Anse."

"You live in town?"

"Sometimes."

"You go to school every day?"

"All I can."

"What stops all you can from being all, period?"

"Weather and distance."

"Care to spit out a hair more detail?"

The boy frowned. "I live 'round here, and sometimes it ain't all that easy to make it up to the school."

It was eight miles from the shop to the high school. Here since late July? Was this kid for real? A year? Holey moley. "Huh," Muley said. "You hungry?"

"You think I was in the bin to work on my tan?"

Muley laughed. Clearly the kid had some sand. "Got a name?"

"I got to say?"

"Yah, cause the wife she teaches up at the high school and she'll know who you are, and if you're bullshitting me."

"I ain't bullshitting. My name's Jeremiah."

"Johnson or Bullfrog?"

The boy grunted. "You don't seem all that right in the head."

"Share that with the wife. She'll no doubt agree."

They walked into the house and only then did the man-boy unnock the arrow. Micarla came out of a bedroom and looked at the boy. "Jeremiah? Is something wrong?"

The boy nodded at Muley. "Ask *him*."

She looked at her husband. "Well?"

"If this young fella living in our dumpster qualifies as something wrong, the answer's yes," Muley said.

Micarla shook her head. "I think you boys are a couple of innings ahead of me."

Muley said, "This boy goes to L'Anse High?"

"He does, but he's absent a lot."

"Good student?"

"Yes, but he could be more consistent. History and English tell me he has the memory of an elephant."

Micarla never used other teachers' names, only their subjects. Muley laughed. "He's got 'em all fooled. Hell, he can't remember how he got in our dumpster or how he broke into the shop or how he helped himself to our things."

"That's not true," the boy said.

Micarla said quietly, "Jeremiah, I have been married to this man for thirty years and not once has he ever lied to me."

Muley said, "Spit it out, boy. The truth might set you free."

"I'm *already* free," the boy said. "I'm my own man."

"You may be closing in on it, but you ain't there yet," Muley said. "Time to man up."

"I only took a little and I paid it all back."

Muley smiled. "It took me a while to get onto you, you sneaky little bugger. You're artful, I'll give you that, but not artful enough. I marked the chocolate milk." He added, "Paid it all back *how?*"

"I need milk for my bones."

"Not what I asked and that's not no answer. I had a table joint I was working on a while back. I couldn't get the damn thing to fit."

"You measured wrong."

"The *hell* you say! I *never* measure wrong."

"You did that time."

"And youse discovered my mistake?"

"Couldn't miss it. Was obvious."

"I left the shop at night and the joint didn't fit. Next night it did. You saying that was you?"

"Seemed the least I could do."

"Spit it all out," Muley said. *Mismeasured? Shit.*

"I've been living in your workshop. You keep the heat on in there all the time."

"Living there since when?"

"Fall for keeps, now and then before that."

Muley looked over at his wife. "He was in school this fall?"

She nodded.

Muley studied the boy, who was lean and a head taller. "Where're your folks?"

"Gone."

"Traveling?" Micarla asked.

"Dead," the boy said.

"Brothers, sisters, aunts, uncles, grandparents, any kin?"

"Just me left. We were driving east through New Hampshire and got in a wreck. I got thrown out and nobody saw me. I saw them put the bodies in bags. I went on my own."

"East to where?" Micarla asked.

"Maine, somewhere to hide. Not many people there, like here."

"Hide from whom?" Micarla asked.

"The old man broke jail and come for mama and took me too. They were all I had, and we were together all the time until the wreck."

"You should have come forward at the time of the accident," Micarla told him.

"We were in New Hampshire. I didn't want to stay there. The old man was a criminal, a counterfeiter, which makes me one too."

"That's not true," Micarla said.

"You come all the way here on you own?" Muley asked.

The boy held up his thumb.

"Why here?" Muley pressed.

"We came through here once and I liked how it looked," the boy said.

Micarla asserted herself. "Twenty Questions's are done, boys. I'm making venison burgers, go wash up. Muley, show the boy to his room."

"Remind me exactly which room that is," Muley said, raising an eyebrow.

"There's three bedrooms. Let him pick. You got clothes, Jeremiah?"

"Out to the workshop."

"We'll worry about that tomorrow. One thing at a time. Room and food tonight."

"I don't belong here," Jeremiah protested.

Micarla said, "In this house I decide who belongs and who doesn't. Go wash up."

Muley watched the boy eyeing the upstairs windows. "You're thinking this sudden change ain't all it's cracked up to be." Muley took a key off his key ring and gave it to the boy. "For the shop. You get that uncomfortable, go on back to what feels more comfortable. But don't hit the bloody road without saying something or I'll put the cops on your butt."

"Cops don't scare me none."

"I think we've already been down that road."

"Why're you and her doing this?" The boy held up the key.

"Beats me," Muley said. "Maybe she thinks I need help."

"I'm good at stuff," the boy said.

"Especially sneaking around."

"I don't take charity."

Muley snickered. "Me neither. Fess up, you like being alone?"

"Sometimes."

Muley stared at the boy. "You know the first thing wolves do when they meet a stranger?"

"If they don't kill him?" the boy said.

Willibald Fish took the boy's hands and leaned forward and touched his forehead ever so slightly against the boy's forehead. "Welcome to the pack," Muley said. "You think I ain't never been on my own and scared shitless?"

"I ain't never been scared."

"Then you ain't paid enough attention. We *all* get scared. It's what helps keep us alive."

"Aren't we supposed to go down and eat?"

"Which bedroom you want?"

"The one I already got over to the shop."

"Fine by me. You can tell the boss."

"I guess I'll take this one," the boy said.

"You're a young wolf looking for a pack," Muley told the boy. "And now you've found one."

"People aren't wolves," the boy said.

"Sure they are," Muley said. "Even talk like us, or we talk like them, I ain't sure which."

"People can't talk like wolves," the boy said.

"Sure they can. How you think you got here?"

The boy looked at him like he was crazy, and shook his head.

Muley said, "Was wolfie told me youse was here. Now let's go eat. Whole point in life is to eat. Don't believe me, ask the wolves."

Dancing the *Carmagnole*

"Tell me the truth, you think my feet are too big? I don't think they're too big. I think they're proportionate, which means just right for my six-five frame. But what do you think?" Pirkko Rautti asked. She had one of her long legs cocked at an impossible angle and twisted her torso so she could look more directly at Jukka Isokoski.

The boy said, "I know what proportionate means, and it doesn't matter what I think about the size of your feet."

"So, you admit you think about them," she said.

"I didn't say that," Jukka countered.

"Coach says they're too big, that it hurts my foot speed on inside cuts in the paint."

Just like her to see her imperfections when she was a woman among girls on basketball courts. "The way you crushed everyone last season I don't see much of a problem," Jukka said.

The two had been friends and classmates since they were six. She had skipped ahead a grade to the sixth when he was in fifth grade and now was a full school year ahead of him, the top scholar in her class, and one of the best basketball players in the upper Midwest.

"Last year was last year," she said, "Coach is looking ahead to my first year in college. He thinks better foot speed will raise my game and bring offers from even better schools."

"What's got into you?" Jukka asked. "You want West Point. Who cares about the other schools?"

"Isn't that the question for the ages," she keened. "The answer's nothing and nobody, which is a sad tale. I'm will end up a virgin full bull colonel in the army, I just know it."

"How can anyone as smart as you be so dumb?" her friend asked.

"Could be the company I keep," she said. "I've given you an open invite to convert me to womanhood, but here I sit, intact, untouched, and with feet too big for the inside game."

The thought of them as a couple made Jukka uneasy. Just about everyone in town, their parents included, assumed he and Pirkko were and had been boyfriend-girlfriend most of their lives. "Only reason you want West Point is that I want West Point," he told her.

She flicked a grass stalk at him and plunked her feet in his lap. "Rub those big puppies, please."

"Canoes with toes," he remarked.

"I'll be at West Point a whole year before you come dragging in, if you get there, so who's following whom, bub?"

Jukka grimaced.

They had learned to talk at about the same age, but he began with single-syllable words, and she with full sentences and endless paragraphs. By the time he was up to tentative sentences, she was deep into soliloquys and speeches, and here in high school he was still behind her, a gap he had resigned himself to a long time ago. There was never going to be conversational parity. Pirkko dominated him, just as she ruled basketball courts across the U.P. and northern Wisconsin.

"You find summer work?" she asked him.

"Same old, making wood for my Grandma Niemi and my folks, and working on my science project." Pirkko's folks were well-heeled, her dad a lawyer, her mom an English teacher at the high school and the district's department chair. His folks struggled. Dad was a cashier and stocker at Polakoff's Grocery in Red Bay and ploughed snow for the county during seven-month-long winters.

Pirkko grinned. "The vaunted and eternal ultrasecret science project with no name. You've been consumed by that stupid *thing* since sixth grade, but you never talk about it. You know I'm no slouch in science," she reminded him. "You remind me of Truman Capote's last book," she added, plowing on. "It's just like Ms. Birch-Rautti told us. Capote talked incessantly about it, told his agent and his editor about specifics he was working on, made it into a real-life, bigger-than-life drama, the biggest thing since *In Cold Blood*, and neither his editor nor his agent ever saw a single page. When Capote died, it turned out there weren't any pages, it was all bullshit he spewed for years." Ms. Birch-Rautti was her mother's professional name.

"You think I'm a bullshitter? I have a proctor for my project," Jukka said.

"And mincy Truman Capote had an editor and where did that go? Nowhere is where. Maybe you're like Capote feeding a line of B.S. to your proctor, and me." She stopped and looked over at him, "Do you think Capote and Harper Lee did you-know-what when they were young? They grew up next door to each other, played together their whole lives. Just like us. You *do* like girls, right?"

"I was wondering the same about you." He told her and she grabbed a handful of new grass and threw it at him, laughing.

"That's mean," she said.

"Maybe a little. Sorry."

"You want company this summer, I'm your girl in science *and more* if it works out."

"You'll be in round-ball camps most of the summer," he reminded her. "Besides, what I've got is a one-person project."

"Two heads are always better than one," she countered. "Two v. one is the ticket to victory, the tactic that wins every time."

"Sorry," Jukka said.

"Why are you always apologizing to me?" she asked. "Got you a guilty conscience?" She wiggled her toes. "More please."

"You're always there tripping me up and making me say things before I can think them through."

"Boo-hoo for you, a little extra oomph on the toes okay?"

He kneaded and rubbed. Her feet were *big*, and even though she was six-five, she was still growing and they might get even bigger. At six-two he sometimes felt dwarfed by her. He was a football player first, with basketball a distant afterthought. But they played one-on-one against each other, and she incessantly pushed him to beat on her and knock her around to toughen her up so she could dominate female opponents.

"Do I have to beg?" she asked.

"For what?"

"To be part of your science project, lunkhead."

"Sorry."

"Stop apologizing. When you've done something that requires an apology I'll make sure you know." She pulled her feet away, put on bright red Nike high tops without socks.

She ran in place, raising her knees above her waist. "You've got no clue what you're missing," she told him.

"If you're the virgin you claim, you've got no way to know that," Jukka told her. "Not enough data points for comparison."

"I was talking about heaven, musclehead." She faked a dope slap and made him duck.

He couldn't possibly take her along, Thirteen years? Had they known each other *that* long? Good grief. Okay, he had had feelings for her, big feelings, but not ones he could yet name or wanted to. All he knew was that they were different than feelings he'd had for other girls, deeper, thoughtful. Whatever these were, they were *strong*.

Words slipped out before he could stop them. "There might be one thing," he said.

She walked over to him and looked him in the eye. "You bullshit me and I will kill you with my bare hands, Isokoski."

"There's a wolf complaint meeting for the public at the high school Wednesday night," he told her.

"Wolves?" she said. "Those things killed Denny Staker's aunt's Chihuahuadoodle last summer. I never did like that dog, but wolves are killers."

"*You* eat meat," he told her. "Does that make you a killer?"

"They kill it and eat it raw. I cook mine. Or mom cooks it. Point is, my meat has met fire and heat."

"Your Uncle Slaw eats raw venison liver and heart from the first deer in camp."

"He *cooks* that junk. What time's this wolf thing, and what's *your* interest? You are so darn secretive, Jukka, why is that?"

"Seven," he said, ignoring her question.

"I'll drive you," she said. She'd had her own Pathfinder since her sophomore year. He still had to beg for mom's ten-year-old VW.

"We better leave early," he said. "I think there's gonna be a crowd."

"Blood sports," she said, clucking. "I'll never understand that."

"And you want to be a soldier? What's the army, a board game?"

For once she had no comeback. He thought she looked disconsolate, which put a lump in his throat.

Acting on an urge he couldn't push back, he said, "And don't for a minute think that one of these times I'm not gonna jump your bones."

She patted his cheek and smiled. "Talk is cheap, pal. See you Wednesday. I'll be going commando."

She ran off laughing and jumping and juking phantom opponents like a rabbit on meth.

—◦—

The cafeteria was painted in school colors, red, white, and blue. A sign on the front wall proclaimed in three-foot letters, "Home of the Bombers," with the black silhouette of a B-52 carefully drawn inside a gold oval. They had arrived a half-hour early and couldn't get a seat, but some younger girls recognized their local stars and gave them their places along the wall. Elementary and middle school students circulated through the crowd past them, most of them greeting Pirkko by her nickname, Freak. They nodded at Jukka Isokoski, whose quiet demeanor and barely restrained aggression on the football field unnerved others, even his own teammates. She was Freak in name, and he in reality, a bookworm and weird guy always working on his secret science project.

She whispered, "Why're we here, Jukka? Really."

"Sam Balcers," he answered.

She hunched her shoulders and sighed. "*Sam Balcers* is your idea of an explanation? Really? You are *so* lame, musclehead, so *lame*."

"Quiet," he said, "I'm trying to think."

"The whole cafeteria can hear your gears," she joked. "Does it hurt when your brain parts rub together? Maybe you need some WD-40."

"*Pirkko*."

"Okay, okay, I thought dates were supposed to be fun." She held up her hands and feigned hurt.

He said, "This is *not* a date."

"Says you. We are in public and we are together. Let others connect the dots. I am totally commando tonight, you know, and this is *my* definition of a date, or at least the front end of one. Besides, Balcers is an asshole creepaloid. He hits on high school girls. He asked me once if he'd need a stepladder to reach my sweet shop. I told him only if he wanted to go through life with his ladder lodged up his ass."

Balcers was at least a known quantity. The wildcard in Jukka's mind was his companion PHK, Peckerhead Kangas, a six-seven logger with an IQ just short of his elevation, and the hair-trigger temper of a brown water snake. Wherever Balcers went, PHK was usually lurking nearby. He could see Balcers tonight, but not PHK. He had to be somewhere close.

Jukka checked his Batman wristwatch. The crowd was getting restless, and it was already ten minutes after seven. Clark Wick was never late, and this was *his* meeting.

Something was wrong. Jukka studied the room.

"What's her name?" Pirkko asked. "Who're you looking for?"

"Him not her."

"Well that makes my stomach bolt," she said. "Truly that's the *last* answer I wanted to hear."

"Clark Wick, the DNR biologist," he said.

"Never heard of him."

"You spend too much time with your hoops. You need to expand your horizons."

Sam Balcers stood up in the front row, stretched, and said so others could hear, "This is the respect the DNR gives the public. They call a meeting and then they don't bother to show up. This is so much bullshit. I say to hell with them. I come here to tell my story, and I'm gonna damn well tell it. Where's a mike?"

"So sorry," a voice barked from the back of the cafeteria. Wick limped quickly to the front of the room. He was built like an oak with about the same range of motion. "Thanks, everybody, thanks for coming. My apologies for being late."

There was a woman with the biologist, tall and slender, wearing a faded plaid shirt, shredded jeans, scuffed boots. She was good-looking in a nature girl way.

Pirkko said under her breath. "Who's the *looker?*"

Jukka had no idea. "Quiet, okay?"

"So *that's* my competition," Pirkko muttered.

"Pirkko."

"I *know. Shhh.*"

Wick said, "I know a lot of you have questions about wolves, and tonight we're going to try our best to answer as many as you have. Remember, nobody knows everything about these animals, but we know quite a bit and we're learning more every year."

Balcers said, "You guys got no answers anybody here wants to hear."

"Point duly noted, Sam," the biologist said with a smile.

Someone in the audience shouted, "Your wolves are slaughtering livestock, sporting dogs, the hull bloody deer herd."

The Wick Jukka knew was always laid-back and thorough. Even now with all the tension in the crowd, he looked passive, almost sleepy.

Someone else called out, "There's a YouTube video of DNR trucks with Minnesota plates dumping off wolves at night in Michigan, in the U.P. Videos, not hearsay. We've all seen it."

Wick grinned. "I've heard about that video. Anyone here have a copy? I keep hearing about it, but nobody ever has a copy and when I talk to YouTube people, they tell me nobody has taken such a thing down and they have no record of such a video ever being posted. So please, could somebody help me? Michigan is *not* transplanting wolves. The animals came back here on their own. It was *their* choice and their initiative, not ours."

"Not *our* choice, neither," a voice in the audience shouted, and this drew laughs, applause, and a few catcalls.

"I seen the video and PHK seen it too," Balcers said. Other heads in the crowd nodded.

"But not a single person here made a copy?" Wick asked.

"*I* know where there's a copy," Balcers said.

"And where might that copy be?" Wick asked.

"In a safe place," Balcers said.

"I'd sure like to see it."

"So youse can make it disappear? No way. Word's out the DNR's been confiscating videos and stuff, and everybody's afraid to talk about anything."

The biologist said, "How about you get the tape and show it to everyone at the same time? That way we can all sing off the same page in the same songbook."

Balcers sneered. "Right, so you can gank it? Dream on, you think we're stupid? You seeing it, what's that supposed to prove?"

Clark laughed, "Well it would prove that there *is* a video—and that would be a good start."

"You calling me a liar, Wick?"

The biologist said, "Take it any way you like, Sam. Here's the bottom line for us. Until others see the video and we all confirm we saw the same one and confirm the content, then and only then can we attest to its legitimacy. You've got a story. You claim this is evidence. If you want the video taken as legitimate evidence, then it has to be made public in order to be judged."

"Buncha legal mumbo jumbo," Balcers said. "Same old state bureaucracy. It's all bullshit."

"Sam, if you've got a story to tell, why don't you tell it right now and here? You'll never get a bigger audience, and we can all hear it at the same time and ask our questions."

"I thought you come to answer *our* questions," Balcers shot back.

"I did, and I will. But you've got a story you've been telling piecemeal all over the county, so why not give it the grand premiere right here?"

"Everybody in town knows what happened. I told it to Channel 6— *on camera.*"

"That was Marquette, it was a fifteen-second report and there were no details other than you stating you had a wolf story to tell."

Balcers ran a huge hand through his thinning blond hair.

Pirkko nudged Jukka and whispered, "Is this for real?"

"Shh," he said, touching her hand. She squeezed his and they sat holding hands, and he could see her looking around the cafeteria to make sure people were watching them. Pirkko loved being the center of attention, and most of the time she deserved to be.

Balcers began, "I had my huskies on the Burned-Black Plains last July. I had leads and bells on the both of them, radio collars, the whole shebang. They were in their crates and had the hots for a good run. See, huskies can't never get enough running. I parked and looked up this two-track and seen this wolf staring at us. Just standing there, like, hey dudes, this is my house."

"It *is* his house," Wick said.

Balcers kept talking.

Jukka could tell that Balcers was having a problem telling his story, but he wasn't sure how he knew it. Wick said learning to listen to people was the hardest part of any job that had to deal with the public.

"Minute or so later," Balcers told the audience, "out steps this second wolf, this one to our left, and I look behind us and see two more. Just like that, they've got us boxed in and I'm thinking, uh-oh, this ain't good."

The crowd sniggered.

Balcers continued. "You know how they move like ghosts?" Many heads nodded.

"Two more came in between the truck and the first wolf and started coming at us. I jumped back in my truck. As you can imagine, my dogs were going apeshit in their boxes. They really wanted a piece of them wolves."

Jukka was listening and thinking. Wick told him that most dogs who unexpectedly confront wolves do not make a ruckus, and Jukka knew this to be true, had seen it for himself. What they would do most of the time was try to disappear. Beam me up, Scotty! When hunters formally reported attacks on their sporting dogs, all the sound came from the wolves, never from the dogs. Did the audience not know this?

"Them last two wolves come running at my truck, jumped onto the bed and began going after my boys, but my boys didn't cower and fought them wolves away."

Fought through the mesh of steel crates? Jukka noted. Balcers had a real imagination, or something.

"You get a video of this?" Wick asked

"I tried, but my camera she didn't work," Balcers said.

"Were you unarmed?"

"I don't never go to the woods I ain't packing. I got my card, it's all legal, but the wolves were up in the back of the truck, and the rest of the damn pack come to help, and there I was behind the steering wheel. I couldn't take a shot and risk hitting my boys. All I could do was quick-fire up in the air outside my window and back the truck the hell out of there. I tried to back over one of the wolves, but they're a nimble lot, I gotta give 'em that."

Balcers concluded, "So, I got down the road a bit, stopped and checked my boys. Those wolves had ripped open the steel crates and both dogs were bleedin' and tore up bad. Took fifty stitches in one's leg and the other one's now got three ears where he used to have two. He's gonna have to have surgery on that."

"Where did you take your dogs for treatment?" Wick asked, "And how long were the wolves in the back of your truck?"

"I done first aid myself," Balcers said. "No sense spending cash with a damn vet so she can buy her a Florida condo."

"You're saying there are no vet records of this alleged event?"

"It ain't *alleged*," Balcers said sharply, "and I didn't say that, but that's right, their ain't no vet papers and there ain't gonna be."

"Where are the dogs and their crates now?"

"Out to camp. No reason to keep crates in the truck with the dogs tore up the way they were. They ain't goin' no place till they get healed up."

"Was there blood on the cages?" Wick asked.

"What the hell do you think?" Balcers challenged.

"I don't know. I'm asking you, Sam."

"I guess probably there was blood. I had to stitch 'em up, didn't I?"

"Did you at least get some pictures of the wolves while they were up in the bed of your truck?"

"You're not listening. I just said my camera went kerflooey. Don't you DNR people never listen?"

Pirkko whispered, "Sounds like Balcers went kerflooey."

"Shh," Jukka told her, and Pirkko rolled her eyes.

Wick walked over to to Peckerhead Kangas, who had appeared in the cafeteria entry. "PHK, were you with Sam that day on the Plains?"

"Ya sure, I seen it all," the giant said, "but I didn't have no eyeglasses on account Sam and me got drunk night before that and he sat on 'em and broke 'em all to begeezers."

The crowd laughed.

"*Ain't funny*," the big man said. "Can't see shit since then."

"You're saying you were there, but you couldn't see what happened in the back of the truck?" Wick asked.

"I guess I seen it all," PHK repeated. "Sam told me."

"You guess, or you know?" Wick pressed. "You saw, or you just heard Sam's story?"

"I seen and heard, I just said."

"*Without* your glasses, without which you just told us you can't see shit," Wick said. "Anything you want to add, Sam?"

"No, I said my piece."

Wick said, "Thanks for sharing."

The woman in the plaid shirt walked into the cafeteria and announced, "Clark, it's cued."

The biologist said to the audience, "We have a video. It's just footage, no sound. I'll answer your questions after we look at it. Let's move to the auditorium."

Jukka Isokoski didn't need to watch the video. It was his, and he had given it to the biologist last fall after Balcers began talking to TV stations and newspapers about his "harrowing" wolf experiences and his "savaged" dogs.

"What bullshit video?" Balcers asked.

"Just something we acquired. I think we'll all find it relevant and instructive." Wick said, and added to his plaid-shirted assistant, "Roll it when everybody gets seated and settled, Shelly."

The crowd rose and began to move.

Jukka said, "Let's go,"

"Think they'll turn the lights off?" Pirkko asked.

"We're not going into the Aud for *that*."

"I am," she said, lowering her eyes and chin. "God this is the funnest date."

"That's not West Point talk," he told her.

"When we're *at* West Point, we'll talk West Point. Meanwhile I'll talk the way I want," she declared. "It's still a free country."

It looked to Jukka like the audience assembled in the auditorium was even larger than it had been in the cafeteria. The thing about people in the U.P. was that they loved a good argument or verbal dustup, and had over generations developed fine-tuned noses and ears for such events. Cell phones sped up the smoke signal gossip network. Next to high school sports, the commonest cause of arguments was verbal scraps between locals, especially between the DNR and anybody else. It was about as good as it got, primo entertainment.

The video showed Balcers with two dogs on leads and one wolf not fifteen feet away. The dogs were cowering, their tails down and both of them turning constantly, trying to find an avenue out. All the while the wolf stood calmly, as Balcers shook a fist and seemed to be yelling at the wolf as he pulled a pistol from a belt holster, but apparently he'd forgotten to load it because nothing happened and the wolf appeared to get bored and eventually walked slowly away.

Jukka Isokoski had seen the video many times. After it ended, Balcers was on his feet shaking his fist at Wick, "This is bullshit, this ain't real, this is faked, it's all lies, it ain't real. This ain't what happened! Fake news! I demand to know where this come from."

Wick looked at Jukka and nodded. The high school junior nodded back and stood. "I made the video. I saw the whole thing. I was there that day. I was fishing brook trout in Cold Creek."

Jukka saw Balcers clench his fists and step toward him, but Jukka was 230 pounds and everyone in town had seen him play football and behind his back called him "Haywire." Balcers stayed put and glared with his fists clenched tightly and shaking by his sides.

Being on the football field was a helluva lot easier than this. "I was there that day and I never saw Mr. Kangas."

The big man said, "I was in the truck, Jukka."

Wick said, "The video doesn't show you there, PHK."

"Well, he was there," Balcers said. "I can swear to that. And that's two against one."

Wick took a deep breath. "See how this business works? Someone makes a claim. Maybe what they saw happened, maybe it didn't. But if they bring in their dogs or ask us to come look at their livestock, we can tell if there's been a wolf attack or if it's something else. Not one hundred percent of the time, but pretty close. And if it is a wolf, we have a state program to compensate people for their losses. Sam has made no claims. Nobody in this county has made a claim this year, for livestock or dogs, and only one claim was made last year. So all the stories you're hearing at the barbershop, in the coffee shops, and in the bars, they're mostly bullroar. One thing about people up here, you mess with their property when there's a legal way to get paid for their loss, they'll line up at your door for the payoff. Only nobody's lining up at our door, so you can draw your own conclusions."

Wick paused to let the words sink in. "It's possible what Jukka filmed is a different time than Sam told us about and that would account for the differences. Sam's already said his camera didn't work that day, so there's never going to be a video from him. And that leaves us with what Jukka shot."

Jukka watched with great interest. Wick had predicted what would happen. Balcers, realizing his hand had been called and crushed in public, raised his voice. "The wolves come back later just before I tried to get the dogs out of their crates and that's when the attacks come."

The biologist didn't try to respond to this. Jukka said, "I followed you back to your truck. I have video of all of it. What we saw is just when the wolf showed up, and all the video's got the date and times recorded."

"You fucking punk," Balcers snarled at the boy, and PHK took a step toward Jukka. Wick yelled, "Leave it, PHK," and the man stopped and Pirkko jumped up, raised her fists, and yelled, "Come on, big boy, come and get *some*!"

Everyone in the audience got to their feet and began to cheer the kids.

Jukka held his hand across Pirkko to block her charge. Her temper was legendary and sometimes got her into foul trouble on the court.

The biologist held up his hands. "Listen people, Jukka Isokoski is sixteen. He's been in close contact with this wolf pack since he was eight. He's seen puppies born and raised and seen new blood come into the

44

pack, and he's found animals killed in fights. He knows these wolves like his own family."

"That's DNR bullshit," someone in the audience grumbled.

Wick glared at the man and said, "It's real as it gets, and it's unique. Jukka's had this long-running science project he calls 'The Life They Lead.' What he's done is astonishing, and he's not done yet. When this program concludes, we will see and learn things we've never known before."

"That kid's nuts to mess around with them wolves," someone said.

"Jukka is a naturalist and a woodsman. He gets only so close, but over the years the pack has come to accept his presence."

"Do you pet the wolves?" a little girl asked Jukka.

Wick answered for the boy. "Never. They're wild animals, not his pets. But they sometimes come right up to him and sniff him all over to be sure its him, and sometimes when he's fishing, they lay along the side of the creek and watch him."

"Sometimes they take my brookies," Jukka said, and everyone laughed. "I don't fight them for the fish," he added. This brought more laughs.

Balcers wasn't one to give up so easily. "That video is fake, all this shit is fake. Nobody gets that close to wolves. This is just more of the DNR's bullshit."

Wick said, "Annamarie Seitz is the science and outdoor editor for the *Chicago Tribune*. She has a camp up here and she's seen the video and shown it to national experts, including biologists at the US Fish and Wildlife Lab in Missouri."

A woman got to her feet. "My name is Annamarie and I have a report from Fish and Wildlife confirming the video as authentic. They say it's remarkable."

"Fish and Wildlife is just a federal DNR," Balcers complained. "They lie through their damn teeth, the whole lot of them."

"FBI techs have *also* authenticated the footage," the Chicago editor said and was soon deluged by the people, all firing questions at her.

A laugh that began softly spread through the audience and grew louder as Balcers and PHK made their escape in the ensuing tumult.

The crowd got to their feet and applauded Jukka, loudly, enthusiastically, without restraint.

Pirkko was quiet during the drive home. She finally said, "This is your science project, and you never said one damn word to me? That hurts, bub."

"Would you have believed me?"

"You didn't give me a chance not to," she countered.

—◦—

A coolish Sunday in July. Pirkko followed Jukka down the bank of a whispering clear stream to a beaver dam. There was a white cedar canopy over their heads and a heavy paper birch copse to the west, with miles of aspen just to their east, the aspen now the perfect size and spacing for pat cover and hunting. The creek was no more than ten feet wide and shallow, with a pea gravel bottom. They rounded a turn and Jukka touched her leg. "Stay," he whispered.

"I'm not Maxey," she said. Maxey was her golden retriever.

Jukka looked around and patted the bank. "Sit."

"Stop telling me what to do," she complained, but sat where the boy told her to sit.

Jukka circled her twice and sat beside her.

They had not talked about wolves since the meeting that night. She was off to a string of basketball camps and he was cutting winter firewood for his folks and his grandmother and working every minute he could with Clark Wick and following his wolves. Wick had come up with some grant money and was now paying him an hourly summer wage as a junior wildlife technician.

Pirkko looked around the grass and made a face. "Ticks. I hate ticks. If I get one, you die," she whispered.

"Shh," he told her. "Ticks won't hurt you."

She smiled. "But I don't like touching *them*."

"For cripe's sake, Pirkko, just shut up for a few minutes."

"But I'm happy, and I always talk when I'm happy."

"Please?" he begged.

It took ten minutes but eventually he saw grass tops moving along the small ridge on the other side of the stream. The air was dead still, no breeze, no movement. Only an animal could move grass like that when the wind was shut off.

Pirkko leaned against him and he touched her hand and leaned close to her ear. "Be still, they're coming."

She stared at him, mouthed, "They who?"

"Wolves," he mouthed back.

"*Shit*," she whispered, touching her throat.

"Don't move, it makes them nervous."

"Makes *them* nervous? Can I at least whisper?"

"They don't like human voices. They just want to look at you."

"Says you," she said.

"I know them."

Jukka thought he saw tears welling in her eyes, a first in all the years they had been friends. He knew she was highly emotional, but she always seemed to hold herself together when the need to do so was greatest.

The pack materialized not thirty feet from them, the two alphas, three other adults, and five pups, ten animals in all, a large pack.

The alpha male stood directly in front of Jukka, and he whispered to Pirkko, "Look down, don't look him in the eyes." She did as he did, and the alpha moved past them. A pup ran to Pirkko and sat next to her.

"Pew, it stinks," she whispered.

"Think how we smell to them," Jukka said.

The pup started scratching itself wildly. "What do I do?" she asked.

"Don't touch, it's wild. They're as curious as we are." A second gangly, long-legged pup came racing by after a yellow butterfly and then a breeze came up and the butterfly shot up into the air and was gone. The wolf sat down clumsily and looked disappointed.

Jukka heard the female alpha whine, and in an instant the pack was gone into the wind. Pirkko fell into Jukka's arms. She was sobbing and shaking and he held her.

Eventually she calmed down. "I can't go to West Point. I can't be a soldier."

"You can," he told her.

"No, just now I felt like I was on a fine line between life and death, at some kind of halfway point, and I knew I couldn't go forward. I lost my courage."

"It was the same for me early on," he told her. "You're with them, and you realize you're powerless. I got so scared I had to remind myself to breathe. After a while they change you, or something does. You start to see and hear and smell and sense things you never knew were around you or inside you."

"I don't know," she said. "This was too hard."

"You didn't like it?"

She kissed him. "I *loved* it, but I was shaking the whole time."

"There was no danger," he told her. "This was purely a social meeting, a gift from them. When you learn their body language, it's almost as easy as us talking to each other."

"That's not so easy," she said with a giggle. "Sometimes."

The boy stood up and proffered his hand. "What?" she asked, looking up at him.

"You need to learn to dance," he told her.

"I already *know* how to dance. It's you who needs to learn."

"I know how," he said.

"Who taught you?" she wanted to know.

"The wolves."

She rolled her eyes.

He helped her up, took both of her hands, and began to skip sideways, hopping as he went, and then he threw his arms around her and began spinning her around the clearing on the edge of the stream. When he let go, he began flinging his arms and feet out, and she tried to mirror him. They went faster and wilder until he tackled her and folded her down to the grass.

"What the hell was *that*?" she asked, breathing heavily.

"*Carmagnole*, the victory dance of Napoleon's men after they did something brave and important."

"I didn't do anything," she said.

"You did everything," he whispered. "You didn't run."

She plucked a blade of grass, stuck it in her mouth, and propped her head on her hand. "I'm commando under my shorts, is there a dance for that?"

Didit Dave

Yooper nicknames are like Indian names. Your ma and pa give you a name or two when you're born. But later, as you start to grow up and do things on your own, you begin to earn other names, some from your family, some from the people in the town where you live, teachers, neighbors, friends, strangers, everyone's free to jump in. The only test is whether the new handle sticks. Up here you can end up with your family name, maybe your mother's pet name, the name your brothers and sisters and aunties hang on you, and most significantly, your town name. There are profound social histories lurking in town names.

To wit, Aino the Ax gave the worst haircuts in the Copper Country, and while he'd never been a master barber, he was a master bullshitter. He could entertain for hours as he put people in the chair and gave them his standard Finnlander square-head chop, which made clients' heads look like hair-sprouting boxes. Stylish it wasn't.

When Aino retired, Didit Dave (aka D-Square, D2, and Double-D) took over the business, and unlike his dad, who stuck to his shop during duty hours, Dave repaired to Ticky Torsky's Underdog Bar across the street to keep an eye out for customers. When Dave saw someone pause at his shop window, he'd blast down his beer and rush across the street to fulfill his tonsorial duties.

Barbers eventually learn the likes, dislikes, wants, and want-nots of their customers, who likewise learn the same things about their barbers. It didn't take long for word to get around that if you wanted a halfway decent haircut (there was no such thing as a wholly decent one) you needed to get to Didit's shop before 11 a.m., otherwise there was no telling how far along the drinky-drink trail Didit might have traveled. When people new to South Range asked others where they got their haircuts, they'd be told Dave Did It, and that's how that name came to be legitimized as his town name. Through most of his youth Dave had been of a high-spirited, risk-taking ilk, and in those days, whenever his parents, teachers, or cops wanted to know who was behind the latest mischief they were investigating, they were just as likely to hear Dave Did It as any other name.

Two weeks after Dave took over his father's shop, Felix-the-Kat Welttenen went into the Copper Country Bank branch in South Range with a .12 gauge Winchester shotgun and an embarrassed smile on his beer-weathered face.

You couldn't call Felix *the* town drunk because there were so many such buggers, and in those days it wouldn't be fair to put the label on just one of them. Remember, this was the early '70s, when drugs were being generously dumped into the stew for local buzz-agendas, which made for widespread and frequent intoxication just about anywhere you went during the day and virtually everywhere after work.

Back to Felix-the-Kat, who we now have standing in the bank sort of pointing his shotgun at the tellers, all of whom he had known most of their lives. Everyone in town knew Felix as a drunkard, a gentle soul, as well as a major mooch, which was an odd combination, but Felix defined odd.

It was just before noon when Felix waved his pump-action Model 12 in the general direction of the female tellers and asked in his soft voice, "Can Felix please, ladies, to have the twenty dollar, please?" He winked. "Don't none of you nice ladies have no worries, dis scattergun she ain't loaded." He held up the weapon to show them.

Simultaneously Jack Nedomansky, Fat Jack the PO-lice Man, entered the premises, breathing like he'd just run the Boston Marathon, when all he had done was waddle a mere seventy-two yards across the street from Ticky Torsky's Underdog, which more or less faced the bank. Ticky himself had seen Felix go into the bank with the shotgun. "Hey Jack," the bar owner called to the cop, "I just seen Felix-the-Kat go into bank with Model 12. You t'ink it's gift for somebody over dere?"

"Drat," Jack said. He was chief of police for South Range, Painesdale, Tri-Mountain, and a half dozen smaller villages, including Sunny Italy, where ancient men spoke broken English and paid young boys with high-alcohol chokecherry wine to bring home songbirds and trout for them to eat. As a one-man law enforcement unit, Jack was largely a reasonable man, but hated to have his drinking and chiefly ruminations interrupted by actual police business.

Having heard what Ticky had seen, he ordered a bump and a beer, hauled out his Colt .38 Python, checked to be sure she had a lead peanut in each hole, gulped down the shot, then the beer, snugged the revolver back into its holster, closed the safety snap over the hammer, hitched up his pants, and crossed the street with the speed of a slug on black ice.

Felix smiled when he saw Jack. "Sorry dere, Chief, but I'm gone bust and I didn't want ask no more borrowments from all da fine people of dis town. Gun she ain't loaded. You want cuff me?"

"No bloody cuffs," the irritated Fat Jack said. "Get on over to the damn jail, Felix, and wait right there. I'll be along. Put that Winchester on my desk. You got shells in your pocket?"

"No sir, I left 'em somewheres, over da house mebbe, hard remember some days, you know?"

"Okay," Jack growled. "Git."

Felix left and Jack pulled out his notebook and took statements and got times and all the details he needed for the arrest warrant. With his draft report, interviews, and all the attendant administrative work finished, the chief ambled back to Ticky's to resume patrol, and first thing, he asked Ticky to send someone over to the jail with a bump and a beer for the erstwhile bank robber. "Tell your man to tell Felix to make himself comfortable, I'll be there by breakfast."

Next morning, Fat Jack let Felix go on his own recognizance, gave him a summons, got the old fellow's promise to show for court, went into Felix's cell, stripped down, and passed out, his patrol in the bar having lasted all night.

South Range mayor Charles Emerson Greenbank (never Charley, Chas, or Chuck, it could be only Charles) was known behind his back as Enema (we shall not speculate why). Enema was said to be kin to distant Czech blood and carried himself as a dandy. When Fat Jack came to Ticky's the next morning, Enema pulled him aside and chided him, "Chief, you can't be sitting in a tavern swilling alcohol all day. Think how bad that looks to the citizenry."

"I don't swill," Fat Jack said in his own defense, "And to be accurate, it's morning, not all day. The fact is, I get some damn good looks and tips from this place. I got that bank robber, didn't I?"

"Wasn't youse seen Felix go yesterday into bank," Ticky corrected the chief from behind the bar. "I seen Felix and passed over to youse da word."

Jack sighed and glared at Ticky. "You want to lose your best damn customer?"

The chief turned to Mayor Enema. "Here's the thing, Charles. It comes down to theological physics: A lone, solo cop can't be everywhere at once all the time like God. It's my policing strategy to locate myself centrally in such a way as to be able to respond quickly to developing events. Had I been down to the jail yesterday, I might very well have missed the attempted bank heist, but I was right here on top of things, hurried over to the bank, and made the apprehension."

The mayor mulled this. The jail *was* three blocks away, and the chief's argument had some merit. Witnesses said it had taken Fat Jack a less-than-competitive six minutes to negotiate the seventy-plus yards from bar to bank. Had he been coming from the jail, he might not yet have reached the bank.

Enema recognized an airtight argument when he heard one and let the issue drop for now. But the mayor, who for thirty years had taught some kind of existential egghead thing over at Michigan Tech up to Houghton, had a long memory for affronts. Anyone who disagreed with him was immediately placed on his long-term list of get-evens.

The judge sent Felix to the county jail for six months and everybody else got on with living.

No mistake, the town and Copper Country, for all their eccentricities, were populated by hard workers, which did not include most of the barflies prominent in this telling. There was the state's dole of course, to help those who were down and out, but most people in this area were too damn proud to take handouts and having a job was back then a matter of pride. The drinkers happily took the dole even while they bad-mouthed it. Some wags said a third of the people in the U.P. worked for the government, another third lived off the government, and the middle third was trying to figure out which third to join.

Enema recognized Fat Jack's lack of physical prowess and energy, and rather than having their man with the badge knocking back bumps and beers in one of the town's taverns all day, he convinced the city council to purchase a used gray Plymouth Fury for the chief. The mayor had a gaudy gold badge painted on the doors and roof and trunk, the idea being that Fat Jack might be encouraged to make his patrols in the Plymouth instead of from the Underdog's front window barstool.

Fat Jack thanked the mayor and declared that day to his wife and barmates that his life was now in valence, whatever that meant. Ticky immediately said, "I seen dat movie with The Duke himself and Jimmy Stewart." Fat Jack snarled and ordered his usual bump and a beer. His arrest rate, despite the newly acquired Fury (which could top out right around 163 mph), remained unchanged.

Jack was not a stupid man and in his way *was* dedicated to police work. Jack also had more than a touch of civic-mindedness. Once he had the Plymouth, he made a point of splitting his time between the town's four taverns, always parking the patrol car closest to whatever barstool he was patrolling from at the moment. Jack thought it judicious to spread around the business, despite the fact that the police chief never paid a bill, which meant there was no revenue to be had from his business no matter where he took it. Who the hell ever heard of a U.P. cop *paying* for a drink? Nobody could or did argue the point because it was true and, if pressed, Jack would explain patiently that he understood he represented zero revenue for the tavern operators, but by moving around he at least spread the loss.

For years Ticky Torsky had absorbed the whole tab, but had never complained because, let's face it, there were times when having a cop on the premises could be a darn handy thing. You keep a cop in uniform at the bar, tempers don't flare quite so much and donnybrooks become dinosaurs. It was cheaper than hiring a bouncer.

There came that day at Ticky's when Vivian and Francis Herlihy, brothers from Donken, stood at the bar tipping down shot after shot. Ticky listened to them tell how their woods boss Wildcat O'Brien had made an off-color remark about the brothers taking twenty-minute lunch breaks instead of the standard fifteen minutes other loggers got. This was when the lads were working back behind Lake Perrault in the Salmon Trout River drainage country. The brothers, both in the neighborhood of six-five and three hundred pounds, had never married and drank up whatever they earned from cutting pulp. They were at the very bottom of the area's social pecking order, being drunks, Irish, and pulpies, the trifecta of Yooper loserdom.

Ticky told them, "You boys need to apologize to Wildcat. How you fellas live you can't afford drink, eh?"

Much to everyone's surprise, Fat Jack came out of the men's room trying to button his fly and announced, "Go easy on these fine lads, Ticky. What's their tab?"

"She go back two month, got them up near thirty-two dollar, they do."

"Tell you what, Ticky, tack these fellows' tab on mine." This said, the chief turned to the hulking pulpies, "Lads, you're now clear as brook trout water. And you can thank the town council for its generosity."

Vivian, the more socially inclined of the brothers, said, "Might, we knew who the hell they be."

"Mere trivia," Fat Jack said. He had that morning gotten a telegram telling him that Felix-the-Kat, gentle-soul bank robber, was coming back from jail. This small detail was a major burr under the chief's professional saddle. Having Felix back would mean continual small irritations from the man's inability to live in any normal manner. Fat Jack sent a letter to the town council requesting that, in the interest of expense reduction, Felix be banned from the Quad Town jail, no matter his transgressions (and as long as nobody got hurt). Knowing Felix, Jack estimated it would be a week, maybe ten days before the old man would do something stupid enough to necessitate jailing him again, and this was a game Fat Jack had tired of playing.

When Jack explained this to Ticky, the bar owner said, "I don't care none 'bout dat Felix. I only care about tab youse run up. Cheezus,

Chack, you got biggest bill dis place ever, and don't not even not count dose Irish brudders."

"I have no bill," Jack reminded the proprietor. "I'm a peace officer on duty twenty-four hours a day and if you are feeling a need for settlement, *Mister* Torsky, I suggest you take your business directly to the city council. I shall speak no more of this, so set me up with a bump and a beer and let bygones go wherever the hell they go."

Bernie Porrier, aka Bernie the Psycho, came into the bar after the Irish brothers and made a big show of his fire-engine-red cowboy boots. He told assembled imbibers that he'd bought them secondhand from a college kid "up the college." They were pretty tight, he allowed, but the kid had explained how cowboy boots were meant to be fit tight, like hockey skates. Bernie, who had been a fine ice hockey player in his day, understood the importance of tight-fitting skates and bought the boots. They had been hurting his feet ever since.

Bernie explained that his current love interest, one Vesuvia Piccolomini, had to help him get the boots off every day, and Vesuvia, renowned for her volcanic temper, seldom got them off without losing her cool and slapping Bernie around. In fact he was sporting a nice yellow-green mouse under each eye when he came into the Underdog. A couple of patrons tried to tag him with Coonie, but the name didn't take. It might have if Bernie had lived, but that was not to be his fate.

The night of the day Bernie showed off his new-used red boots at Ticky's, he and Vesuvia were in his red Fairlane headed south to Toivola when a deer ran out on the road. Bernie swerved, and the Ford went down a steep embankment and bit hard into a huge ironwood, throwing Vesuvia and Bernie through the windshield and out of the vehicle.

When Fat Jack got word of the accident and finally reached the site, Good Samaritan passersby presented him with two dead bodies under a bloodstained and tattered Green Bay Packers blanket.

Jack noticed Bernie was sockless and bootless and asked where the dead man's boots were. The Good Samaritans went with him and when they got to the wreck, Jack found Bernie's boots wedged under the clutch and accelerator, and it made him wonder if the boots somehow had been involved in the fatal crash.

Next day at Ticky's the boots were on display with a hand-lettered sign proclaiming, "Don't' drink and drive if your damn boots don't fit."

The day the sign went up, which was the morning following the commencement of Vesuvia's and Bernie's eternal dirt naps, a relaxed and reformed Didit Dave came home after six weeks at White Pine, where he had gone through an intense drinking-cessation program the wife talked their health insurance company into paying for.

Dave was in some ways a changed man, but the change wasn't easy for most to detect. He stopped at home to pat wife Cindy's fanny, which precipitated a one-minute variation of their regular two-minute drill. Domestic duties discharged, Dave ambled downtown to open the barbershop for the day's business. Shop open and left unlocked, Dave drifted over to Ticky Torsky's to catch up on local news.

Fat Jack noticed that Didit didn't order a drink, which was astonishing, maybe a first.

Ticky showed Didit the red cowboy boots and related the tragic death of Bernie and Vesuvia, but his story got interrupted by Ante "Loco" Nevala roaring up Main Street on his 1973 Honda CR250 Elsinore. Nevala did a wheelie the whole five blocks, and one of the patrons remarked, "Dat crazy bugger making 'is rice-burner stand right up, hey. He's on knobby tires too, ain't easy ride dose t'ings."

Ticky saw the scene differently. "That damn kid's leaving nasty black tire marks down whole bloody street and won't be long till July fourth the parade. Somebody ought to make that little son of bitch clean up dose marks before the parade."

Didit looked up to see Fat Jack, beer glass in hand, waddling into the street, his face all puffed up and red like a ripe tomato. The Nevala kid came flying back up the street and Jack held up his beer glass as a signal for the biker to stop, but Loco snatched the beer from the police chief's hand, chugged the remains, and threw the glass to the street where it popped like a .22 round.

"Litterer," Ticky remarked in the bar. "Oh boy, Jack *hates* littering. Watch dis."

The Nevala boy spun around and was coming back for another pass. The entire clientele hurried outside to witness what lay ahead. They heard Jack yell, "Ticky, add another bump and beer to my tab." Jack then unsnapped his holster, pulled out his Colt Python, yelled, "Stop, I'm the *law!*" Jack got off a single round, which missed the motorcycle rider, but blew out Mayor Emerson's Chevy windshield, the shot making the Nevala boy swerve and crash directly into Fat Jack, sending both of them sprawling, and the bike spinning and careening out of control.

As a kid Didit Dave had been no slouch on a motorcycle, and when he saw the bike spin away, he quickly reached over, grabbed the left handle bar grip, jumped on the seat, pulled the nose up into a wheelie, dropped it, made two tight spins, and stopped, dropping the kick bar. By consensus of all hands on the witness deck, Dave's bike routine beat the hell out of the Nevala boy's, who broke both arms and his nose in the crash.

Jack had too many injuries to catalog on the scene and was taken by ambulance over to Houghton. Enema Emerson came out of his office on the main drag to see the final confrontation, the impact, and the bike save. He called the the hospital for an ambulance and made sure to tell the ambulance driver to tell the doctor to get word to the judge that the chief was drunk on duty and needed to be remanded by the judge over to White Pine. "Tell the doc to let the judge know, I'll call him later."

Enema Emerson did not miss Dave's little performance and went right over to him. "Haven't seen your shop open for a while, David."

"Put myself through the spin dry, over White Pine."

"It work?" the mayor asked.

"Better have," was all Didit said. "Weren't no picnic."

"I saw what you did with that bike. You've got nerve and we need a sober new police chief."

The mayor was staring deep into Dave's eyes and Dave was thinking how much he disliked policemen. "Jesus, Joseph, and Dropkick Mary," Dave said. "*Not* me!"

"Perfect," the mayor said. "Come over to my office this afternoon and we'll get you sworn in."

"I ain't been no police school or nothing."

"A mere detail."

"I'm barber, not a pig."

"You can be a barber *and* a cop. Beats hell out of having our police chief working out of the lushlunchhaus."

Dave moped home and told his wife what had happened.

She laughed out loud. "Youse come 'ome from da spin dry, grab a quickie, go see chums at bar, and come home chief of da PO-lice. How much you drink dis morning?"

"Not a damn drop," he exclaimed. "I don't never want go through the spin dry again."

Which is how Didit Dave became police chief of quad cities' law enforcement and earned his latest town name, Wheelie.

Booley's Gift

IT WAS 1958 AND IN SOME WAYS ICE HOCKEY WAS A BEAUTIFUL THING to watch, in some ways not.

All the boys called him Booley, which some claimed came from the Old English *bula*, a bull, and *leah*, a grove, meaning a place where the bull grazed. This surely described the lives of journeyman hockey players, who were bulls if nothing else, but this isn't where the name came from. One of the word's definitions says it means to get one's way by intimidation. And this pretty much, sort of, kind of, described Booley, who was known in certain circles as an expert at getting his way, which the player himself defined narrowly as winning games by doing those things he could do best.

This was a time before hockey players wore helmets. Cornishman Taryn Blydh was a lawyer and a hockeyman, working for a resource investment group out of Boston, but living in Lansing and making regular trips to northern Minnesota, Wisconsin, and the Upper Peninsula of Michigan. His company invested in mining properties and sent him out from time to time to report back on how things were going up north with their iron and copper holdings. Blydh's father had moved the family to western New York when the Yooper-born Blydh was four and he'd grown up a New Yorker with occasional visits to grandparents and other relatives in the Keweenaw Peninsula of the U.P.

Blydh's inspection trips north took him into hard-core ice hockey country, where professional hockey had gotten its start, and being an old hockey player, this made him a happy man.

On the trip being reported, the lawyer had an extra day and some of the boys in the hotel dining room let him know during breakfast there might be a pretty good game between Yooper town teams in Calumet, fifteen miles north of Houghton.

Blydh traveled north by train from Lansing and stayed at the Shelden Hotel in Houghton. He used taxis to get around and arranged one north for the game. Taxis were at a premium on cold days in January in the Copper Country and Blydh, being pretty handy with words, talked his cabbie into staying with him for the game. A fellow Cousin Jack (Cornishman), Cabbie Jacca Tredwyn, was Hancock-born and also loved hockey.

The Calumet Colosseum was built in 1923 as an ice rink, turned over to the National Guard in 1942, and renamed the Calumet Armory.

The rink had been an architectural marvel in its day. Most towns in the far north had roofless, outdoor ice sheets. Even without heat in the armory, the lack of wind made games easier on players and spectators alike, and inside ice could be better tended to and repaired as games went on. Most teams across the U.S. and Canada played outside in the elements all winter, and when winds blew, players learned to keep their shifts short, jumping onto the bench every minute or so to get back to the warming stove in the bench shed between the times they had to be outside.

Hockey in the far north tended to produce a hardy lot of players and fans. This day the temperature hovered around zero, and the armory's ice was hard, black, and fast.

Blydh was bundled up and had a flask of rye stashed in his inner coat pocket. The flask, he guessed, helped convince taxi-man Tredwyn to stay for the game.

Soon after the opening puck drop, a player wearing number 14 caught Blydh's eye. He was not tall, but built wiry-rangy and deceivingly fast, with quick feet and soft hands, and he was quick-eyed with the puck. His age was impossible to determine. He looked like a boy, but played like a man.

Number 14 fought four times in the game and in Blydh's opinion lost every scrap. Late in the game, with the score tied at five, and with less than one minute remaining in regulation time, Number 14 broke away alone, cut aggressively from left to right eight feet in front of the goalie, and snapped a fast, hard wrist shot through an opening under the goalie's catching glove, a space no larger than a playing card. Goal. The goal judge turned on the red light and the player's fifth fight broke out, but this time the refs were quick to get the fighters apart. Time ran out, and the boy's teammates carried him off the ice on their shoulders like a trophy.

Blydh shook his head. He was seated at such an angle that he had a keen look at the tiny opening and watched openmouthed as the player flicked the puck through the miniscule opening. Skill or luck? Because hockey happened so fast on the ice, it was often hard to separate skill from luck on any given play, but over time certain players would repeat certain feats. An ancient man in a heavy woolen peacoat was one row down in the bleachers and smoking a cigar redolent of green mold.

Blydh tapped the man on the shoulder, "Might you know the lad who just scored the goal?"

"That would be Booley," the man said. "Hundred fifty-seven pounds of rock 'em sock 'em hell."

"Family name's Booley?"

"Can't say for sure. The kid's an imbecile." The man tapped his head. "Not all there upstairs, fight fight fight. Story goes that as a little kid some adult beat the hell out of him and he told his mama he wanted to grow up to be a bully."

Blydh chomped his cigar. "*Did* he?" It wasn't a question. Smug bastard, this one.

"By definition, bullies intimidate people," the lawyer, Blydh, asserted. But he only nodded, turned away, and resumed puffing his cigar.

"Sir," Blydh said. "Sorry to interrupt you again. This Booley's club: They're from where?"

"Trout Lake," the man said. "East side."

Lawyer Blydh knew of Trout Lake, which was close to 300 miles from the Copper Country. The team went by the name of Pulp Dogs, at least that was the name embroidered on their game sweaters; like most amateur teams, they had threadbare sweaters, but they were at least all of a color and that's what mattered most.

The whole logic of Booley and his view of his role on the team defied anything Blydh had ever encountered in the game, and lawyer Blydh had deep experience. The lawyer had dinner alone at his hotel dining room that night and afterward walked down Shelden Street to The One-Man Drill for a libation. He was surprised to see the Trout Lake players in there singing and carrying on.

"What's the celebration?" Blydh asked the barkeep.

"Best team from the eastside U.P. just beat the best of the west," he said. "West team ain't lost a game in five years, but the eastern boys brought them some dandy players."

"Fella named Booley one of the dandies?" the lawyer asked.

The man nodded. "Yah, I t'ink mebbe that's what dey call him."

Blydh later found Booley sitting quietly in a chair while his teammates carried on nearby.

"Mind if I join you?" the lawyer asked.

"Free country," the boy said.

"How old are you?" Blydh asked.

"Ain't allowed to say, Mister."

"Who won't allow it?"

"I ain't sure," the lad said.

"When do you fellows play again?"

"Tomorrow. The cup's best two of three."

"Cup?"

"Upper Peninsula Cup," the boy said.

One of Booley's teammates pushed his way over to them. He was drunk and in a mood to brag. "Ain't no eastern team never won this cup," he said. "Till us."

The lawyer didn't point out they hadn't won it yet. "Have you fellas lost a game this season?" Blydh asked.

"Nary a one," the player said, sticking out his hand. "My name's Bodoni, out of Chippewa County."

"Blydh," Blydh said, "Lansing."

"You're a long way from home," Bodoni said.

"Up here on business." Blydh turned back to Booley. "How many fights you had this year?"

"I ain't kept count," he said.

"How many have you won?"

"All of 'em."

"You won all your fights today?"

He smiled. "You bet."

"How many goals have you scored this season?"

"Never kept count," Booley said. "Some, I guess."

Bodoni chipped in. "Ain't Bool's job to score but once in awhile."

"What *is* his job?" Blydh asked.

"Tell the man," Booley's teammate said.

"I don't never quit," Booley said. Then he beamed a smile that showed a gap in his teeth.

"Your job is to never quit?" the lawyer asked the boy.

"Yessir, that's it."

"And this helps the team how?"

Bodoni butted in again. "Booley ain't never played in a losing game."

"Never?"

"Not one."

"How old is he?"

"Beats me," Bodoni said. "Who the hell cares?"

"You and your teammates seem to treat him like he's a prize pet or a Steinway. What time's tomorrow's game?"

"Same as today, one p.m. You gonna be there, Mister?"

"Name's Blydh, and yes, I think I will." The lawyer decided right there to change travel plans and take in the game.

The kid's speed and accuracy with the puck? The kid was the quickest on skates Blydh had ever seen, pro or amateur. Two strides and he was in full flight. It was breathtaking and astonishing. Blydh had seen enough to called his pal Amo Bessone, head hockey coach at Michigan State. He called the coach at home.

"Amo, Taryn Blydh, I'm up in Calumet and I've seen this kid. You aware of a player, name of Booley?"

Amo carried prodigious quantities of player stats and evaluations in his head and had almost immediate and full recall. "Hey Wolfie, how's tricks? No, can't say I know the name. Why?"

Blydh was Cornish for wolf and the lawyer was known in certain hockey circles as Wolfie.

"Dunno, but he's got pro speed and great hands."

"Size?"

"Five-seven, one sixty max, nothing special."

"Age?"

"Don't know yet. He looks like a kid but he's playing with men who're a lot older and he's the one who dominates."

"Where'd you see him?"

"Here at the Armory, game against Houghton, first leg of the U.P. Cup. Trout Lake beat Houghton."

Amo gasped. "Houghton's not lost in five or six years. Some of my boys played up there. Are you sure it was Trout Lake? There's nothing in Trout Lake but woods, trains, bears, and bobcats."

"One of his Trout Lake teammates is a guy named Bodoni."

The college coach laughed. "Be *damned*. Bullhead Bodoni came up through the Soo Greyhounds, in Soo Canada, and played four seasons with Boston's big club. Checks like a truck. If he's playing for Trout Lake, they must have a fair club."

"Second leg is tomorrow. I'm going. You interested in this Booley kid?"

"He scrappy?"

"Five fights yesterday and with a minute left in the game he put one under the goalie's armpit. He was moving across and away from the keeper with two defensemen chopping at him like firewood."

"He win the fights?'

"I wouldn't score it that way."

"Sounds more thug than scrapper. We're trying to get fighting out of the college game, put the emphasis on skills, not fists and goons. He got some sort of emotional problem?"

"He seems pretty mellow," Blydh said, but he knew that some of the game's most violent and hotheaded players on ice were the gentlest off ice.

"Okay, Wolfie. Theoretically, sure, I'm interested, but here's the thing: Can he get into college? And can he stay in once he's here? Has he even finished high school? Is he American or Canuck? How old is he? You look around all the leagues in North America and you find a shitload of transient hockey bums moving around, playing for teams here, there, and everywhere, and getting paid cash on the side. I don't like picking up players who've been paid to play. They don't adapt well to college life or our college game, but sometimes it works out and if a boy's got great skills it might be worth a gamble. I'd love to see him on the ice. Find out where they'll be playing next so I can take a look with my own eyes."

Blydh wondered if a player who lost five fights in a game qualified as a thug or fool. Blydh engaged his Cousin Jack cabdriver Tredwyn again for the next day, had a glass of tawny port at the bar, returned to his hotel room, and called it a day.

———

Blydh got to the rink early and saw Booley racing around flicking pucks about and then he swerved and cut over to the warming bench. A few players from both teams were on the ice, slapping around pucks, and skating their stretches. No goalies yet. Temp right around zero again, and hard, fast ice.

The lawyer stood behind the player. "You fellas ready to go?"

"Always," Booley said, with a grin.

"Is it true what your teammate said, that you've never played in a losing game?"

"Yup," Booley grinned.

"So you assume you're going to win before you step on the ice?"

"I don't assume it, I know it. And I love it that the other side doesn't know they're gonna lose, you know?"

Blydh had no idea what the boy was talking other than nonsense. Everyone lost, sooner or later. "You're fast and you've got soft hands," Blydh said. "If you fought less, you could score a lot more goals."

"Not my job to score goals," the player said. "I never quit."

That again. "If you lose all your fights, someday you're going to get seriously hurt."

"You've got it wrong, Mister. A real hockeyman would know better. See, you've got to watch closer. In a fight on the ice, watch the skates. The one in control is planted, the one out of control has his skates all over the place—like he's running on marbles."

"It's not the feet that are going to hurt you."

The player shrugged.

"Booley, I've talked to a coach friend. Have you graduated from high school?"

"Yah, sure."

"What sort of marks?"

"Not bad, not great. I liked most subjects, but not school, you know?"

"Your team, are you guys playing any more games or tournaments this year?"

"Down to Sarnia later this month, I think."

"My friend, the coach, would like to see you play, Booley."

The boy shrugged, said, "She's a free country."

"I'm talking about college hockey, Booley, everything paid for four years. Are you American or Canadian?"

"American."

"From where in the states?"

"Iron Range in Minnesota," the player said.

"One other thing," the lawyer said, "There's no fighting in the college game."

"College boys don't fight?"

Blydh had been successful his whole life by anticipating. "No fighting in college and no fighting today. We need to know what sort of self-control you have."

The boy stared hard at him. "This is the championship game, eh?"

"I know that," Blydh said.

"Four years, everything paid, and I can choose what I want to study?"

"That's how it works, if your grades and tests get you in."

"Only if I don't fight?"

"Right, that's the deal, and you don't win any of your fights, so it shouldn't make much difference to you."

Booley glowered. "You're not much of a hockeyman."

The player skated away and joined his teammates as the two goalies came out to begin the formal pregame warm-up routines for both clubs.

Blydh scowled. *Not much of a hockeyman?* He'd grown up in Rochester, New York, played on scholarship for Colgate, been assistant captain in his senior season, gone to law school there, and served as a graduate assistant with the team while he went through. He had graduated at the top of his law school class, and he knew a player when he saw one. This thing about a fighter's feet was new to him. He vowed to pay attention to it during the game and went to get some coffee and join his driver companion in the bleachers.

The Houghton team's tactics showed early. Less than one minute into the game the team's biggest defenseman piled into Booley behind the Houghton goal. To his credit, Booley tried to spin away, but the bigger player had too good of a grip on his sweater and Booley's options were few once he was in the man's grasp. The aggressor's fists looked the size of Booley's head.

The referee and his two linesmen let the bout go on too long. Despite the spate of fists raining on Booley's head there seemed to be no blood on his face or head. When the refs separated them, the combatants skated gingerly to penalty boxes, where Booley blew a kiss to the big defenseman. There were perhaps a thousand people in the stands, and being hardened hockey types (who else would sit in near-zero temperatures?) they liked the little exchange, small player to large, and cheered enthusiastically.

Blydh had watched their feet during the fight and when it was finished, realized Booley had been set in one place, unmovable by his larger opponent. Not a single wobble, and no matter the look of the punch (some looked powerful enough to break bricks), Booley remained almost bored, so calm, moving his head only slightly, but definitely moving to cause some punches to miss or make only glancing blows. When it was over, Booley was grinning and hardly sweating while the big man looked like he'd been wearing a fur coat in a sauna.

By raw punch count, Booley had lost the fight decisively, but by the count of actual damage-doing blows, maybe not. The psychological winner, Blydh thought, was clearly Booley. Strange and a stupid darn way to play the game.

Fifteen seconds out of the penalty box, Booley hammered the same big defenseman from behind and put him on his face, and the defender came scrambling up to recover his lost dignity, fists going like windmills.

Booley went into a stone-still turtle position and did not move while the other player whaled at him for all he was worth. Blydh did not miss the fact that the sharpness of the big man's punches was gone.

Five more minutes in the sin bin for both men.

Ten seconds back on the ice, Booley took a short pass from a team-mate, cut directly to his two-fight opponent, danced around him with the puck cupped on his blade, veered sharply between his defenseman and the goalkeeper, and when the goalie leaned slightly right, Booley snapped a shot into the upper lefthand corner of the net. 1–0. Trout Lake and the defenseman lost all control, and the latter chopped Booley across the back of his legs with his stick. The defenseman got a ten-minute misconduct for intent to injure and was thrown out of the game.

Blydh sat and thought about it. The game was now not 13 minutes old, and Booley had spent 10 of the game's 13 minutes in the penalty box, had two fights, and scored a goal.

With 58 seconds left in the first period, Booley got speared as he floated past the Houghton net, and as naturally as rainbows follow rain, Booley lit into the offender who was more his size and commenced to turning the opponent's face into bloody mush. From the bleachers and the bench, if Booley's teammates' enthusiasm was any indication, Booley had emerged the winner, and when the ref sent the players to the penalty boxes, they headed to the warm dressing rooms, their penalties to run into the next period. With four seconds remaining, Trout Lake's Bodoni bowled over a defenseman and snapped a low shot inside the left post to make it 2–0.

Three fights in one period? Astonishing, but this was backwoods amateur hockey, not college or pro where three fights in a game put you out. Apparently no such rule existed at this level, if even a level this could be called.

Second period, Booley on the wing, a left shooter on the right side, which struck Blydh as odd until he realized that with every stride the left-shooting right wing took toward the opposing net, his shooting angle improved. Was this an accident or planned? If the latter, it was subtle and brilliant. Booley had been a left shot on the left side in the opening period.

His third shift in the new period, the referee called for a face-off at center ice. Trout Lake's center easily won the puck and snapped it forward onto Booley's blade as he broke past his defending winger and split the two defensemen, who tried to scramble back to clog the center, but they were too slow, and Booley accelerated even more, leaving all behind him. He swept in alone on goal, gave the keeper a couple of stick-and-head fakes, and shot the puck through the five hole to make the score 3–0 Trout Lake. Both teams changed personnel and within 30 seconds, Trout Lake scored again. East 4, West 0.

Next time out, Booley was attacked by his winger, but spun away from the confrontation. The Houghton wing drew two for roughing and lost the subsequent face-off.

Booley stole the puck from Houghton's center and broke in on goal all alone and this time cut straight across in front of the keeper, moving right to left, and lifted the puck over the opposing goalie as he slid to block the space in the net, East 5, West 0. The period was over. Two periods in the books, one to go.

The final period began quietly enough and Booley on his first shift on the ice took a pass, deked his defending winger, shot between the defense pair, and sent a stiff shot right on the ice just inside the right post. Instead of celebrating, he swerved and charged the winger who had tried to inveigle him into a fight earlier.

The fight began with Booley in his turtle, but in an instant changed as Booley wiggled loose, and then the other man was trying to cover up and Booley got in one monstrous punch that made the opponent go googly and slump to his knees. Officials had to peel Booley off his victim and help the dizzy Houghton man to the penalty box. Booley sat grinning in the penalty box while his teammates skated past him and saluted him by whacking their stick blades on the side boards.

Halfway through the period Booley corralled a loose puck off a defenseman's skate, took a couple of quick strides, and let loose a slapper that was past the goalie before he could react. East 7, West 0. Game over for all practical purposes.

Pro speed, heavy shot, resolute, fearless. This kid would be a star in college, an All-American for sure.

Two more fights in the game for Booley, and two more goals, a total of six fights, five goals, three assists. Good lord.

Booley's teammates swarmed him after the game and he led them around the ice with the U.P. Cup held high over his head.

No showers in the locker rooms. The team repaired to the tavern in Houghton and Booley was smothered with attention. Blydh drank alone. It was over an hour before Blydh got to talk to him.

"Six fights and you got in one punch? That's it? What the hell's the point of getting your ass kicked over and over? Your face looks like you got rubbed with an ice scraper."

"You never played, hey?"

"Played varsity three years at Colgate."

"The toothpaste company got a team?'

"The sixty-sixth oldest college in the United States," Blydh said, and immediately regretted his pride. Damn hubris.

"I only know the toothpasters," Booley said. "You ever have a fight?"

"No, we tried to stay *on* the ice, not in the penalty box."

"Then you didn't play. Ever afraid when you were on the ice?"

"Afraid of what?

"Getting' hurt, getting beat up, losing . . . looking bad, you know?"

"Not really."

"Like I said, Mister, you ain't played much, not really. See, in real hockey everybody's scared shitless all the time, you know? You've got to find a way to think and act as we, not me. That's why I fight."

"You're making no sense, son."

"I'm the street dog."

"What?"

"Street dog, shit disturber, agitator, rabble-rouser, provocateur. Period one, it was team against team, see, only I got into their big boy's head and then in the second period they put their fighting winger on me and they stopped thinking about winning the game because they all wanted to kick my ass. They all started coming after me, and it didn't matter because they couldn't get me and I just did what I always do, and let the boys take care of business."

Was this kid seriously (as in clinically) disturbed?

Booley asked, "How much they pay when you play that no-fighting college game?"

"They pay for your education, room, board, books, tuition. There's no salary, son. It's not professional hockey."

"They pay all that for four years, and she ain't professional, eh?"

"Legally it's not professional." Nothing wrong with the boy's brain.

Booley smiled and patted Blydh's shoulder. "They pay me here hundred fifty every game we win. Maybe someday I go college. Meanwhile, a man got make a good living while he can. Nobody gets to play this great game forever, eh?"

"But you only got in one punch."

Booley smiled. "I could win every fight easy enough, but what's the point? The boys need somebody to follow, see, a guy the other side hates, a guy who don't never back up or quit. What's that worth? One fifty a win this year, next year might land with club pay me two fifty easy."

Bodoni was drunk and grabbed Blydh as he tried to leave. Blydh had a train to catch in the morning. The big winger pinned his shoulders against the tavern wall and stood nodding and slobbering happily, finally managing to mumble, "Champions, wah. . . ."

Blydh conceded, "Champions for sure. Tell me something. How old is Booley, really?"

"Secret, don't like t'say when drunk," the winger slurred to the lawyer. "You guess."

"Nineteen, twenty?"

Bodoni grinned, sniggered, and pointed upward with a finger.

"Mid-twenties?"

Bodoni vigorously shook his head, smirked, and vigorously pointed straight up.

Keeping Secrets

Camelot "Cam" Wakes was the paper's star investigative reporter, full-time for the Detroit morning daily for twenty years and also freelancing for the *New Yorker*, *Rolling Stone*, and the other remaining serious money markets in the slickmagbiz. Wakes was a hot commodity in the words-for-sale game and found it easy to get published and have his newspaper pay subsidized. No whore to the buck, Wakes didn't jump on every story that floated past his considerable news nose. Wakes preferred to pick and choose his stories and his girlfriends.

What a fucked-up year 1995 had been. Wakes still couldn't wrap his head around the past year's sheer and vast weirdness. He remembered disparate things: American astronauts sponging off the Russian space station; religious eight balls launching a sarin gas attack on a Tokyo subway; and thousands of Rwandans hacking each other to death with machetes. A sick damn world to be sure.

In October, O. J. Simpson was found not guilty after an agonizing and overly reported über-expensive nine-month trial. An estimated 150 million Americans watched the verdict be read out on the TV and cheered or cursed and shook their heads.

The number-one song for the year was some rap crap called "Gangstas in Paradise," which some claimed was ripped off from bat-blind Stevie Wonder, the story went, who had scribbled something on a notepad, which some groupie asshole allegedly lifted and sold out of the back of a truck, or something like that. America, forget ethics or honor, was about business as usual, and money was the only economic fuel.

Something even stranger happened that year in December. Unseasonably heavy early snows closed down the Upper Peninsula of Michigan's Lake Superior coast. Wakes's phone rang too early one morning, and he knew it could only be Jaap "King David" Silver, aka K. D., a former editor of *Playboy, Esquire,* and *Atlantic Monthly, and* currently the features wallah at *Rolling Stone.*

"Yo, Motor City Yutz," Silver greeted Wakes.

"Fuck off, K. D., I'm busy."

"Doin' what, countin' baby Ford Broncos jumping fences? Mustangs fucking rams, wildcats fornicating with whatever passes for sexy out that way? You're not even out of the sack yet. Don't all you folks out there got cows to milk before breakfast?"

"What the hell do you *want*, K. D.?"

"You won't remember this, you being a snotnose kid and all, but decades ago the Feds charged Teamsters president Jimmy Hoffa with taking kickbacks. No surprise, right? A jury acquitted his ass, but on the last day of the trial he was accused of intimidating jurors. This brought new charges, a new trial, and *su-fricking-prise*, a fuck-you guilty verdict snugged up his ass with a sentence of up to eight years inside. I think that verdict is what the Lit types call symbolic or whatever. Not long thereafter they also nailed Jimmy Boy on mail fraud and this got him thirteen more years—this courtesy of the Feds, but Tricky Dick the Nixonoid pardoned Hoffa in 1971—after only four years of butt-buddying in Lewisburg."

"There a point to this tedious and cobweb-filled days-of-yore fairytale?"

"There was another asshole, name of John Smith, worked as a GM lawyer. He was a whistleblower on the pension fund-slash-mail fraud deal that put Hoffa into L-burg. Word is Hoffa didn't feel a lot of love for Smith and put out a contract on him."

"I'm going back to sleep," Wakes said.

"Get this," Silver continued, "Slick Willie, our *new* POTUS, wants to award Mr. Smith the Pee-Em-Oh-Eff, a very tony, swishy-swanky medal for civilian heroism, only nobody seems to know if the man's under dirt, or vertical, afoot, and alive."

"I don't know either," Wakes said.

"NBD, asshole. Here's the point: It . . . don't . . . fucking . . . *matter*. Get it? This gewgaw can be awarded posthumously and this so-called Presidential Medal of Freedom is a very big fucking deal, awarded to roughly one person in 20 million, the country's highest decoration for civilians," Silver said

"The US government has already looked and they couldn't find the asshole. They prefer to not be in the position of having to tell President Fast Willie that they've tried and up-fucked the pitbull. The Feds have a joke. Find Hoffa, find Smith. Har-har."

Wakes smiled. Jaap Silver was a card-carrying, full-metal-jacket, hair-on-fire liberal, like his close pal and latest boss, *Rolling Stone* founder Jann Wenner.

Wakes took a moment to mull. The country's new chief executive had crawled out of the slimy clay of Arkansas where he had been controversial as a governor—with an alleged insatiable predilection for the ladies, any and all, and apparently not so much his wife. Wakes had done a short piece on him after last year's election and the piece had drawn a lot of attention and not a little criticism. The hed on his piece read, "Perot knocks ball lose from GHWB's second term; Bubba recovers fumble and now what?"

Silver continued, "My employer and I would like very much for you to locate Mr. Smith, dead or alive. If alive, you will of course interview him. If dead, get a photograph of the remains and a death certificate, etc., and write a long shiny obit."

"I've got an employer, a beat, and plenty of other assignments."

"Dead or alive, this will be a cover story for *RS*, with, of course, commensurate remuneration, and even a bonus to double your check, our way of thanking you, once again, for doing the impossible."

"If I find him, you won't be able to say it's impossible."

"*Nit-picker*. First you have to find the man."

"How long do I have to make this weighty decision?"

"While I conclude smoking my one nicotine installment of the day," Silver said.

He had less than one minute. His reporter's interest for magazine jobs was solely in his wallet, but with no deadline to nail him down, it was tempting. "Previous articles?"

"Our morgue file has been copied and is in the mail as we speak, special delivery."

"Let me look through your stuff and get back to you."

"You fucker!" Silver said with a heavy sigh. "Bandit! You're already on the story!"

"I didn't say that."

"You don't have to. I *know* my people, their voices, their brains, how they think."

"I am not *your* anything," Wakes reminded him.

"Self-delusion is unbecoming of a great reporter," Silver said and hung up.

Bill Clinton wanted this? That fact alone fattened Wakes's interest in Mr. John Smith.

The phone rang: Jaap again. "My dear boy, my friend, my colleague, Mr. Smith made some *very* powerful, disagreeable, and unforgiving enemies."

"Like the Feds joke, he's probably with Hoffa, which is why the Feds can't find either of them. You know what my gut says, K. D.? They're both long dead, fully decomposed and past stinkerdom, decades into the dust-to-dusting process. Thirty years is a Kelvin-cold, cold trail."

━ ⌣ ━

As promised the file came, and Wakes learned Smith had been fifty-two in 1962, which would make him eighty-two-ish now. The reporter augmented the stuff from Silver with an expensive Lexis-Nexis multiple-subject search and dump to his *Free Press* office on Fort Street. He learned little off the newly spawning Internet, much ballyhooed among the young and early adopters, but to his thinking, not much more than an electronic toy.

Wakes learned that Smith hailed from Red Tape, West Virginia, and he quickly discovered it had been a real place and later a ghost town in coal-mining country. Smith went to high school in northern Wisconsin and worked for a logging company that operated in northern Wisconsin and all over Michigan's Upper Peninsula. He served in the infantry in the US Army in Korea at age twenty-five, got out in 1955, and went to law school at the University of Detroit. No valor awards, but Smith had a Combat Infantryman's Badge and an expert ribbon for marksmanship. He joined GM as a divisional personnel lawyer in Flint, but transferred at the end of his first year over to their corporate litigation office. Hmm.

Almost a year after Wakes began working the Smith story the reporter took some days off to hunt ducks in Tawas Bay on Michigan's so-called Sunrise Coast. After a day of hunting, he walked into the closest bar, where he overheard a conversation that forever changed his life.

One grizzled participant, purporting to be a retired game warden, informed his two companions that "The guy who busted Jimmy Hoffa's balls is living as a hermit in a remote U.P. swamp." He added, "For years game wardens, including me, been serving as Smitty's go-betweens with the outside world."

Smitty? Reporters developed certain skills not taught in journalism schools: how to read upside down or over somebody's shoulder, how to read lips, how to eavesdrop without seeming to, how to sort a single voice out of a social crowd in a public place. An intriguing eavesdrop to be sure, and probably beer-induced bullshit, but if you wanted to succeed long term as an investigative reporter, you developed an ear and sense for wheat vs. chaff. This obscure little tale had a wheaty scent wafting off it. Smitty? Geez. The final tidbit was that the hermit was somewhere in northern Schoolcraft County, near the Alger County line, a quite remote and daunting area.

There was a chance. Maybe this was just wishful thinking, but it didn't cost much to run down certain leads and this he classified as a lead while others might quickly write it off to gimlet gossip.

Everyone Wakes talked to, from Seney up to Grand Marais, seemed to have some sort of infectious lockjaw, which was typical of two things: U.P. denizens and, more importantly, people who knew something and were trying to paste over it with silence. He could smell the scent of a secret gasping for air.

Ten days after the duck hunt, reality and practicality forced him back up to Tawas, where he found the house of retired Conservation Officer Earl Marx, popping in on him with a no-notice visit.

Wakes didn't fool around. He told the man he was going to make the story public unless the man leveled with him and told him what he actually knew, not at some bullshit future date, but right-the-fuck now.

Wakes drove his own Jeep to the U.P. and on Earl Marx's directions, followed a spaghetti route of trails and two-tracks to a dilapidated house trailer set back along a small, clear stream that dumped into the headwaters of the (to some people) famous Fox River. Thirty of the nastiest-looking dogs he'd ever seen greeted his Jeep's approach. A dust devil of barking, snarling, whining curs followed him en masse to the door of the trailer. They never once tried to block him or bother him, but he nevertheless had the distinct feeling any diversion from going straight to the trailer might bring different reactions. The dogs were of all sizes, colors, shapes, and breed mixes, droolers, snarlers, whiners, barkers, silent ones, everything imaginable.

Wakes's research yielded only a single photograph of Smith. GM Personnel told him that the Feds had cleaned the company files of all evidence of Smith. Wakes had several times tried the Freedom of Information Act route, to no avail. FOIA had been passed in 1966 and here it was with Lib Democrat Bubba in the White House and extracting information, unclassified stuff, was still like pulling teeth from cockroaches.

The photo showed a slightly hunched-over slight-framed man with a tonsure of classic male-pattern baldness. Wakes found himself stammering when a short square-shouldered fellow with a massive mop of white hair came to the door and cracked it open, barked "Hush, you" to the dogs, and got instant compliance. The man had a beard, long, wiry, and squared tit-to-tit across his chest like Moses himself. His eyes were old and a bit rheumy, but as intense and alert as a kid's. His movements were a bit jerky, but Wakes had a feeling the motion thing was partly for show. At first the reporter put it down to nerves and fear of being discovered after so long—a stranger showing up unannounced and brazenly calling him by name.

"Mr. Smith, I'm a reporter with the Detroit *Free Press*. There are a lot of people wondering if you're okay. More to the point, they wonder if you're alive."

The man looked Wakes up and down, obviously trying to decide his next move.

Wakes added, "Marx gave me directions. He didn't want to, but I had a job to do, and when I muscled him, he told me where to find you. He cares a whole lot about you."

"How *is* Earl?"

Just like that, admission of identity. "Getting long in the tooth, but he's alive and kicking down in East Tawas."

"Mmm," Smith said and smiled, opened the door, and held it open. "I know where Earl is. He got word to me you were likely to show up in my swamp. You'd better come inside. The skeets out here are cannibals."

There was a small circular table with two chairs, a half-dozen dogs of indeterminate parentage boiling nervously around his legs and all of them keeping an eye on their alpha. Wakes also noticed an uncased rifle standing in every corner, and several semiautomatic pistols and revolvers (all loaded, he guessed) on counters and shelves. The reporter sat down and tried to ignore the dogs sniffing at him. Eventually they withdrew and lay down to watch the stranger.

"Call me Smitty," the trailer man told his uninvited visitor. "By the way, that's my real name and isn't that rich? Everybody thought it was an alias the government gave me, the stoolie with the plain John Smith handle. This country is beset by its own ignorance, I wish I knew why. I was born John Smith and over time I changed it to Jon, Johannes, and Jahn, but it never mattered a damn bit what my first name was, because everyone called me Smitty. I moved out here to the swamp partly to be shed of useless crap: schools, city councils, corporate boards, company politics, union crap, neighbors, hell, even families are fouled-up messes these days. If someone had been able to describe me in one word I guess fair or blunt would do the job."

"That's two words," Wakes pointed out.

"I said 'or,'" Smith corrected him. "Don't be confused by my humble surroundings. I was a lawyer . . . a damn good one. You need to listen in your job, son, not play the nitpicker with the eyeshade counting meaningless beans. Are you a dog for details, son?"

"No more than the next man."

"Get this straight. I'm no fan of what you call the next man, and by that I mean the so-called average Joe. What's your name? I know you said it, but it seems to have flown on by."

"Cam, Cam Wakes, Detroit *Free Press*."

"I see," Smith said. "Mr. Wakes, papers aren't political parties, or their mouthpieces, though some like to think they are. We ever get to the point where one paper's a puppet for labor and the next one for management, we will all be royally screwed, blued, and duly tattooed as a country. Only thing keeps the bums in power honest are stubborn honest reporters running around with their own agendas and big noses. You got a big nose, do you?"

"I'm here," Wakes said.

Smith smiled. "Indeed you are. There's no such thing as an organizational news slant." Wakes said, "The reporter's only test is news, whether technically it is or isn't. . . ."

". . . You think I'm news?"

"You are."

"Seems to me you need to get out of your newsroom and spend more time circulating in the real world."

"I don't work in a newsroom. I'm an investigational guy, and I stay out of the building as much as possible."

"Wakes, huh? Why am I news?"

"You've been missing for years. Hoffa's gone and nobody knows where. The auto industry had to be bailed out by taxpayers. The Russians are a third-world country. There's no need for you to live up here like this."

"Hoffa was a giant story and still is," the reporter went on.

"People sure don't have much taste in such stuff," Smith replied. "Jimmy? He hated the spotlight, you know?"

Wakes didn't know and felt this was the time to go easy on talking more.

Smith asked, "Why would you care how I live?"

"I *don't*. You testified against the Teamsters, and that started Hoffa's downfall. It took guts and that alone makes you a real-life hero, something we are way short on these days. Your living like this just makes you eccentric."

Smitty grinned crookedly. "And look where all that got me."

"My morgue research shows you had your own plane, that you're a licensed pilot."

"Still got that bird, but I doubt the engine will even turn over. Isn't the morgue for dead things? Near as I can tell, I haven't yet joined the lengthening list of lates."

"Sorry, morgue's a newspaper term, an unfortunate one. It dates back to the nineteenth century. It's our repository of old stories, previously published stuff, even reporter notes from some old and important stories. You don't fly anymore?"

"In my head sometimes, but not through the air in an airplane."

"Your plane's hangared somewhere?"

"Why, you looking for a bargain buy?"

"No sir, I'm only interested in getting all the facts. So it's in a hangar?"

Smith smiled. "Might say that, only not in one piece. I chopped it up into parts that serve me now in other ways, not stuff that serves me only when I need it to fly. Kind of like taking your deer to the processor to get it all cut up for the freezer and the year ahead."

What was Smith talking about? And where was West Virginia in the man's accent? Wakes prided himself on his ability to quickly identify where people hailed from, but Smith was giving no hints.

"Except in my head, I guess it's not an actual airplane anymore," Smith said. "Was once a Beechcraft Bonanza I bought thirdhand and pretty cheap, all things considered. Twin-engine job, had real pep off the ground and she was real easy to fly. Had lots of cables and wires and components, metal wires, sheet aluminum, a six-passenger cabin sweet as home sweet home. I just couldn't bear to part with that cabin, and that's the truth."

"You kept it?"

"Don't strain your eyes trying to find it. It's not where the likes of you will ever see it."

The man seemed wound up. "I don't mean to offend you with my questions."

"No offense taken, but if you don't have half the sauce I once had, all your snooping around will take you nowhere. Me, I got lots of juice left. I may be edging into the cult of catnappers, but that doesn't make me dead, not yet. You've got business with me, let's get down to it and move on. Anybody sits too long in the same place risks getting run over—or blood clots."

Wakes had trouble concentrating when one of the dogs would stand, walk over, and stare at him. The stink on the animals was almost noxious and several of the nappers were snoring and whining with dreams. Surreal. How would he write this? Focus on facts, not your senses.

"You were in GM's legal department."

"The suits called me 'the experiment.' When they transferred me over to the Litigation Department, I was a lawyer in name and license only. Most of my time I had spent jawing with and at unions, speaking to them in a language they could understand, and I got along good with most of them. I saved GM shareholders a heap of money. Fred Lee Klein, our corporate attorney, noticed my contracts not only always got signed, but were always on time, and he called me in one day and asked me to help his Ivy League contract negotiators and litigators learn things I picked up in dealing with unions. I knew how to talk plain to the union's biggest pricks."

"Including Hoffa?"

"Not until later—a couple of years after I joined Litigation, Klein called me in, stuck an illegal Cuban cigar in my mouth, and said, 'Get that S.O.B. Hoffa and his truck drivers out of our business.' Turned out I got on just fine with Jimmy. He was a rough-edged odd duck to be sure, but once he understood you couldn't be pushed or intimidated, he was okay. Over time I worked all sorts of our unions' financial books and then I began looking at our pension stuff and the union's pension stuff too and I saw how fucked up the whole thing had become. I don't know what Hoffa was thinking, and I told him so and he wasn't happy with me, but he was the kind of guy didn't make or take business personally. Over time I learned that he let the mob have access to Teamster pension money and the bent-noses took Hoffa's guys' money and stashed it all over the place."

"You were that close to Hoffa."

"*Nobody* got that close to Jimmy. We talked, had drinks sometimes, a cigar, played a few rounds of golf at Oakland Hills. Not great friends, but business-professional associates. Why am I telling you this? This was all in the papers. Walter Cronkite talked about it, praised the work I did."

Wakes was trying to figure out what Smith was thinking, spouting off like this, and talking so loudly. Was he going deaf?

"After I left, Personnel took the scalpel to the department and renamed it human resources. You can always tell there's shit afloat when they put the flensing knife to the language. You know what a flensing knife is, Wakes?"

"Not exactly."

"Trappers use them for skinning. Got a thin, a razor-sharp edge. Buffalo hiders were good with them, and lawyers and attorneys use them to squeeze all the fat and extraneous words and meanings out of contracts and such. GM dumped 'personnel' because it was too impersonal and then they commenced to ship tens of thousands of jobs out of the country—all to improve shareholder returns. And to hell with human life, families, communities, all that baloney. People went from assets to expenses and out came the accountants' flensing knives. In my day we hired damn good people and hung on to them and got our money back many times over with their loyalty. Win-win, see? That feeling's all gone, erased by eyeshades. Everything's all gone."

"When did you move up here full-time?" Wakes asked the old man.

"August of 1975."

"The company approved your move?"

"None of their damn business. After the Feds got Jimmy, I didn't have much to do, but people were making noises, and the Feds were telling me they couldn't protect me forever. I got a permit to carry concealed and Klein called me in and told me I couldn't have a firearm on company property, and I told him his bodyguards in suits were carrying and he got hot and said, 'You're not security, Smith.'

"I said, 'You're right, Klein, I'm not anything,' and I quit.

"'How will we protect you?' Klein asked me.

"'*You* protect me? From whom? Hoffa's not *my* enemy.'

"'Well," he said, "we're not wasting any more company resources protecting you. I hope you know how to dig yourself in."

Smith continued. "After I retired, the Feds came to see me and made it clear there was a contract on me, though they weren't exactly sure who was issuing or holding. I told them go take a flying fuck, converted everything I had to cash, bought the Bonanza used, found this property, had the trailer towed here from Manistique, did all my deals for cold cash, not a damn link on the books, anywhere. The locals have been good to me. Most of them hate Lansing and Washington, D. C. equally. I pay my property tax through a local, who appears on paper to own the property. I've got no mailbox, no traceable phone. I don't exist, except to the dogs."

"You sure own a lot of them."

"I don't own them, not a single one. They hang with me. Nobody owns dogs, just like nobody owns a person. Some stay here all the time. Others stop on their way through, and come back every year or so."

"Your game warden friends and dogs, that's your security these days?"

Smith smiled. "A real man takes care of himself and doesn't have to depend on others. Any shit lands here, I've got a hundred ways out, even if there's ten feet of fresh snow on the ground. I've tested all the routes, at all times of year, night and day, in all kinds of weather."

"You feel pretty secure?"

"There are no absolutes, but I've got a hundred firearms and ammo, gear and food, which can hold me a year, all in caches. I can bug out from here and never look back."

"There's no reason to live this way anymore, Smitty. You can come out now. It's all over. People want to meet you and thank you. The new president wants to decorate you with a medal."

"I don't much care about tin and ribbon and I choose to live how I live, Wakes. Free country and all that, right? I got my own reasons the public ain't got a right to know. You go to good schools, son?"

"Good enough."

"Book-learning isn't life, Wakes, and real life's so-called games don't ever end."

"This isn't real life," Wakes told the man.

"There's all sorts of life on this puny planet, living every imaginable kind of existence and many of them in places smart folks are certain can't possibly support life, and yet they do. It's about finding your niche and sticking to it. There's no story in Smitty, Mr. Wakes. I'd allow there mighta been a small one once, but that was a long time ago, and if you write something about me being here, I'm sure as heck gonna be overrun by kooks and the curious just looking to shoot the breeze so they can brag to folks they were here. Nothing good comes from getting your name in the paper. Celebrity's a death knell for folks like me. It's up to you what you do with this," Smith said. "I don't like putting the burden on you, but welcome to my world."

Wakes knew there was a story. Not just the obvious one but something more, and he couldn't get a line on it.

"Where you parked?" the man asked.

"Top of the hill to the north."

"Good place, can be a bitch to get back up that hill."

"Will the dogs give me any trouble on the way out?"

"I neither read dog minds nor speak dog," Smith said, with a grin. "They won't be a problem, just as long as you head straight to your vehicle."

"Thanks for your time, Smitty."

"Liked meeting you, Wakes. You've got depth and a heart. I can feel it."

———

Three years later Wakes got a phone call from Earl Marx. "Smitty's dead, thought you'd want to know."

"When and how?"

"Not sure. Eck Filoret wants you to come up and talk."

Eck Filoret was the current conservation officer in Grand Marais, one of the tiniest men Wakes had ever met, especially for such a physical job. Size aside, Earl Marx called the man a giant.

Filoret lived in a cabin off a bad dirt road that ran 15 miles east to Deer Park from Grand Marais. Wakes talked to the game warden on the phone and made arrangements to meet him at his house.

They drank coffee, "How'd Smitty die and when?"

"Won't know till we fetch the body and the M.E. does an autopsy."

"You haven't seen him?"

"A trapper found his camp door open. This was three weeks back, but it's damn near impossible to get back there and we've had one big-muscle snow dump after snow dump since. I think we can run my snow machine back on the two tracks and get the rest of the way on snowshoes if we have to. You got your own?"

"Nope."

"No matter, I've got plenty. We'll get you set up. Smitty thought you were a good fella, appreciated what you did for him, keeping your mouth shut. Hope you have a strong stomach. This is likely to be real messy and not everybody's made for such work."

"I barely knew Smitty, met him just once. This gets too nasty, I can always walk away," Wakes said. "Is the county medical examiner going with us?"

"This isn't Below the Bridge," the game warden said. "We have to be more informal and more efficient up here. Most agencies and outfits up here know how to cooperate and share, and I'm empowered to declare death for the official record and legal paper trail. Smitty said you walked right through his dogs. That nerve impressed hell out of him."

"Had to eighty-six those skivvies later."

Filoret laughed.

The machine was not the snowmobile Wakes expected. Instead it was an awkward-looking, high-cabbed, tracked vehicle, like an anorexic tank. Filoret said, "Brand's Dallee Sneaker, my White Dirt tank. Can be real helpful, got heated cab and the whole deal."

"You and your guys were Smitty's lifeline."

"Much as any man can be for another. Smitty was paranoid and getting worse every day."

"But there was no reason for the paranoia."

Filoret looked back. "You think?"

Wakes said, "Did he tell you about all his guns, his caches, his escape routes, and all that?"

"Tell me? Hell, he ran me through some of the routes to check them. Saw one cache with automatic rifles, not semi, but full-dance auto. No idea where he got all that crap, but we've got more than our share of gun nuts and collectors up here in the boonies."

"You never told BATF about the automatics?"

The game warden grinned. "Nah, Smitty wasn't gonna start a revolution or anything like that."

"How long to get to his place?"

"In this rig? Three mph on even gravel or snow. With this snow's depth we're talking a full day if we're lucky. If we can't get there, I've got keys to several camps out in that country. We'll be fine. Eventually we'll get to him."

"You make this sound routine."

"It's not. Nothing about Smitty has ever been routine."

"Let me get something straight," Wakes said to the game warden. "Am I on this trip officially or unofficially?"

"I guess that's up to you. Smitty told me if anything happened to him to be sure to call you."

"Photos, free to publish?"

The game warden shrugged. "Makes no difference to me. Smitty's dead."

"That Lansing's view too?"

"Lansing doesn't know anything about any of this, just us few game wardens who've worked this area. Not even the other guys and gals in our district know. Loose lips and all that, right?"

They spent almost all day on the Sneaker and plunged slowly through deep sloping snowdrifts into the man's camp after a two-hour nap, coffee, and sausages in a cabin six miles from the dead man's trailer.

First thing the two men noticed when they came down the hill to the trailer site, no dogs. And thick winter silence, the kind that swallowed men. The game warden offered Wakes a Colt .357, grip-first, and said, "Don't see any dogs now, but with Smitty dead they'll have gone feral. It happens fast, that going feral business. Nobody can predict a feral dog."

Wakes took the handgun and let Filoret lead the way. The early morning sky was dull-gray, the sun behind heavy clouds, but despite the thick overcast, there were bizarre purplish-blue streaks on the snow. Filoret saw them and said, "Stains from shadows," and laughed.

The door to the trailer was open and a snowdrift blocking the way. Inside there were little dog canyons winding around like a labryrinth.

The game warden pushed inside and popped right back out, looking peaked. "No need for you to look. Wasn't my job, I sure as hell wouldn't."

"It's my job too," Wakes told him. "Any indications of violence?"

"Plenty, but is it foul play or just violence? Death can sometimes get violent and messy all on its own. I can declare him dead and take lots of pictures of the remains, but the M.E. will have to figure out the science side."

"What if it's a crime site?" Wakes asked.

The CO handed the reporter his flashlight. "You tell me."

The dead man was on his back, naked, his arms folded, hands and forearms deep blue, almost black. He was clean shaven, at least on that part of the face that remained. The dogs had been at him.

Filoret was right on Wakes's shoulder and prompted, "See the face."

"What there is. Dogs, right?"

"Dogs indeed. Wolves wouldn't come inside."

"His dogs?"

"Always claimed he didn't own them."

"He told me that too," Wakes said. "I don't see blood."

"It's here, somewhere below, frozen. I'll make sure we get samples for the ME."

"He didn't have to die like this," Wakes said.

"Who?" Filoret asked.

"Smith."

"You think this is *suicide*? What do *you* think?" Filoret asked.

"I'm a writer, not a med-tech or cop. You think Smitty killed himself?"

"Smitty? No quit in that man."

"This guy's shaved."

Filoret said, "Yeah, I noticed that too." He squeezed past Wakes and went to work getting the remains into a black Kevlar body bag.

They spent all day at the site, brewed tea over a fire they made on a flat log, ate sandwiches, and eventually loaded the remains on the Sneaker's trailer. And not a single dog.

They took a route that let them see the Fox River from time to time. "He shaved?" Wakes said to his companion as they agonizingly bumped their way northward. Why shave?

"No more need for all the beard, I guess," the game warden said. "Go figure."

"Eck," Wakes said, "Smitty was bald. The guy in the bag behind us isn't."

The game warden stared straight ahead.

"I only met Smitty once," Wakes said. "But I don't think that's him in the bag."

"DNA will tell all," Eck Filoret said. "Always does." The game warden lit a cigarette, offered the pack to his passenger, who took one and lit it. "If it ain't Smitty, who then?"

"Beats hell out of me."

"Guess that's the M.E.'s question to answer. Looks like there's plenty of teeth. Only thing is, our M.E. isn't all that competent or dedicated, and he used to fish for brook trout out here all the time."

Wakes weighed what he was hearing. "He and Smitty were pals?"

"Could say that. Most likely the M.E. will make an assumption based on where we found the body. That logic seems clear, doesn't it?"

Wakes nodded and said no more. He knew they were not retrieving Smitty's body.

"How's someone end up way the hell out here with Smitty?"

"*You* came out here."

"Not in winter I didn't. You want to stop the Sneaker? Let's take a look."

Filoret did as asked. They opened the body bag, shone their lights, poked around. Wakes suddenly understood. He dug in his pack and pulled out two photos, one of Smitty.

The game warden lit another cigarette and exhaled after a deep puff. "Nope, not Smitty. Gotta agree."

Wakes showed him the second photo. "Look at those cheekbones."

"Son of a bitch," Filoret said. "Sort of poetic, ain't it, America's two most famous missing men not missing at all, least of all to each other. You gonna write this?"

Wakes shurugged. "Who'd believe it? You gonna say the other name out loud?"

"No fucking way. Not under penalty of death. This has been my albatross for decades and now it's done, game over, no more babysitting."

Wakes said, "His middle name was Riddle, did you know that?"

"It's on his sheet."

"This a federal deal?"

"Seems like. They milked both of them like farmed snakes over the years. Smitty helped him and them. He was their go-between."

Wakes wrote a moving obituary and eulogy for the late John Smith. *Rolling Stone* ran it as a cover and paid a nice bonus.

Only one name got mentioned. The other name died in the snow.

⬤～⌣

Life went on, and once Wakes heard from the doctors his own time was finishing, he hoped he'd run into Smitty on the other side, even though he knew it wasn't Smitty who died in his trailer. Wakes told his wife, Siggy, to put a single word on his gravestone: "Secret Keeper."

"That's two words, she said.

"So hyphenate it." Everybody was a damn copy editor.

"You going to share your secret with me?" Siggy asked her husband.

"What, and ruin my inscription?"

Win-Win

Fort Des Roches thought the lumbering Dr. Pat Pathanos of Nephrology LLC showed the herky-jerkyness of motion and conversation of a tin robot. Pathanos was invariably mechanical and unimpaired by human emotion. He reaped, what some speculated and others insisted, a fat six or seven figures yearly. He never worked in the glitzy snip-snip world of cosmetic surgery. His wealth came from the mass transplantation of life-preserving kidneys, swapping out dying slabs of gray meat for the almost-fresh viscera of the barely dead. Fort Des Roches knew the doctor only from a distance, which is to say not at all. They would nod at each other at Little League games, if the doc happened to be there, which he rarely was.

The surgeon's wife, Aksinya, claimed to be fluent in eleven languages. Her English, near as Des Roches could tell, was not one of them. In reality, few folks could understand a word the woman said. Partly it was her rapid rate of delivery, words pouring out of her like enriched uranium twenty mike-mike rounds from a Warthog's cannons. Her words came so fast they sometimes sounded like a flyover by a 20,000-pound hummingbird.

Fort regularly saw the woman at the Marquette Little League fields, or got emails from her announcing his time for "Sweets Doody," by which she meant it was his turn to sell candy at the concession stand, to raise money for new uniforms, team equipment, and field maintenance.

The Little League complex had begun life as a series of livestock pastures and the volunteer ground-keeping committee back then had sworn to make their playing fields shining examples for other leagues. Though most of the original developers were now dead or homebound, their field committee inheritors continued to claim the fields had not come far enough from their crude natal condition. Unadulterated bullshit, Fort knew, but striving for grass excellence continued to take the lion's share of the league's funds.

The current fields certainly didn't look like pastures. Ford knew: He had played his high school football on a converted pasture, where cow and horse patties had a nasty way of announcing themselves as they plugged one's helmet ear hole, or face mask. When he and his fellow Bulldogs announced they were going to make the visiting team eat shit, it wasn't idle talk.

By contrast the kids here played on putting-green grass and the magicians who had converted the pastures to such lushness seemed to resent the kids daring to trod on them at all.

Negative thoughts of the field keepers were not meant to demean either the league or Aksinya, whom he saw sitting alone on a yellow and red Mickey D drink cooler, smoking a long thin grayish cigarette. Fort's first notion was to avoid her, but this felt unneighborly, and what was this town and him, if not friendly and welcoming to all?

Aksinya *alone*? This was preternatural, almost unimaginable. The tiny and quite attractive Russian woman insisted people call her Ya in order to spare them embarrassment in trying to pronounce her given Russian name, which as Fort had heard it from others, had been her great-great something or another's relation from before the revolution (which one not specified) and a patronymic as long as a snow scoop handle. He didn't really want to talk to her, but finally decided he had no choice. *Why avoid her, Fort? You hardly know the woman, and she's always there for the kids.*

Usually she was surrounded by others, but with her doing almost all of the talking and gesturing, overwhelming all listeners, no matter how badly outnumbered she might seem to be. Fort guessed she could single-handedly kowtow a full house at Michigan Stadium into mass mutism. Life presented few dramatic decisions and stopping to disturb a quiet in the presence of Ya, if not a comfortable stop on the way to the top of the hill that was his problem, was surely a safe place to pause.

Why was it so unsettling to find her alone? The cigarette in her left hand had an ash that hung down like a congenital, dysfunctional sixth finger. The look on her face suggested that she was drifting somewhere between gobsmacked and inadequate R.E.M. sleep, her lids opening and closing slowly like a lizard's trying to catch the last shavings of a day's dying sun.

"Everything okay, Ya?"

The woman's dark eyes rolled slowly up to look at him. "Ya, Ya is excellent, Ya is good, ya, she is."

"Well, I'm sorry to intrude into your privacy but you do look a bit in."

"It is Pat," she said, not in her usual light-speed gibbershite, but in astonishingly clear, concise precisely enunciated English, all in a simple and succinct declaratory sentence.

Fort thought, so she *can* do commendable English when she chooses to take her time.

"He is ruined, you see. We are ruined. Ya is ruined," all these words said in an even, emotionless voice that hit the precise subtext of the words she chose.

"What's the problem? An accident, a malpractice suit, something like that?"

The surgeon's wife pressed the back of her hand to her mouth. "There is also an accident, malpractice this is so? Tell Ya, please. Ya *must* know this."

She seemed to have been taken off guard by what Fort considered a pretty bland question.

Aksinya sighed, her shoulders slumped, and her voice turned a low grumble. "Is it that we have too much, or perhaps it is people such as you who have not enough?" she asked. "We work hard for everything we have make into accumulations. Ya's dear husband does ten kidneys a day, day in, and day out. There is no time or place for personal time in life and death matters, so yes, we are well compensated with little chance to enjoy the fruits of our labor. Accident or malpractice?" She curled her lip with vulpine precision. "What do you mean, please. Ya is not hearing of these things before."

"Pat has a problem?" he ventured in an attempt to redirect.

"Yes, it is the bloody diagnostic criteria board that rules this country, those heathen bureaucrats in Washington. They are Soviets reborn, apparatchiki, you see, no hearts, no minds of their own, only orders to follow . . ." she said, standing up and lighting another cigarette.

"Got an extra?" Fort asked. "And yes, I am highly suggestible." He said, "I'll pay you a dime."

Ya frowned. "One cannot purchase even a small sweet with a dime," the surgeon's wife scolded. "Cigarettes of this flavor are now nine dollars a pack at the Eleven and Seven. You will to give me one dollar for one, please, which is quite fair as I profit not from this sale."

Profit not? With 20 smokes in a $9 pack, the cost of a single smoke would be 45 cents, which meant she was pocketing 55 cents off the one-butt sale. He almost hesitated on some kind of unarticulated principle he couldn't clarify into words. He forked over the buck and lit up. He then pulled his own yellow and red barrel over closer to hers and sat down, and there on their perches they inhaled and exhaled in unison, saying nothing, avoiding even looking at each other.

The woman broke the moment with an uneasy giggle.

"What?" he asked.

"Ya is thinking like the good-sex times when the two bodies are in complete harmony and precise timing. Ya push, he push, Ya push, and so on and up the curve of energy we make travel together, like that, yes? It is nice, Ya thinks. Yes?"

He could do no more than nod faintly. Where was *this* going?

She turned and looked him in the eye. "Does your spouse, very sorry, Ya forget her name, does she make with you most satisfying sex?"

"I'm a widower," he said. "No wife at the moment. Just the kids."

"Ah, poor man. Ya forgets your name as well. All this concern for Ya's husband stifles all competing thought. Ya is normally clearheaded in the face of all challenges."

Des Roches said, "I'm called Fort."

"Like the automobile?"

"No, like Fort Drum."

She made a sour face. "No, Ya does not know this Fort Drum. These were your progenitors?"

"No, my family name is De Roches."

She nodded. "This means rocks in French. You Americans are such a mongrel people with your naming conventions."

"Yes," he said, "Fort De Roches, that's my name."

"And your wife is deceased, leaving you how many progeny, and why are you not married again for their sake? The normal development of children necessitates two parents, you must know. The literature on this is massive, the conclusions unanimous."

"I've not yet met the right woman," he offered.

"Beggars, you know . . .," she said.

"I'm not in a hurry, the kids and I are fine."

"You cannot possible know this for certain for many years to come. This is like hitting a *yakyu*, sorry," she giggled, "you say baseball, and waiting ten years to know if it is caught or a hit."

"Well, it seems fine for now. The kids and I are good to go."

"Appearances deceive," the woman said. "Look at Ya's happy-go-lucky Pathanos."

Pat might be many things, but happy-go-lucky was not a quality Fort would *ever* attribute to the surgeon. Morose and weary, yes.

"It is off-season for baseball," Ya said. "Why are you here? There are no games, no practices, no work in concession stand."

"Same as you maybe, just looking for a quiet place where I can think."

"Ya should have your problems and you Ya's," she said, exhaling a faint smoky blue racer.

"All right," Fort said. "Done. Sure, why not?"

She stared at him. "Yours first, please."

"Our neighbor next door. He is always on a rant, scaring half the neighborhood's adults, and he screams and shakes his fists at everyone, even the kids. The dogs hate him, the mail carriers won't go up to the house, FedEx and UPS leave packages on his sidewalk rather than deal with him face-to-face."

"Have you express your concerns to this individual?"

"He drinks heavily all day, every day."

"Have you confronted him? Ya thinks it is barbaric to scream at children."

"That's what I came here to think about. I don't want to start a neighborhood war over this. It's not that serious a thing. More like annoying. I'm sure he's a regular guy. He just has a lousy attitude."

"I see," Aksinya said. "You seek a diplomatic solution, to coexist peacefully with your enemy the way the Vichy French arranged with their Nazi invaders? The way Stalin sought peace with the evil Hitler?"

France? Stalin and Hitler? Good grief. "No, *nothing* like that. This is just a neighborhood issue, a minor irritant, nothing more." Her assessment should have been a red flag for him, but he was too astonished to think clearly, and then her very shapely, extremely long right leg came over to his leg for a perch. She said, "Have another cigarette, Mr. Fort, this time and only for you, 60 cents."

She was still making a nickel profit. He gave her another dollar bill and she gave him a cigarette, but no change. "Consider the change a tip," Fort told her.

She pushed at his knee with her foot. "Rub please, Mr. Fort?"

The surgeon's wife pronounced his name "fart." Which made him want to smile.

"Which part?" he asked.

"Any, all. Ya concentrates better when Ya is being actively stroked. Do you recall this feeling from your dead wife?"

Yes, no. "I guess?" he ventured.

"Ya finds herself strangely attracted to you, my dear Mr. Fort, may I say that or shall you be offended?"

"No offense taken," he said. "But let's get back to your problem, your husband's problem," he said, rubbing her ankle and starting up her calf.

"It is this way, you see, the government had arbitrarily changed diagnostic criteria. Forever, surgeons have checked a certain box on the state insurance form, and presto, the transplant is instantly and magically approved. It was so automatic that surgeon can check the box and schedule the surgery simultaneously, very efficient, an exquisite paper production line. Surgeons in other specialties were quite envious."

"And now?"

"This special box no longer exists. Thousands of kidneys exchanged under that one box over all these years and poof, no more box, no more transplants, no more kidneys." She looked over at Fort. "The government is of the misguided opinion that too many kidneys are being transplanted. They want to retard the practice, which they do without talking to surgeons or patients. It is tsarist in its unilateral expediency. They think only in fiscal terms, these people from the *apparat*. The result is that Ya has never seen her husband in such a frame of mind.

"Keep rubbing," she said. Not a request.

There were things about life that Fort personally found daunting, one of which was to think you were starting down one path, only to discover almost immediately that you were not at all on the path you thought you were on, and worse, there was no obvious turnaround to retreat, or to get around and continue safely forward. Fort found such phenomena in life quite disconcerting, to wit, this moment.

"Pat seems to have control of the matter," Fort offered.

"In appearance only. You see, Ya must dole to him her magic in small portions, and at great cost to Ya, a factor he does not recognize. The reality is that if Ya allowed him all he wanted—and at his will, how would we live? Someone must assume the onerous responsibility for income generation."

What? Wasn't Pat the one bringing in the dough? Fort decided that nice as her leg was, and good as the cigarettes were, he had had enough. He decided to steer the conversation in a new direction, toward deeper, safer water. Every sailor knew deep water was safety and the ragged rocks along shore sure disaster. "What diseases are most likely to cause kidney failure?" he asked.

The question levitated between them and she cocked her head. "What business are you in, my dear Mr. Fort?"

"I'm a poet, a teacher at the community college."

She said, "Diabetes, of course."

"Diabetes always leads to a transplant?"

"Of course not, but often, it depends on the patient, age of onset, type, severity of disease, symptoms presented, many factors."

"Can Pat just check off the box for diabetes without assigning a severity level?"

"Faster," she said, pumping her leg against his hand. "Diabetes, of course, yes!" Her entire body lifted off the plastic cooler and literally bucked and arched as she fell forward against him, and he had to grab her to keep her from knocking him off his cooler.

"You are *genius*, dear Mr. Fort," she whispered from somewhere in the vicinity of his shoulder. "Diabetes, *of course*. Why did we not think of this, the power of the naïve to solve complex problems? You see, this is *pure* genius." Her chest was heaving. "So obvious, yet neither Pat nor Ya could see the truth and there you have shown us the way."

"Are you okay?" he asked, helping her stand.

"Far more than pedestrian and mere okay," she said. "Thank you, dear Fort, and as for your problem, it will be taken care of."

"I don't understand."

"You have no need to understand the method, only the result to come. The strategy in such things is planned deniability."

"I think I could use another cigarette," he told her. He was taken aback to learn that the price had returned to a dollar.

Ya dug in her purse and Fort thought he saw her shudder.

What did one make of such an encounter? Fort had no idea, despite having the kind of orderly mind that liked lists and names for things. "Not even a hint vis-à-vis the neighbor problem?"

Ya looked at him. "Have you ever taken a good look at my husband?"

"No," he said. This was not quite true. Pat was one unhealthily ugly and apelike creature.

"He was stevedore before medical school, truly a *khishchnik*, this word means beast in Russian, and I think this was Ya's Pat by all definitions and measures."

"Pat's going to take care of my problem?" This was disturbing. "I didn't mean for you or him . . ."

"Yes, of course, but there must be a *quid pro quo*. You took care of ours. Now we shall take care of yours."

"Your problem, or his problem?" Fort asked, confused, and wanting this conversation to be over.

She laughed. "His, Ya's, they are same, *da*? This is the Russian way, you see. Better a hundred friends than hundred rubles."

"We're not in Russia," Fort reminded her.

She grinned. "We are closer than you think, dear Fort." She sat down and put her other leg on his leg. "Please?"

A week later Fort came home from the grocery store to an enthusiastic hug from his eldest, seven-year-old daughter Marny, whom he had always called Junior.

"Dad, dad, a meat wagon just hauled off Mr. Prinkipyle on one of those wheelie stretcher doodaddy thingeys."

"What happened?"

"Shelley Rubick says somebody gave Mr. Prinkipyle a big-league butt-kicking. One of the ambulance dudes said it's so bad they're going to have to take out one of Prinkipyle's morgans."

Shelley Rubick lived next door to Prinkipyle. "You mean an organ," he corrected his daughter. She was precocious if not precise.

"His kidney, I think," Junior said. "What's a kidney, Dad?"

Alone Mostly, Not Entirely

THE THING ABOUT FLYING WAS THAT NOBODY BUT THE PILOT REALLY knew what the hell was going on, especially in a B-17, especially if you're the tail gunner, the sucker wedged into the ass end. It's just a stupid routine training mission, for Christ's sake! Geez, we whipped the damn Krauts in the Big War and now we gotta go back and do it again? What a frigging world this is.

Carlo-Giuseppi (Cee-Gee) Faffenborgia was disgusted, afraid, angry, and seriously confused. Worse, he was in the middle of a combat training flight, when suddenly it looked like the only people about to die were him and his own damn crew. Fuckin' Bob, now where the fuck was the justice in this *shit*? What's our damn altitude? One fricking intercom call, and nobody's said shit since. Punk pilot told us there's an engine fire in number three, voice like a farmer with a straw hanging off his bottom lip. Like hey fellows, we cannot seem to tune in the dad-blamed ball game today. *Dad-blamed*? Damn hick. No fricking emotion is this guy. Same tone, engine on fire, no baseball on the radio, no difference?

So we're in or about to be in the shit, and what does the damn pilot give us? Freaking silence. The hick's gone mute. Emergency sort of declared lazily, and then, nothing more, not a word. Silence from forward and above. Okay we get it, this shit happens in mechanical junk heaps built by the lowest bidder, but pilots got ways to deal with such shit, right? That's what those assholes are taught to do, why they get to call the shots, little pimpled gods swaggering around, bragging like they actually control fate. Bullshit! The rest of us depend on those stupid looeys, and what do we get? Information? Encouragement? Anything? Bupkes. Fuckin' Bob. Asshole haunts this crew. Jesus Moses Mary.

Heard the damn alarm bell warning: Prepare to bail out. No question it was the alarm signal. *Heard it for sure.* Since then? Nothing. Where's the execute signal? Whole plane is quiet as a whore's church on Sunday morning. No final bell, no decision bell, no get-the-hell-out-of-this-piece-of-shit-bell, and here we are with our thumbs up our butts.

Straining to hear, finally they make out the pilot's squeaky-dick voice. "Bail out," he says, with no emotion whatsoever, not a shred of encouragement or energy, like the hick's saying pass the freaking salt or something. What is *wrong* with these kid pilots? It's 1943 in the forever war; they'll kill our asses our first week in Europe. What do their flight school instructors do, drain their brain cells and blood, swap their brains for sponges? They don't talk, these kids. What *clowns.* No emotion. Just fire. Bailout. Bailout. Like Our Father Who Art in Heaven, fuck us not.

Of course my rear escape hatch is jammed shut. Naturally, we never do drills that require us to actually open the damn hatches during flight, so who the hell knows if the hatches would ever work up here at full speed and altitude, which in this case this hatch ain't. Fuckin' Bob.

Gonna be the last man out? No way! Don't want *that* shit. Bailout? Okay, wise guys, where the hell are we, or *were* we, anything . . . something?

He had heard the copilot mumble something about Lake Superior but couldn't remember what he said. It's April, for God's sake. What's the point of jumping over the lake, if that's where we are? Even if you're lucky enough to land on the ice. If you land in open water you'll have maybe a minute of life left. Stop thinking, get the hell out. *If* you can get out, *if* you can open this damn hatch. Which you can't. Fuckin' Bob!

If you get out—no, *when* you get out—keep it positive, jerk-off! *When* you get out, *then* what? The fuzz-faced navigator Vairo never said boo about where we are and now *I'm* supposed to take a blind-ass leap into the freezing black night? Wanted to be a pilot, ended up a tail gunner. Great. The tail gunner's the crew's last thought and the enemy's first. Would've been better off in the Navy or even the dirt-sucking gruntfantry.

Stop bellyaching, Cee-Gee. *Think.* You can't get out your hatch. Crawl your scrawny ass up the tunnel to the waist, see if anybody's there, use one of those hatches if you can. *Do* something and do it quick, asshole.

———

In a *tree?* Fuckin' Bob and Jesus Moses Mary! *Geez.* No stars above me or ground below. Okay, is being in a tree still considered part of in the bailout deal, or is this a new stage, a new category? We did not train for this *shit.* The Army Air Corps will have a term and a form to fill out. Bet your ass on that. Calm down, Cee-Gee, re-sack your nuts, take a deep breath, light up. You ain't going nowhere until you've got some daylight to see with. Relax. You're still alive. Right?

Or is this how death is? Who the hell would know? Maybe morning light comes and you see all those other assholes from the crew trapped up in trees and trying to figure out where they are and what they'll do next. Would that be Hell, Heaven, or more shit on earth? Smoke one, stop thinking.

Hanging in a tree, like a suckling pig in Pauly Ponozzo's meat cooler. At least you're not upside down. You, a city kid, stuck in a frigging tree in the middle of who frigging knows where? You *hate* all outdoor shit.

Ma yelling. "Cee-Gee, get outside and play and get you some fresh air, it's healthy." Like hell, Ma, I *hate* all things outside, *all* of it, bushes, bugs, dog shit, bees and birds, sun, wind, all that crap. Grass makes me crazy. "Give it a chance," she whines, "give it a chance, you'll learn to love it. We Germans adore the outdoors." God. I ain't no frickin' German, Ma! I'm a toe-of-the-boot southern eye-tie and I hate everything outside the house. Stop thinking about Ma and home. You just bailed out. You're in a tree. Concentrate on now, here.

No use. The mind has its own mind. The folks decided to move out of the city to get free of the coloreds. But you wanted back on Fort Street, downtown in the frigging city, your city, *any* city. People *belong* in cities, black, white, whatever, who cares? *You* belong in a city. But are you in a city? No. You're in a damn tree and what's below you? Can't see anything, but there's some snow piled on all the branches. Was it snowing when the chute opened? Can't remember. Too frigging scared then to notice anything. Snow? *Snow!* I hate frigging snow. There ain't no more snow on the ground back at the base in Iowa and last letter from Ma, she said there ain't no more snow outside Detroit. But up here, wherever the hell this is: snow! Perfect.

Listen Cee-Gee, it was you who wouldn't wait to be drafted, you dope. You volunteered, you knucklehead! Had to be the hero, cash in on the girls, so how did that shit work out? Air Corps, you told yourself, life inside an airplane, a few hours in the sky, then back to base, and not living in the mud like infantry or Marines. Air Corps, clean, slick modern life, not living with a bunch of stinky country boys shittin' in the woods. Now *this*? Jesus, when did I pull your pud. God? Fuckin' Bob.

Stuck in a tree and got no sidearm to signal with or defend yourself. Holster's empty. Jesus Moses Mary, I see that navigator again, I'm gonna rearrange his baby face, officer or not. Court-martial for punching an officer? Fuck that! Who cares? Nobody has to bail out of a brig.

Look at the bright side, wiseguy: Least you got some smokes, two new packs. Good. But one pack is Luckies and they taste like rat shit. Disgusting. Next pack is Camels. Women like the Camels, don't know why. Sophistication, maybe, what was it Aeleni Malani said? I'm gonna puff on something I wanna puff the best. Aeleni, she was one great gal. Don't think about that stuff, you dope! Aeleni ain't near puffin' on nothing, Cee-Gee, so cut the crap.

So, you're in a tree. Deal with it. You know there's snow below, and you're stuck up here, nowhere to go. If you don't keep your head in this game, you won't never be squeezing on Aeleni's big tits again. Forget the broad. You're stuck, same as Jesus, without the nails. Hey, no offense, Lord, but you didn't have no frigging snow to deal with, and I'm real sorry those Roman assholes nailed you to sticks. Been southern Italian, none of that shit woulda happened, and Lord, somebody came and took *you* down and I do not mean to minimize your shit, man, but you had help and there's frigging nothing here but this tree and me. The Air Corp's always going on about the team, crew, the force, all that group-song crap. And here I am alone. What are you? *Sopressatta*? You're on your own. Forget team, forget corps. Where's the frigging team *now*?

What team? Say you're back in your pod and an ME-109 flares in on the Liberator. What, you're shooting your twin 50s for the team, God, and country? Bullshit. You're shooting to save your *own* ass! You shoot for yourself first, forget the frigging team!

What the hell time is it? Your watch musta come off when the parachute opened. You thought your joy boys got ripped off too, thought you had that harness good and tight like they told you, but here you are, balls still in place, yes, but your watch? Gone. Getting lighter yet?

The problem is the fricking Jonah crew you got stuck with. Somebody dumped you with nine jamokes, the *incompetenti*. Their last tail gunner lost his nerve during a shooting drill and they brought home his whining, cringing, listless ass, his dipstick not even close to touching oil. Next thing you knew, you got stuck with these losers. All they'd say about the other guy was Fuckin' Bob, and nobody would say why. Just Fuckin' Bob. They never said hello, welcome to the crew, none of that shit, just Fuckin' Bob, and they all give you the cold shoulder. Nobody cares about tail gunners, and nobody says nothing about nothing, just gives you their icy stares and a mumbled Fuckin' Bob.

Way you heard it from another crew, Bob was the crew's rock before he blew his head gaskets, then blooey, no more Bob, no more glue, no more crew. They were all scared shitless after that. Fuckin' Bob? Frigging flyin', frickin' shit airplanes, frigging B-17 Flying Fortresses, *flying my ass*! Frigging Army Air Corps, friggin' punk officers, fricking engine fires, friggin' no good crew, frickin' Bob, frickin' fuckin' fuckers, all of 'em.

A gust of wind suddenly tore through the branches around the tail gunner. He could still see snow on branches above but there were holes now and he could see it was snowing hard. *Great, perfect*, stuck in a tree in a blizzard in a parachute. Which reminded him. Was he still connected? He'd felt the harness and felt shrouds drooped down and got nervous. What if he detached the chute from the harness and fell out of the tree and killed himself? The thought made him laugh out loud. He disconnected the chute from the harness and cleared the clutter away. *Much better*.

Cee-Gee, snap out of it. Stop your pissin' and moanin'. You're alone, which makes it *your* problem, just yours. Rest of the boys have got their own troubles and problems—if they're even alive, which probably they ain't. Fuckin' Bob! Sleep. You ain't going nowhere till you can see where you can go.

Nobody said nothing in training about gettting hung up in some frigging giant-ass tree, or about bailing out in a fucking snowstorm? What, they don't got no snow in Europe? Fuckin' Bob.

Ma, your son's gonna be worm food. "I love my flier," she tells you, whispering in her voice like she's doing Stations of the Cross, and you tell her again and again, Ma, ma, I'm a friggin' crewman, a gardener or something, not no flier. "Nonsense," she says that morning you left.

"You young fellas are all up there in the sky together, which means you're all fliers. Who operates which contraption on the plane is only a technicality is all. I'm so proud, the whole family is so proud, our boy the flier."

Jesus, Ma.

Aeleni the night you came home on leave . . . opened her blouse and looked like she was gonna unsnap her bra, only there wasn't no bra, and she said, "Go on, Cee-Gee, the girls ain't never had no squeeze-up by a flyboy."

You ain't no flier, you tell her. You're a gunner.

She just laughed. "I guess we'll be getting to that gun part pretty damn quick, bub."

Yo, pay attention here, Cee-Gee. You're not squeezing Aeleni's tits here, you're in a tree, just you. There ain't much wind now. Is that good? Got no damn looey here to tell you, Cee Gee. Decide for yourself. Yeah, less wind is good, okay? This is gonna be okay, or not.

You're in a tree, you're cold, you have no idea where you are or what shape the other guys are in. If you had a sidearm, you could swallow a round and be done with this shit, but you ain't got you no gun, so you want out, jump. One step and it's all over. Cut your own throat? Fuckin' Bob.

Can't do that. Lost your damn knife too. Ain't no wind in the branches. The breeze went away, thank God. Sound, something moving upward, climbing? Shit, how come you got the *agita*? When's the last time you ate, knucklehead? Where's your extra rats? Supposed to be in your gear. Box lunch in the bomber, that was last. Dry chicken drumsticks and an apple you couldn't eat. Not real food like Ma's.

You swear you can hear something climbing the tree, and something moving around close to your limb. "Guys? Is that you, guys?" No answer. Oh shit, do you ever got the *agita* now. Burns bad. Fuckin' Bob, his fault you're in this shit. His fault this happened. Fuckin' Bob.

———

Blowden Hode had trapped the Porkies his whole life, save two years in France during the First War. He especially loved winter when a man could concentrate on work and not run into fools on picnics and other folderol. Tonight he was home in White Pine, wishing he was up in the mountains in the snowstorm that was starting to build, a major dump cranking up, maybe the last of the season. But suddenly there's bloody pounding on his front door and Old Dorothy, his bloodhound, she don't sing a single note of warning.

Opened the door to find 75-year-old Sheriff George Airgood at the door, his hat in hand. "Hode, the Army Air Corps has lost one of their B-17s over the Porkies. You hear anything?"

He hadn't.

"Ten men had to parachute. We've found nine of them so far, but not number ten—the tail gunner."

The sheriff showed him a rough approximation of the dying craft's flight route.

"Could be up in the Lost Creek area," Hode told the sheriff. "Worst place God made around here. Big snow's coming down, and she won't stop soon."

"Can we even get up there?" Sheriff Airgood asked.

"West–northwest from here to the old Nonesuch Mine on skis and north from there up the old camp road, and northwest into the woods on snowshoes from there." The old mine had played out in 1912 and had never yielded much copper.

"I'll deputize you to lead the search, okay? The dog going with us?"

Hode shook his head. "Dot's too old, got a poor nose in the snow. I'll lead if you want." The trapper got his gear together, took the old man into the storm, and led him west toward Nonesuch.

Hode had no idea how long they trekked, but the sheriff's eyes were sunk back in his head and his beard entirely iced over, and not once did the old fellow complain. Had to admire Airgood, even for all his strange ways. The fresh snow was soft and falling on a layer of spring scab, which made for some tricky footing in places. Hode tried to keep them on the fresh snow, to avoid the icy crust as much as they could. If you slipped on crust, you could end up a hundred feet straight down, and broken in winter was as good as dead. No mistakes allowed up in this country, not in winter. And no trails. This was a place few men visited. But Hode trapped the creeks and boreal ponds, knew his way around.

Sometime after daylight, Hode saw fresh bear tracks. Likely a damn fool young male, out of the den early and looking for easy pickings. Hode used his eyes to follow the tracks, which led to the base of an oak tree where he saw not one bear, but four or them sitting on their haunches, looking straight up, monkey-see, monkey-do. Above them 50 or 60 feet up he could just make out a greenish-white parachute hanging down like a theater curtain.

"Stop," Hode told the sheriff, and pointed.

"Maybe he got hung in the tree and fell?" the Sheriff said, thinking out loud.

Hode yelled and the bears scampered into the dawn. Snow still falling.

The two rescuers circled the base of the tree below the parachute, searching. No body, no nothing.

They both looked up.

"Hey!" a muffled voice yelled down at them.

Too much snow and not yet quite enough light to see detail above the fabric hung in the the branches. Airgood yelled up, "Who's up there?"

"Sergeant Faffenborgia, Army Air Corps, tail gunner. I ain't sure how to get down."

"You hurt?"

"Just sore and I'm almost out of smokes. It's friggin' cold up here!"

The sheriff said, "Patience, son, Deputy Hode is coming up to get you. When we get you down here we'll take care of whatever ails you and make some hot tea."

"I need a damn cigarette," the airman yelled down. "But no fucking Luckies, I'm almost out."

Airgood yelled back, "Relax until we have you."

Hode said, "I've got six tree spikes in my ruck. I can climb up, rope him, and lower him."

"You got the energy?" Airgood asked.

"No choice but find it. We've got to get the man down or he'll be done for. This storm ain't done yet. Spending the night up in that tree can't have been good."

When Hode drove the first spike, there was a commotion above and a loud crash as a pile of something hammered into the deep snow six feet from him and made him jump back. It was a man in a flight suit and leather jacket, dead.

"Jesus, he was just talking to us!" the Sheriff said.

"I thought he sounded fine, didn't he?" the trapper said, staring up at the dark tree.

Airgood said, "Well, he's not talking now and by the looks of him he hasn't talked for a long damn time."

A frantic voice called down from above, "Tree to ground, are you guys still coming up here? What the hell's the holdup down there?"

The rescuers looked at each other and at the unexplained body in the snow.

Hode yelled, "Yah, I'm coming up. Stay put until I get you secured. Don't try to help me."

"No worry," the tail gunner yelled back.

"I'll make a fire for tea," the sheriff said. "Got chow in my pack. Let's hope he isn't injured too bad. Wonder who the heck this dead man is."

Hode shook his head. A half hour later he had the tail gunner on the ground and they had him wrapped in a blanket and seemingly all right.

The sheriff pointed to the body of the dead man. "Was he up there too?"

"Fuckin' Bob," Faffenborgia said. "Fuckin' Bob."

St. Certain's F.C.

"Sure you're up to this?" Ek asked. Knute Sjogren had only recently returned from Korea after spending eight months in San Francisco's Letterman Hospital. When he finally got home to Ironwood, he clomped up to his old bedroom, closed the door, and hunkered down, venturing downstairs only to eat. Had Ek not called his mom, Sjogren knew he might still be in his room.

When Coach called, his mom insisted her son come downstairs to answer the phone, and Ek asked him, "You ready to come back to work? Pauly and me sure could use your help." Ek had been his high school football coach and his summer boss when he dug graves. He had joined the Army right out of high school and been sent to Korea. Sid "Backstraw" Ek never seemed to age, had always been around, always quietly in charge. Knute knew Ek meant "oak" in Swedish, and the name described the man. Ek had survived World War Two, including Omaha Beach, and made it all the way into Germany. He had been wounded four times, and afterwards never talked about the war.

Knute shrugged. What was there to say, that he'd lost count of all the bodies and body parts they'd buried in the Korean muck and stone ground? Chosin frostbite left two of his fingers numb and on fire, depending on the moment and who the hell knew why, certainly not the arrogant, hassled cutters who, when it came down to it, were nothing more than body mechanics using meatball medicine like it was some sort of magical spell.

"I'm ready Ek," Knute said.

Ek had taught and coached at Ramsay High School. His Highlander teams were renowned for their lack of size or technique, yet somehow they had managed to win seventy-seven straight football games, then both the state and national records.

Opposing coaches called him the magician. But his players called him Ek and tried to do whatever he asked them to do. Ek never suited up more than twenty players. Most games there were only two or three subs on the sidelines and everyone played in every game. Some years there were not even enough players for decent scrimmages, and Ek devised a series of precision drills as choreographed and complex as a Russian ballet. Noncontact drills taught his players to read the field as space, and when game time rolled around, his players hardly paid attention to their opponents. Mostly what they saw was the playing space, which in their minds was a kind of chessboard. Ek's teams in games were always many moves ahead of their opponents.

"*Sure* your hands are okay?" Ek asked.

Knute wiggled his fingers. "See, peachy."

The crew was made up of Knute, Coach Ek, and "Clubfoot" Pauly Kangas, whom the army refused to take into World War Two becaused of his deformed foot and maybe because he was thought a bit slow mentally, but Knute knew his friend could physically outwork any man on the Gogebic iron range. Coach and Pauly had employed several thirds while Knute was in Korea, all temporaries.

Coach flashed his sly smile and showed the boys the plot map for the Ironwood Riverside Cemetery, which Ek and his grave-digging crew called St. Certain's F.C. Coach had once seen a piece in the *Ironwood Globe* about an English football club, F.C., but to the digging crew it meant Final Curtain. St. Certain's Final Curtain. Death was like graduating high school. You went through the door and never came back.

Knute had first reported to the F.C. on Monday, three days after Coach's call. Of the temporaries who had filled in for him during the Korean mess, Pauly said only, "They was all just second stringers." Knute knew these were not the coach's words. Ek never thought in terms of first or second strings. Everyone played, everyone contributed, and they won or lost together. Pauly was a snail between the ears and a lion in the heart, a man incapable of lies and a man who loathed all confrontations. Grave-digging suited his introverted personality and relaxed manner.

Knute had always liked the cemetery work. Some winters the frost line sank down eight or nine feet, and with such deep frost, graves couldn't be dug, and bodies couldn't be buried. In those years the dead were stacked high at Koko's Beer Warehouse over in Wakefield. Not until the Koko family complained in spring to the county board would Riverside management do anything about actual burials.

Ek and crew preferred to wait for full spring, which might not come until mid-May. Weather in the western Upper Peninsula being impossible to predict from year to year. Some winters so many old people died, there was no choice but to dig graves and plant the newly departed in semi-frozen ground, which sometimes led to downstream problems during the spring ice-out.

Riverside was like a lot of other Upper Peninsula cemeteries: It didn't matter if the deceased believed in some flavor of Protestant god, a Catholic deity, whoever Jews prayed to, or if one had a hard time believing in a god, or decided there was no god to believe in. To come to the attention and care of the F.C. you had to be dead and beyond worrying. There were social classes and divisions in life and in town, but Ek made sure everyone who died rested together and he put a lot of thought into where each new client would be placed. If Ek had a prejudice, it was toward and for his former players, who got what Ek considered to be the best available gravesites.

The Chosin Reservoir had taught Knute a hard lesson as stiff piles grew higher daily—on both sides, with American and U.N. troops madly retreating and the damn communists relentlessly swarming after them, pushing them farther south. Each day felt like death and for many men it was, especially soldiers who ran out of emotional gas and couldn't or wouldn't hang on and adhere to the fighting retreat. Knute thought of these men as "empties," and when this happened, the empties often curled up like newborns and died right by the roadway or rough trail. The enemy didn't even have to spend a bullet.

Not one of the empties ever cried out for his mother or god, and Knute took note. His time had been close more than once, but unlike the unlucky he seemed to have the right combination of luck and no-quit. After all, he was a Backstraw guy and Backstraw guys never gave up.

Knute thought the best place in the cemetery was the grassy shelf that sloped gently down toward the Montreal River. In early summer the slope was filled with forget-me-nots. In winter, before the spring burial push, Pauly and Knute trapped along the river and Ek helped them brain-tan hides. The three of them split the take when they sold the furs to the Chicago buyer who came through Ironwood twice a year.

Spring traditionally was the crew's busy time as they planted the beer warehouse's winter overrun. Summers and falls were more on an even keel of departures, and generally lighter, depending on what sort of communicable diseases were making their way through the area.

Pauly patted Knute's arm. "You want, Knute, I can do this one, okay? I don't mind."

Pauly had a work ethic to shame most men. Tireless and always cheerful, he never complained. They lit their last cigarettes before walking out to Row 38 Echo, Grave No. Nine. Knute used his thermos to fill Coach's cup, and Pauly held out a cup too.

"You weren't drinking coffee when I left for Korea, Pauly."

"Yah, I guess I changed," Pauly said with a grin.

"We all do," Knute said.

"You sure you're okay, Knute?" Pauly asked. "You know, your hands, and all? I heard they got froze up, Knute. They unthawed yet?"

Pauly was hundred percent Yooper. Unthaw was Yooperese for thaw. Knute flexed his fingers. "Good as new. Who's our first customer this morning?"

All the dead were customers or clients to the three-man F.C. because it made the work seem less ghoulish. The F.C. Gravediggers, unlike the cassocks and collars who took care of parishioners, dealt only with the dead. They seldom ever saw any survivors, and they rarely watched graveside ceremonies.

There had been no such niceties in Korea, where the dead were all just stiffs, most of them without names, just icy, muddy, bloody dog tags that got tossed into bags if there were bags available, and twenty or less minutes to bury a man, which some days there wasn't even that much time.

One night yellow wolves barged in and dug out some shallow graves and Knute heard them, and he and the two other men had gone out with their entrenching tools and hacked at the starving wolves until they retreated. Knute sometimes wondered if the wolves also ate Chinese and Korean dead, or was their preference strictly Westerners, who had more fat on their bodies?

The North Korean and Chinese Armies, near as Knute could determine, didn't give a shit about their dead, just left them to rot where they fell. In summer the smell would have been toxic.

The Korean War veteran knew when his mom called Coach she had also shared her concern for her son in her unobtrusive Swedish way. That had been enough to get Ek to the house.

Knute stared at the grass at location Row 38 Echo, Grave No. Nine. He toed the frozen turf with his boot. Wouldn't be real spring for a while. There had been no grass in Korea. The ground there was rock, and mud, ice and snow, bones, smells. Dark.

"Czerna Fjetland," Coach said in his flat voice.

Knute's heart jumped, and he realized it must've shown.

"You didn't know?" Ek asked.

Knute shook his head.

"This is Czerna's grave, Knute. New Year's Eve she and her schoolteacher boyfriend ran off the road outside Hurley, went down a deep gully, and got all smashed to smithereens. The Ford caught fire. I talked to Ned, but all he'd tell me was that it stunk bad."

Ned was Ned Fjetland, who worked as an embalmer at a local funeral home and had been one of coach's finest players. He was also Czerna's father.

"It stinks," Coach added, shaking his head.

Knute was silent. He and Czerna had briefly been a couple until Korea separated them. As for stinks, Knute had swum in the stench of a a stew of toasted, rotting flesh for more than a year, ate in it, drank water from it, slept in it, breathed it, and shit it out on the battlefield, which was wherever you were. Eventually the stink got so familiar he didn't even smell it, but he did wonder from time to time if it would ever leave his pores or his bowels if he survived.

"I'm real sorry about Czerna," Pauly said. "She was a nice girl."

Coach gave his muscleman a friendly shove. "Pauly. I don't think Knute knew."

Pauly hung his head. "I didn't mean nothing."

Knute patted his friend's back. "It's okay, Pauly, I know what you meant."

"You did?" Pauly said.

Ek said, "Okay lads, we're burning daylight."

"Air burns," Pauly said. "I seen it, or maybe I read it in the *Globe*, I can't remember."

The *Globe* was Ironwood's longtime newspaper, in operation since the heyday of iron mining in the Gogebic Range. Ramsay was too small for its own paper, but nowadays there was a weekly Ramsay news column. Not like back when Ek's teams had dominated the gridiron, Ramsay was front-page news then, all football season, every season.

Knute learned in Korea that air would burn, and when it burned, all life near it died. He could still hear Navy jets diving on Commie positions, dropping tanks of napalm, sometimes so close that the heat seared American flesh. Most of the napalm dead died of air starvation, not fire, not that this mattered to the dead.

"Czerna write to you over there in Korea?" Ek asked as the three men got ready to open the grave. Coach, as crew boss, had a pick and shovel and the official tape measure.

"We were over before I shipped out," Knute said. He didn't share that she had walked down to the bus station with him and, just before he got on the bus, told him, "Might be better if we go our own ways. You don't need distractions where you're going." He had tried to feel something, loss, sorrow, anything, but nothing registered, and she had been right. Over there he had not needed distractions. Ironwood could have been the moon or Mars for all he cared.

Coach Ek gave Knute the blasting kit. "You use this stuff in Korea?"

"Daily."

"With this little freeze half a stick per end should work good on the ice-grass."

The explosive thumps seemed familiar and not personal. The small blasts created nice holes on the ends of the new grave. Knute and Pauly carefully cleared the holes, squared the sides, and set up the stiff-planter, which is what Pauly called the device used to lower coffins into the grave bottom. Ek called it their remainsevator.

The three men stood by the new excavation. "What's it mean?" Knute asked.

Ek shrugged. "Burial? Bodies corrupt in air. They don't stink if you put them deep enough in the ground. We bury them to protect the living, and so critters can't get at them."

"Not that. I mean God?"

Ek shrugged. "Who knows and who cares? By the time folks get to us they ain't full of beliefs no more."

Pauly asked, "You kill Commies over there, Knute?"

"When I had to."

"It was fun, right? John Wayne, right?"

"No fun, Pauly, and not John Wayne. It was just like clearing Czerna's grave, just another job to do."

Pauly said, "I think it might be fun for me."

"You could be right, Paul. A few guys seemed to enjoy it."

Pauly flashed a bright grin. "See, I think they should send all us slow guys to kill Commies. We'd have us some fun, you know, win the game, wouldn't we, Knute?"

Knute said, "I don't think so, Pauly. You don't like to hurt anyone."

"Killin' ain't hurtin' nobody, Knute, it's just killin' them."

"It hurts them, Pauly; it hurts them real bad."

"But you killed 'em, Knute."

"I'm not the man you are, Pauly. You care about people. I don't."

Coach said to Knute, "You remember your first game, your freshman year?"

"Against Iron River."

"You didn't start. Five-foot nothing, a hundred and twenty-eight pounds, including equipment. You walked everywhere I walked, my second shadow, kept begging and insisting, 'put me in, put me in, put me in.'"

"You did."

"Not until the second quarter. And I put you in at right guard, figuring you'd get your bell rung. I told Tombo to run the mass sweep right, so that you would have to pull and lead the charge."

"I remember."

"Made four blocks on that play and followed Tombo the whole eighty yards, looking backwards for something to turn and attack." Ek added, "I laughed out loud, told myself, this little shit can play."

Ek added, "I kept you out on the ensuing kickoff and you flew down the field, knocked the ball loose from the ball carrier, picked up the fumble, flipped it over to Tombo and he ran forty more yards for another touchdown. And I thought, thank you God, you've sent me a weapon who looks like a choirboy. But you know what, Knute? It was your brain that made you such a great player. Never once did I see a lapse in concentration, no mental errors ever. Coaches can't teach that, Knute. I'm thinking things got pretty ugly over there in Korea?"

Knute nodded. No details were exchanged. Coach had seen what the boy had seen, and now they were no longer coach and player. They were brothers. Not heroes, but brother survivors.

Coach Ek said, "That hero stuff is all bullcrap. There was failure of discipline and leadership at all levels, too damn many men trying to look good rather than do what was good and right. Disgusted me, the whole damn bunch of 'em. I made up my mind to stay alive, do what I was told, ask no questions, just go along, and keep moving, and keep my butt down, and if I got killed, I got killed." Coach shrugged to close his thought.

"Same here," Knute said.

"You're a thinker, Knute. You've got no business digging graves with Pauly and me. You need to be at college, use your mind, learn to ask questions for the rest of us who can't, or are too damn old, lazy, or afraid to ask."

Pauly said, "But Knute can come dig with us on his vacations, right Coach?"

Ek nodded. "Anytime he wants, Pauly."

"You firing me?" Knute asked his coach.

"Not until you finish college. Until then you've got a job whenever you're home, but once you've got that sheepskin, you're done digging graves."

"What's next?" Knute asked.

"Row Eleven, Grave No. Eleven. It's on the south side of the river lip. Elmer Blom. His liver finally gave out. Lasted fifty years more than I figured he would. He bought another site, but I decided to put him in No. Eleven. It's got a nice view of the river and he was a good honest player who led an unlucky life."

Knute drove his pick into the ground and an earthy scent rose up. He stopped and looked at his friend and mentor. "How long?"

Ek nodded. "Until you're all the way here and not back over there?" the coach said. "It's different for every man. It will take a year or so if you're lucky, but some of you is never coming back, Knute. It just can't."

Knute went back to work. He had killed and watched men killed for a year and buried men and fought wolves trying to eat the dead, and somehow it had all seemed routine.

Today they had dug Czerna's eternal resting peace, now one for Old Elmer Blom, a nice man and a drunk. Knute felt happy for the first time in a long time. He felt his fingers tingling and smiled.

Dead River Rats

THE LILAC AND HAWTHORNE HEDGE WAS, IN THEIR MINDS AT TIMES, the Great Wall of China, Hadrian's Wall, the Green Monster at Fenway, and Gibraltar. They hid in its shadow, not wanting to linger long. They saw that all the tall shutters of the imposing house were closed tight, forcing them to check each gabled tower for any sign of life.

The faded lawn was overrun by invading weeds and had gone wild. Feeble moss roses strained for the sun. The whole fortress was perfectly parked near the edge of a sugar maple forest that lay on a finger that pointed south toward swamps and quicksand. The forest dark, the forest secret, provider of forts, hidey-holes, secret ponds, a wolf pack, and Jilly Kiltner's red-hot scarlet panties.

The ornate frame house, nineteenth-century Greek Orthodox, was a grim, unpainted way station between the light of civilization and the black veil beyond. Just over a series of rock buttes, there was a dirt road that led nowhere in particular, a grass-centered two-track with the collective pull of an unopposable gigantic magnet on boys of a certain age who sweated with the need for adventure, driven by the collective urge to confront their own terrors.

Checkers Holzapple, in unlaced, tongueless high-top sneakers, was compelled to take one last look, his job as he saw it. Checkers snuck a quick peek through a small hole in the hedge, exposing his head no more than a partial second. "Don't give the enemy a target," he lectured his mates. "You can't give 'em no time to aim."

For Checkers, the enemy lurked behind every poison sumac (all sumac was poison to the boys), every stone wall, even in the stagnant ponds and catch pools where the black monster polio lived, turning sweetwater to killing water. The woods and swamps were dangerous in an unspecified way, but ponds were the worse by far. They killed and crippled these invisible demons who lay flat on the bottom, sucking air through hollow reeds, hiding in weed beds and piles of rotting railroad ties once cut and discarded by the CCC almost twenty years ago. Demons waited for kids to swim so they could strike without warning.

With daylight fading, Checkers strained to get his eyes adjusted, and as he waited, he spied an unprotected window, not exactly a clear and easy target, but partially open, shutters slightly ajar. The North Marquette Dead River Rats, losers of six straight years of Little League games, chucked stones with all the vigor they could summon. But their stones missed their marks and struck planks on the side of the house with a thunk, the rattle of a lone snare drummer at work. Only one puny shot found its way to the mark and struck glass, shattering the quiet of coming night.

Heart pounding, die cast, Richie "Polio" Denucci, once stricken with a "light dose" of the dreaded disease—in his butt, seriously—separated from the others and squiggled toward their escape route across the mustard plant meadow. This was not an act of cowardice on his part, but a tactical gambit endorsed by the group.

Richie ran with a weird wobble and needed a head start. Although he was slow and looked unsteady, Polio was not helpless and was in fact endowed with an exceptional power: Richie could outswear US Navy guys, Big Lake sailors, commercial fishermen, river rats, and all the nasty-smelling trappers who stumbled around taverns on the fringes of town. Some believed Polio probably could outswear anybody in the county and maybe the entire Upper Peninsula, which was no mean reputation for an eleven-year-old.

Safely out of range with his head start, Richie would become the group's megaphone, their long-distance envoy and propagandist against their chosen enemy.

Who was where? They had attacked, and gotten no response. Their lean bodies reeked of young sweat, and this smell intensified from their never-washed sneakers in their collective adolescent hormonal-fug. An enemy in pursuit would have to have serious sinus blockages in order to miss the smell, or come at them from upwind.

Seeing Polio in flight, catlike Gene Koon couldn't take any more stress. Nor could Jimmy "I-Ain't-No-Relation-to-that-Asshole-Michigan-Morman-King" Strang. Jimmy was keeper of the gang's sole switchblade, his Uncle Howie-the-Frog having brought it up across the Straits from Toledo. But Jimmy swore to everyone that he had taken the weapon off a city kid on a visit to Ohio the summer before last, and everyone knew Jimmy couldn't not lie and the truth was that the blade came from his Unc, whom they had all met and universally laughed at.

"Where the hell's he at?" one of the gang asked. "Where?"

Taters Tourangeau said, "Loading his faracking shotgun with faracking double-ought buckshot is where he's at."

Taters considered himself an almost-equal to Richie in swearing acumen, and even Polio's better in the art of creative invective, but he was just fooling himself and the boys all knew it. Where the term faracking came from was anybody's guess and every time he said the word or one of his other eight-ball creations, the others tended to grin or laugh out loud. All things considered in a group where collective vocabulary was inappropriate to the psychological need of the moment, a second loud voice never hurt in an impending confrontation.

One of the gang members said, "Not a shotgun, you asshole. He wunt kill us. He'll just pound rock salt up our keesters."

Not that they had ever suffered this from the old man who owned the place, but it remained possible, which was enough. And they had heard plenty of tales from older brothers attempting to steal pumpkins and sundry produce, who had been butt-shot by old farmers with rock salt loaded in shotguns they kept handy for such intruders.

"He's already killed boatloads of people," Checkers announced. "What's a few more stupid kids?" It was Checkers who first brought his gang the story of Zadravic, the Croatian-born Nazi who murdered Jewish and Catholic kids, and had somehow ended up in Marquette. Checkers, sources uncited, as they always were, insisted Zadravic had even been one of Hitler's closest pals.

For reasons undiscussed, the rules of the contest required the throwers to wait on the edge of the street like Olympic sprinters until they spotted Old Man Zadravic. Then and only then could they try to catch up with Polio. Tonight however, time was crawling on broken legs.

Two of the boys were assigned flank positions to keep the old bastard from surprising them from aside.

"It was common tactical military sense," Checkers argued. Nazis never do what you expect them to do, thus caution was advised and flankers the answer. This was not the gang's first mission and having been peppered in their behinds and backs with rock salt was adequate motivation for not doing anything riskier than that already committed to.

A scream split the coming night and they all panicked. Near the light pole across the field they saw Old Man Zadravic manhandling and shaking Richie Denucci. The old man was wearing a gray wool hat and a cape. Even from such a distance in shrinking light they could see Richie's eyeballs bulging like golf balls. Checkers told the others in a hushed tone, "That son of a bitch Zadravic wasn't in the goddamn house at all. He's been outside, waiting for us! We've been ambushed, boys!"

Taters Tourangeau stood tall and yelled, "Hey Zadravic, you faracking Nazi, leave that kid alone! He's had the polio!"

Checkers punched Taters. "You dumbass, the Nazi ain't got no reason to keep Richie alive if he knows he's had the polio. He's already no good for working in the camps. Remember the newsreels, how they gassed the ones who were too old or too young or not fit to work."

Taters hung his head. "I didn't think of that."

Meanwhile, the old man still had Polio by the shoulders and seemed to the boys to be violently shaking him. Only occasionally did Richie's feet touch the ground. Gene Koon said nervously, "When he's done with Polio, he's coming for us!"

This said, all but one of the gang scattered like leaves in a powerful gust. Like the experienced soldiers they were, they knew to keep to the young shadows and avoid the night weeds where there lay pockets of quicksand, the most dreaded and unreadable of unseen menaces. They all knew of people who had been swallowed by quicksand, times and names now forgotten, but the danger forever lurking close by: Step on the wrong spot and shploop, down you went! Gone forever, to some lair of the devil. Good Catholic boys all, they knew that God would never kill a man in such a cowardly way.

Such information passed from fathers to sons to their sons, and just last year some geologist from Northern had written a piece for *The Mining Journal.* "Expert Rejects, Debunks Local Quicksand Myths."

The boys had read it and rejected the rejection. What the hell did some damn egghead know about a contest with the devil? If the evil one could make quicksand, he could sure as hell make it so some four-eyed, slide-rule-carrying college professor couldn't find it. The nearest quicksand, asserted the professor, was below the bridge, way down near the Indiana and Ohio borders.

Bull and bunkum. They knew stupid science when they heard it, like Jules Verne and his story about the *Nautilus*, that could go forever without refueling. All bull too. Everybody knew a sub had to surface now and then to get air and recharge batteries, or something. This was how it had been in the Big War. They'd seen newsreels, heard the old navy guys talk. No quicksand here? Like hell. Folklore was best guarded by those who treasured it most.

The only soldier not to flee was Robert "Bussy" Orr, aka Bingo, aka Lumpy, aka Blinger. The man-sized Orr was the biggest of them and always a step behind most of their thinking. He was a perpetual grinner, like he knew stuff the others didn't. Tall and sort of puffyish, he stood watching as Old Man Zadravic shook Richie. He thought it might be fun to dance like that, so why were the guys running away? They were so darn hard to figure out sometimes. Some moments he could tell if they were happy, or mad, but he could never sense when they were afraid, in part perhaps because he never feared anything and looked at everything as an adventure. Like Gilly Kiltner. The others were scared of her, but not Robert (she always addressed him by his given name and this perplexed the other gang members). Robert and Gilly had some really keen fun. The other guys all claimed to have kissed her and other stuff, but only Robert actually had. He loved playing with Gilly, but not when he was with the other guys, who always got kind of silly and stupid around her.

The only person Robert feared was The One, who sometimes came around and beat on mama and him, but The One had not been around for a long, long time now, almost forever, which was good, because this was summer, his favorite time of year, when he could play outside all day with his friends, and not just on weekends, when they had to go to school.

Robert was schooled by Mama at home because he needed what she called special help. Summers the boys collected him from his house every morning and he made them all toast and butter and Welch's grape jelly and they all stood around the big kitchen and talked about the day's mission. Mama worked early many days a week, but she had taught him to take care of himself, get up, wash up, dress, make his bed and his breakfast, wash the dishes, all the things grown-ups were supposed to know how to do. School was at night or on days mama didn't have to work.

On days when Mama was gone to her work, Robert spent most of his time alone, squashing frogs with big flat stones that he and Mama brought from the quarry south of Marquette. He liked the sound of frogs popping when you got them just right. Sometimes grown-ups would run into him on the street and ask, "How's the frogging business, Lumpy?"

He'd smile the way mama taught him to, and answer, "Real fine," or "Mighty good."

The boy, townspeople would tell you, was different, and harmless, and, in any event, one of their own, even if his old lady left him alone all day and didn't miss many nights at Flynn's Dew Drip Inn.

Robert hadn't always been this way, but one night this man, who blew up things for the railroad, got real mad at his Mama and caved in Robert's head with a chunk of firewood. After that he was in hospitals for a long time until his Mama finally brought him home. His head still hurt something fierce at times, especially when he had a lot to think on or figure out. This always brought bad head pain and sometimes tears. It was like he had a big wad of oatmeal stuck between what he was trying to think and what he was actually hearing inside. Over time he came to trust feelings over his blocked thinking. His feelings were rarely wrong.

Some in town called him Dopey or Loony, but Robert learned over time as his size passed his contemporaries that all he needed to do to stop hurtful words was just grab a hunk of skin from his tormentor and twist hard. They tended to leave him alone after that.

With his friends, the name Lumpy was an affectionate one, a name of respect. They knew their big friend was slow-minded and slow-moving, and terribly awkward, but he went everywhere with them and even when the rest of them were feeling the spookies, Lumpy always stood steadfast, their anchor.

Before he got to know Gilly, he had had for a time some girls who were friends, but they kept pulling down his pants to look at him and once he peed on Laura Leeber's hand when she was touching him. The girls all squealed and pelted him with dirt clods and ran away. Boys were more fun to hang around with, and he liked to tell them about the girls and how they had "messed him up." Couldn't figure out why they'd call girls pussies, because they sure didn't look like any cats he'd ever seen, but if that was the word his friends wanted, it was okay by him.

Starting last summer, other girls began to show up summer mornings at his house, not in groups, but one at a time, and every girl who came said he had to promise to never tell the other girls, or his friends, or his Mama, or Father James in the confession box, that they had been to his house when no adults were there. He had no idea what they were talking about, but readily agreed because taken one at a time the girls were fun and nice, easy to be around, and sometimes they smelled real good.

As Lumpy stood watching Zadravic and Polio, his mind wandered, and when his mind finally focused on the fact that Old Man Zadravic was making his way toward him, he wasn't sure what to do. He didn't feel afraid, because he was taller and stronger than the old man.

Robert looked past the approaching man and saw Richie Denucci crab-crawling (that's what Checkers called it) down the street in retreat. The sight of Richie on the road made him think Polio was going to tear his pants and how his mama would be unhappy about it because Denucci's mother could scream so loud she could break glass.

Meanwhile Polio saw the old man reach for Lumpy and his sense of duty took hold and he popped to his feet and began hurling the nastiest invective his mind could fashion. Usually he liked to have his best stuff written down so he could get it just right. His friend was in trouble and there was no time to delay. The old man had nearly shaken out his own brains and never said a goddamned word to him!! "Dirty fucking dog fucker!" Richie screeched at his foe, this insult a blunt yet vague allusion to the bevy of coonhounds and beagles the old man had chained to dog houses over by the woods behind the house. It was Checkers who first revealed that the old man fucked his dogs and that was the only reason he had them. Denucci raised a fist and kept the stream going, "Shit eater, Geek fucker, Old Jacker-Offer, Tree humper, Pimple sucker!"

When Richie got fully wound up, he was something to behold. Eventually he would run out of epithets and breath, usually simultaneously, and if they were hanging around Marian Conklin's Sugar Bowl, they'd all go inside and have an ice cream or a candy while Richie got his muse and wind back. Having exhausted his epithets, Denucci picked up a chunk of something and flung it with all his might toward Zakravic and Lumpy, but to his great disappointment and shame, he saw the projectile skip off his big dumb friend's head and it was at that moment that he turned toward home and ran with all the energy he could summon, not that anyone would be home to provide protection for him. His mother Francie would spend most nights at the Marquette Hotel bar, called Clams, where she'd drink herself stupid with some downstate sport fishermen, Great Lakes sailors, the occasional golden-tongued sales rep, and once the older brother of a famous movie star.

"Come with me," Zadravic told Robert, who had expected a shaking like Richie had gotten. Instead, the old man stuck out his hand and Robert reluctantly accepted it and they shook hands the way grown-ups did. Zadravic looked old, his skin kind of yellow like an onion skin and wrinkled, but his hand shook and still it was *strong*. Robert wasn't sure what to make of that. Usually when things looked a certain way, like old and weak, they were old and weak. But not this time, and he didn't understand.

They marched through the hedge where the old man said, "You've got a cut from that stupid boy's rock and we need to fix you up."

Zadravic went inside, leaving Robert alone with his own thoughts, which were few. Where did the guys go? What would be for dinner tonight? Was he going to be late? It never occurred to him to run. They had shaken hands. That was good, right?

The old man returned with a damp cloth and gently blotted at the cut on the big boy's head, and when he was satisfied it was clean, he placed Robert's finger on a fresh gauze over the cut and said, "Hold it tight right there, okay?"

"Okay," Robert said. "Tight."

"Good boy, keep it tight. I don't want you bleeding all over my house." Zadravic guided the boy by his arm into the house, the inside of which was enormous, and all Robert could do was gawk.

The inside of the house was warm. Thick carpets on the floors. The carpets had purple flowers. Robert liked flowers and looked down by his foot and said, "Got some like that down by the swamp over by the river."

Zadravic said in perfect English, "I know the place. I used the flowers there to instruct my carpet maker."

"Your rug's not from the Sears and Roebuck?" Robert asked.

"No, I have a man who makes them for me. I give him a design and he makes the design into a carpet."

"That's . . . neat," Robert said. *People* made carpets?

They went into the kitchen, which was long, with a ceiling so high Robert wasn't sure he could even see how high. The old man made coffee. "Are you old enough to have coffee?"

Robert said. "How old *is* that?"

Zadravic smiled. "I think you're old enough. We shall take coffee in my special room."

"What makes your room special?" Robert asked.

The old man chuckled. "You shall see. What is your name, boy?"

"Robert."

The boy followed his host into the next room, where he stumbled to a halt. The room was filled with dozens of sailing ships, all sizes, majestic shiny things. Robert loved ships, and trains, and planes, and cars and trucks and buses and green Jeeps, anything that moved like magic.

They sat side by side on a long brown leather couch with a table in front of them and drank their coffee. The old man's hands were wrinkled with maroon-colored spots, his fingernails cracked, but his hands clean. The old man produced another bandage, took off the one Robert had dutifully held in place, and started blotting again. "Yes, very good. We shall apply a small butterfly and you will be just fine."

Robert said, "Mama used a leech on a boil on her leg one time and I watched it grab on, but she had never used no butterfly for nothing I remember."

"It's not a real butterfly," the old man said. "It's like a Band-Aid or tape—I trim to a real small strip so it has two sides. I lay one side over each part of the cut so it looks like a butterfly's wings. I invented it and Johnson and Johnson bought it from me."

Zadravic had white stubble on his chin, same color as his full head of hair. Robert had no idea who Johnson and Johnson were. He was pretty sure they didn't live in town.

The old man held up his coffee cup. "Drink, drink, Robert. Coffee is good for you."

Robert studied the cup with the coffee and the old man seemed to read his thoughts, "Yes, it *is* lovely. My wife loved genuine bone china."

"China's made from bones?" Robert had heard of China. It was a place where people ate rice and wore funny hats. He'd heard of bones too, found them in the woods sometimes, brought them home.

"It will be when Mao is gone," Zadravic said.

Robert had no idea what the old man was talking about, but this was nothing new. When adults got talking he couldn't follow them after a while.

"You like ships?" Zadravic asked the boy.

Robert lipped a toothy smile and nodded his head so enthusiastically that his bandage felt like it would come loose. Coffee done, the old man pointed toward the ship room and Robert moved eagerly.

The North Marquette Dead River Rats gathered at Marian Conklin's until they grew bored with comics. The proprietor carefully kept the boys away from the covered-up adult section of magazines.

Polio Denucci was last to join the group at the Sugar Bowl. He arrived huffing and puffing and out of breath, face red, and they all wanted to know how he escaped. He said, "I don't know. He was right there in front of me, but I couldn't see him and then he grabbed holt of me. It was scary."

"How'd you get loose?" Checkers asked.

Richie described his escape, embellishing his story in ways only Polio could, including a brutal fight scene in which he resorted to his jujitsu to defeat the evil Z, the jujitsu learned after careful study of Blackhawk's comic book adventures.

"Bullshit," the others called out. They all knew Richie never fought. He swore and that was the extent of his resistance.

The boy dropped his head and said, "I guess he just kinda let go and told me he was sorry, and I got the hell out of there."

The others booed him. "The Nazi let you go and told you he was sorry? That's your biggest damn lie ever!"

He didn't tell them that he had seen Zadravic grab Lumpy. He'd thought about telling the gang how he was wearing his rosary around his neck and that this had forced the Nazi Zadravic back, like a werewolf, but he was too weary to put much meat on such a plot and stuck with the jujitsu, which he liked. It was quite rare for Richie to not work rosary beads into his stories, and the boys noted this omission.

All gang members, except Lumpy, were Roman Catholics, part of Father James Anthony's flock at Bishop Baraga's Cathedral. All the boys were card-carrying altar boys, taking turns in the weekly Sunday mass schedule. Whenever two of them drew the same assignment, the others watched as the boys in front traded SBDs, arm farts, and flying rubber bands.

Each River Rat carried a rosary as a talisman against evil. They were handy implements for young lads with active imaginations. They had at times been sling stand-ins, cat-o-nines, marble bag carriers and headbands used to put foliage around their faces for camouflage. Occasionally they used them to pray, which was generally required after they made their weekly partial confessions.

Checkers put his comic back in the rack and signaled for a huddle.

"Where the fuck is Lumpy, Polio? He's slow, but he should've been here by now."

"Don't know," Richie lied and shifted his attention to picking his nose. He had been so busy describing his own escape that he neglected to tell them about Lumpy's capture. The others all gave him the business over his nose and Checkers wiped an imaginary booger on Polio's arm and they called him snot-sucker and worse and they all laughed and only then did Richie tell them what he had seen.

Checkers said, "We can't leave Lumpy there with that old man. We have to rescue him. He's one of us."

"He ain't so smart he can even figure it out." Richie came back, and Taters Tourangeau pinched his left nipple hard and made him squeal and squirm away.

"We need to know where he is now," Checkers insisted. "He's our friend."

Richie hung his head. "They looked like they headed to the old Nazi's house."

Silence was broken by Coon's whisper. "Old Man Z's gonna will *kill* Lumpy!"

Taters said, "He'll kick the crap out of him."

Checkers said, "Nazis are capable of *anything*."

They burst out the door like a posse and spied local police chief Gnat Murphy, who was parked by Stahl's General Store. They ran to his squad car, all trying to talk at once, jostling each other to be first and loudest, and Gnat, who could do ten one-finger pullups at the age of 62, looked at them, held up one hand, and smiled. "My river rodents," he said. "Whoa, what's the hurry here?"

"Zadravic's killin' Lumpy, ya gotta hurry, Chief!"

"Lumpy?"

"Robert? Robert Orr?"

The chief nodded. "Yah, the dummy. What about him?"

"Zadravic grabbed him off the street," Checkers said.

"Were you boys annoying that old man? I know how you guys are."

"We didn't do nothing," they insisted.

"He attacked us too but we got away and he took Lumpy," Richie said.

Chief Murphy knew Zadravic, a strange old coot who kept to himself. He'd heard somewhere that the old man worked his whole career for the CIA and people like that tended to all be loners and goofballs. There were complaints of the old man's baying hounds once in a while, but nothing else. The old guy's wife had died last year. When there were dog complaints the chief went to see the old man, who always met him on the porch with a double-barrel shotgun and answered all questions calmly in spare monosyllables. Each time he told himself that someday the old bird was going to cause some real trouble. Was this the day? Damn.

The chief loaded the boys into his Plymouth Fury and drove to Zadravic's imposing house. The boys bailed out and charged en masse toward the tall hedges surrounding the place. One of them was screeching a dit-dit-dih cavalry charge sounding like something coming out of a badly warped bugle.

Gnat Murphy shooed the boys to the side and walked slowly up to the house, unsnapping his holster, just in case. When he reached the door, he hammered the brass clapper.

The old man came outside and looked around, locking his gaze on the jiggy-legged Dead River Rats. He smiled at them and watched them tremble and shift their bodies to run. Robert came outside behind him, carrying a four-foot long ship, a perfect replica of the frigate USS *Constitution*, Old Ironsides. The ship had been named by George Washington himself.

Robert said with a grin, "Hi guys."

Checkers yelled, "Look at Lumpy's *head*, Chief."

Gnat Murphy saw the bandage, realized it was fresh and clean, with no apparent blood. "What happened to you, young fella?"

Lumpy said, "Got brained by a rock." He held out the ship for the chief to see.

"A rock? Somebody threw a rock at you?"

"Yah," Lumpy said and nodded toward his pals.

"All of them?" Murphy asked.

"Was Polio got me, but he didn't mean to. He just throws real bad."

Gnat Murphy sighed. Boys.

"The one with the foul mouth," Zadravic said, pointing.

Murphy sighed again, said, "That's Denucci all right. He swears like a 30-year Navy man, and his old lady is even worse, foul, nasty, and mean." What chance did the boy have, and a dose of polio on top of a nutcase mother?

"They all got a mouth at that age," Murphy told Zadravic.

"Most kids," Zadravic said, and added, "But the one with the rocks is *je virtuoz*."

Gnat had no idea what the old fart had just said, but nodded to keep him happy. This was turning out a lot better than he'd anticipated. "Sorry for the trouble, Mr. Zadravic," the lawman said. "I'll have a talk with the boys and their folks. They shouldn't be bothering you again."

"No apology needed," Zadravic said. "Just doing your job. They are just boys and boys are always unruly in groups."

Gnat stared at Lumpy's ship model, whistled sharply, asked, "Who made *that* beauty?"

"I did," Zadravic said. "Can you drive Robert home? It's a long way and it's dark."

"I walk all the time," Lumpy volunteered, and tried to hand the ship model to the old man, who pushed it back. "Take it, Robert. And come see me and we'll build a ship together."

"Mine? Build?"

Zadravic smiled.

Lumpy said with a hiss, "Holy *shit*."

"Yah," Checkers yelled, "a *Nazi* ship."

Gnat shot Checkers the Irish evil eye and the boy shrunk back.

"*We'll* build a ship, you and me?"

Zadravic said, "Yes, of course. One must start learning when one is young. You are the right age."

Robert grinned. "I'm kinda simple."

"Good," Zadravic said. "So too are my ships. Take Old Ironsides home with you. It's my gift to commemorate our first meeting."

"Memorize what?"

"Chief?" Zadravic said with a nod toward the patrol car.

Murphy said, "C'mon Lumpy, let's go."

Zadravic caught the lawman's sleeve and whispered, "It's *Robert*." The old man's grip was steely and Gnat's arm was still aching when he crawled behind the steering wheel of his car. His passenger slid into the back seat.

The River Rats stood by the back door. "What about us?" Checkers asked.

"Walk home, the exercise will be good for the lot of you. Next time you fellows report a crime, make sure it ain't one that you dopes perpetrated." Gnat looked around for Richie, but he was long gone. "Tell Polio I'll be seeing him real soon."

Last Annual

THE FIVE FISHING FRIENDS AND WORK COLLEAGUES OF THE LAST FOUR decades sat around the poker table. There was a porous red placemat in the center of the table, and on it a chromed Colt .44 magnum with a four-inch barrel. They were all nursing a glass of red wine. In the early years they'd already have put away a bottle of Jack and three cases of beer, but that time was long past.

Showtime pointed at the revolver. "It belonged to Richard Brautigan, remember *Trout Fishing in America*?"

"Is it about us?" Canuck asked. "We're trout fishermen."

"No, it's got too much reality in it to be about us," Showtime said.

The Admiral, always the willing interpreter, said, "It's a book that's not much about trout fishing."

Canuck looked perplexed. "Why the hell did the guy name it that if there ain't trout fishing in it?"

"He's from California," Showtime said, by way of amplification.

Canuck was not easily checked off a thought. "Then what's the damn book *about, eh*?"

The Admiral said, "There is some trout fishing in it, but it's not about trout fishing or America."

"They'd never publish that kind of crap in Canada."

"No surprise in that. There's only thirty-seven people up there who can read," Showtime said.

"That's not true," Canuck said. "I read all the time."

"Thirty-eight," Showtime corrected.

"Canadians all read all the time," Cheffy said. "But clocks are one thing and books another."

"Was that a shot?" Canuck asked.

Cheffy said, "Yeah, but it wasn't close."

"Then what is that damn book *about*?" Canuck demanded.

"Anything you want it to be about," The Admiral said. "And nothing, and everything."

"Geez," Canuck said.

"Brautigan was part Canadian," the Admiral added.

Canuck made a snuffling sound. "No way."

"He played for the Rangers in the late '50s," Showtime said. "Long hair, liked to fight."

Canuck looked out the window, "Yah, I think mebbe I played against that guy in the Lumber League over to Sudbury. He couldn't fight for shit. No wonder his book sounds so dumb."

Showtime said, "That's part of the point of it. He wrote it when Vietnam was on and anguish and anger ran wild across the country. The book makes something out of nothing and nothing out of something. Like that war."

Canuck asked, "Why didn't the guy just call it 'War in America'?"

"He did," the Admiral said. "But he substituted trout fishing for war."

Canuck said, "What's all that gibberish got to do with us, eh?"

Cheffy pointed at the poker table, "That's the writer's guy's gun on the table?"

First Swede had been silent until now. "We all got guns, no biggie."

Showtime said, "Not like this one we don't."

Cheffy, sometimes called Second Swede, added, "Well, I don't see no p'ints about that frog that's any better'n any other frog."

"Frog?" Canuck said.

The Admiral said, "Thank you, Mr. Clemens."

Canuck looked at both men. "Clemens, frogs, what the hell happened to the hockey player writer guy?"

Showtime said, "Second Swede just changed the subject."

Second Swede explained, "What I was getting at it is this: The revolver on the table is nothing special. Barry had one exactly like it, but

Dad wouldn't let him have it in the camp after he shot a hole in the chalet roof and swore it was unloaded."

Barry was Second Swede's late grandfather. Over the years Barry had been as much a part of fish camp as the men at the table. The stories about the man invariably involved either gun mishaps or old-time Detroit attitudes. To his credit, Second Swede never repeated a single tale. Each was unique, a long-term cavalcade of fucked-up-edness in action.

The Admiral technically owned the camp on the Dead Priest River, where he hosted the others every year for a week sometime between the last Saturday in April and the last day of September. He drove all the way up from southwestern Missouri every year. First Swede had for years come west from Buffalo, and more recently north from Florida, Canuck came north from Indiana, and Swede Two and Showtime north from Kalamazoo.

The Admiral crossed his arms. "Okay, I'll bite. Why is said gun *here?*"

Showtime took a pull on the bottle of two-buck chuck, wiped his lips with the back of his shirt sleeve. "Anniversary gift. This is our 40th, from us to you and the wife for putting up with us all these years."

Age was beginning to crowd and erode their lives with shrinking borders and this was to be their last camp, none of that last-man-standing baloney. Over and done, a nice clean cut, and thank you for the memories.

The Admiral's sushi brow danced like killdeer nerving up for takeoff. "Well, thanks, guys, I guess. There's no need for a gift."

Showtime shrugged. "It has a history, a provenance, which makes it an artifact."

"Like an antique?" Canuck asked.

"We know there're lots of antiques in Canada," Second Swede said. "You're one of them."

"Guys, I ain't *in* Canada," Canuck pointed out. "I'm a Hoosier now."

"You shouldn't tell people that," The Admiral said. "They might get the wrong idea."

"*What* wrong idea?"

Showtime asked, "Did you see *Full Metal Jacket?*"

"Damn right," Canuck said.

"Remember what the drill instructor said, 'Only two things come out of Indiana, steers and queers, which one are you?'"

"I 'member, he was talking bout Texas, not Indiana. *You* guys!"

"Actually, he was probably talking about England where the movie was made."

Canuck looked confused. "They made a movie about Vietnam in England? Where they got the jungle there, eh? I seen jungle in the movie."

"It's the landscape on the Isle of Dogs."

"In Vietnam?"

"No, in the River Thames near Greenwich Palace, like in London, sort of."

Canuck said, "Where that timey thing comes from, what they call it, Greenwich Meaning Time?"

"Right, the prime meridian," Showtime said. "Zero longitude, starting in Toronto."

Canuck leered.

"I bet it's right there at Anne Murray's house," First Swede said. Canuck alleged that years ago he had dated Anne Murray (talk about fantasies)—a lumber yard rat from nowhere Ontario and the world's Canadian croonoodling queen, an unlikely pairing.

Second Swede began singing "Snowbird," but the others cut him off.

"That's right, "Canuck said. "Make fun. It's zero longitude, right at her house."

"We thought she lived in an apartment building," the Admiral said.

Canuck sighed. "Geez, you guys nitpick everything."

Showtime said, "Stop giving us ammo."

The Admiral said, "Okay, let's hear said story about said pistol."

The Canuck leaned over and stared at the Colt. He had lived a good deal of his youth in the remote Canadian bush doing highly technical ore surveying and living and working with First Nation aboriginals. He had grown up eating beaver tail and bear paws and scraping salt from between his toes to put on his food. He *knew* about guns. "What's that dark crap on the cylinder?" he asked, squinting.

They all leaned down to look closer. Showtime said, "Guess."

Nobody did. For years they had played all-night poker games, usually drunk, stupid games like Blind Baseball, 2–22 Inside Red, 7–27 black, six-card maverick, high-low. Nobody ever lost more than ten bucks in a week, but the wild imaginations in the group sometimes took them far from reality, the result being that none of them wanted to volunteer anything the others could run with. In some ways they were still in the fifth grade. But there had been no poker in eight, ten years, not a hand, the need for sleep replacing whatever it was that had driven the card games.

"Brautigan was unique," Showtime said.

"Unique my ass," Canuck said, "wrote a book about trout fishing that's not about trout fishing."

Showtime said, "Brautigan was not a particularly good writer, but he had Hemingway's knack for living high and hard, and making sure everyone knew about it, more performance artist than actual writer, though he published a lot."

"The gun?" the Admiral said. He had always taken it as his job to keep the ship's navigation on course, or close to it.

"Brautigan had a place somewhere near San Francisco and another in Montana's posh Paradise Valley," Showtime said. "He was periodically depressed and despondent, and sometimes he'd go off the air for months at a time. When he got like that, nobody, not his friends, kin, kids, neighbors, agent, *nobody* knew where the hell he was. He'd just dive into his own little aural null and that would be that until one day he'd wander back into the others' lives. Came a time when he gave up his fly rod and went really dark. Later people described him 'spooling up.'"

"We had an Indian used to spool up like that and talk to trees," Canuck offered.

"The trees talk back to him?" Showtime asked.

"They're just trees," Canuck said. "Trees can't talk."

First Swede asked, "Not even in Canada?"

"Some can," Canuck said, "but they don't bullshit with dumbasses like this trout-fishing writer guy."

"Was he diagnosed manic?" Second Swede asked Showtime.

Showtime said, "I don't think so. But he got the attention of his circle and he milked it for all it was worth. Well, this one time he went off the map and the grid and after four months his old lady finally got worried and started calling his buddies to see if any of them had seen her old man. They hadn't. One of them volunteered to drive out to Montana and look for him."

The Admiral asked, "Why didn't his wife just call a neighbor in Montana?"

"Who is telling this story?" Showtime shot back.

"It's not much of a story," Second Swede said.

"I've got a good story about Anne Murray," Canuck said.

"*Heard it!!*" the others yelled in unison.

"Don't got to yell guys, that's rude, eh."

"Brautigan," The Admiral said, prompting again.

"Like herding cats," First Swede told the Admiral.

"A lot easier than herding this lot," the Admiral remarked.

"Why didn't this writer guy just carry him an answering thingey?" the Canuck wanted to know.

"This was back in the eighties. They weren't widely available yet."

"We had them in Toronto. Anne Murray carried three of them."

Showtime said, "Okay, they had them in Toronto, but not in Paradise Valley, Montana."

"Canada's had them even way out in the bush since World War Two," Canuck said.

"Good to know," Second Swede said, rolling his eyes.

Showtime finally recaptured the floor. "One of Brautigan's pals drove to Montana and canvassed neighbors. Nobody had seen or heard from the writer, so the pal and a couple of neighbors went to see the county sheriff and the whole lot of them drove out to Brautigan's place, which was pretty much snowed in, with no sign of anyone having been around recently, at least outside the premises."

"Was the trout guy's pal famous too?" Canuck asked.

"Not yet," Showtime said. "The sheriff broke a window to let them into the house."

"Got keypads in Canada for that," Canuck said. "Even got them in Indiana."

Showtime went on. "The sheriff headed the expedition, flashlight in his left hand, Wap-9 in his right." Showtime took a drink of wine.

First Swede said. "We don't have all night here. My Fitbit says I've still got a thousand steps to do today."

"They found him," Showtime said.

"He have a stripper with him?" Canuck asked.

Showtime stared at the man as if he were an alien. "There's no stripper in this story."

"Could have been, Montana's like the Canadian bush. They got strippers in places you wouldn't' believe up in Northern Canada."

"You're right," the Admiral said, "We wouldn't believe; let the man finish his story."

"Had eaten his gun," Showtime said quietly. "Parts of his head were all over the place."

Silence in the room, all eyes on the revolver on the table.

The Admiral spoke. "Uh, a Colt .44 mag, I presume."

"Ayup."

"And the Colt on the table is the very gun."

"Ayup again."

"No way, Bozo."

"Is indeed, there's provenance in the box."

"And *you* came by this how?"

"I just did. How is unimportant."

The Admiral said, "I'd think how it came into your possession would be part of the provenance."

"Who cares?" Canuck said. "Sounds to me like this guy had your, what do you call it, the bipoker disorder?"

"Could be so," Showtime said. He took an envelope from his shirt pocket and placed it on the table beside the gun. "The last thing the man ever wrote. Remember how he was said to be spooling up. This time he was spooling up for suicide."

"Long note?" the Admiral asked.

"Three words."

Showtime let them stew on this while he took another slug of wine. He opened the envelope, took out a yellowing piece of paper, and started it around the table. He said, "A cautionary tale, lads. This is what can happen when a man stops trout fishing."

The Admiral was last to see the note. He read it, and grinned crookedly. "This is your idea of an elaborate joke, right?"

"No joke, it's legit."

The Admiral dropped the note on the table. "Get that sick shit out of here before my wife sees it."

"It's our gift," Showtime said. "It has historical value."

The Admiral went upstairs.

Showtime had another sip of wine. Just ten years ago, the boys would have been all over this deal, but tonight they just drifted away and into their own thoughts. He picked up the note and read it. Brautigan had written, "Messy ain't it?" Showtime refolded the note, tucked it into the envelope, and put the envelope under the Colt. Messy, like camps and friendships that endure 40 years.

Best Baseball Man Ever

Houghton County Sheriff Soren Wallen sighed when he saw the black plastic body bag. He was in the basement rec room of one Donald "Cuckoo" Olivanti.

Acting medical examiner Dee Dee Ivory unzipped the bag and showed Wallen the face. "J. J. Halusky," he sighed.

She nodded. "Aka Bugoo, in the flesh."

He stared for a while. "Holey moley, where're his eyes?"

"Evidence bag," Ivory said. She sounded weary, distracted, disgusted. Ivory was the county's acting M.E. and newly retired from her family practice. He knew she was anxious to be done not just with M.E. work, which she loathed, but all things medical. He couldn't blame her. There were days when he felt the same way about law enforcement. Cop work was ugly, even in a small town. Emotions up here lay deep as the bottoms of icebergs and rarely got to the surface, but if they did, more often than not, his people had to unroll body bags. Days like this. Bugoo? Geez.

J. J. Halusky and Donny Olivanti were lifelong pals, a brace of nutcases, a pair of loose cannons, sidekicks, and not-infrequent combatants. Wallen had seen a sad-faced Olivanti upstairs in the kitchen in handcuffs, his head slumped. Normally Wallen didn't visit homicide sites, but Detective Abel Herman had called him and urged him to get up to Overidgeton, a onetime mining location just north of Houghton.

Wallen looked over at his detective, who had quietly joined him downstairs. "What's Cuckoo got to say?"

"Says he did it, straight up. But you'll want to hear his story for yourself."

Wallen thought his detective and two deputies, and even the M.E., seemed to be biting back smirks, and this annoyed him. "What's so damn funny here? This is no joke. We've got a homicide."

"Talk to Olivanti," Detective Herman said, "fighting again."

"Book him first. He had Miranda?"

"You bet, right off. And he wrote a statement."

"Then get him out of here. I'll talk to him at the jail. No statements to the TV and radio jokers. I'll call Korba at the Urinal and tell him we have a suspected homicide, one suspect in custody, investigation under way, more information when we're done." The Urinal was what some cops called the *Daily Mining News Journal*. It was a lousy rag, but heads above local electronic clown work. Korba was the publisher, his daughter Elise married to the sheriff's son Monty, which made them kin. Sort of.

Detective Herman gone, Dr. Ivory said, "Victim has a broken tibia and fibula, left leg. Blunt instrument I'm thinking, say third of an inch in diameter, like that fireplace poker over there on the floor."

"Blood on it?"

"*Beaucoup*. It's all set for an evidence bag."

"Have you ever seen anything like this before, Dee?" Ivory had been an assistant M.E. in Duluth, Minnesota briefly after med school. This had been many years before she moved to Houghton to open her own family practice.

"Nope, this is a first for me," she said. "You know the deceased?" she asked.

"Hell, everybody in town knows the both of them."

"I never even heard of them until today," she said. "Local characters?"

Character was a category reserved for eccentrics and the socially unstable, a classification not unlike that of pets, but with less intimacy. "In the making. Neither or them is yet 24."

"One less candidate for characterhood now," she said.

The sheriff met Olivanti in an interview room at the county jail late that afternoon. The man was sobbing and could not, or would not, stop. With Olivanti you never knew. "Pull yourself together, Donny. We need to talk."

"But Bugoo's *dead!*" the man blubbered.

"No shit. You told Detective Herman you killed him."

Olivanti flashed a forlorn look. "I didn't want to, honest."

"How'd you get from didn't want to, to did?"

"Dude," Olivanti said. Wallen hated the word, wanted to dope slap the man, but the town's university libtards didn't like cops dope-slapping halfwits, even killers.

"Bugoo knew everything there was to know about baseball," Olivanti said. "Him being dead could kill our national pastime."

Baseball? What about the man's family? Wallen took a deep breath and exhaled slowly. "Baseball has survived steroids, the Black Sox, segregation, integration, several expansions, and Pete Rose. I think it will survive this too, Donny."

"See, this is *just* like all them things you said," Olivanti said. "Only worse. He was *my* best friend." More tears.

Good God. "Your best friend, who you just killed."

Olivanti said, "I know, but was mostly on accident . . . ya know?"

"No I *don't* know. You're telling me you mostly accidentally killed your best friend? How exactly does that work?"

"My best friend *ever, wah!*"

The last sound made Wallen cringe. Wah was a local sound, a sort of imprecise utterance for surprises, good or bad. He loathed it.

"You want tea or coffee?" the sheriff asked the prisoner.

"Yah sure, tea's good, six sugars and white milk."

The sheriff left the prisoner, went over to the jail kitchen, and returned with a teapot, sugars, and milk. He watched Olivanti's tea ritual. All coffee and tea drinkers had their own little routines. The boy sipped the mix, made a sour face, and said, "Perfect."

Wallen cringed. This boy just gouged out his best friend's eyeballs, and murdered him, and here we sit having refreshment, like a late afternoon high tea among the hoity-toitees.

"Take your time and tell me what happened, Donny."

"Ain't nothing happened."

"Bugoo's dead?"

"Oh yah, that."

"What happened?"

Olivanti said, "Remember when the Gremlins entered a team in the state sports trivia quiz bowl and won the whole state?"

Where the hell was he going with *this*? Gremlins was the mascot name for the teams at Houghton High.

Olivanti said, "J. J. answered all the questions got asked and never give nobody else a chance to answer. He didn't need them others. He was one of a kind."

The sheriff remembered and cringed. There had been a huge rhubarb over the specialized quiz bowl, especially when the final match in Lansing focused exclusively on baseball, and later it turned out that a retired Houghton High administrator had chaired the committee that picked the subject and approved all the questions for the final.

"Tell me what happened," Wallen told the prisoner. "With Bugoo."

"I just told you, he won state all by himself," Olivanti said.

"Not then. Here, today, Donny. *Focus.*"

"Wah, right. So . . . Bugoo went JFC on me and I couldn't shut his ass up. We were drinking tea and coffee and some Faygo one minute and the next minute he's gone full JFC. This one time, was maybe a year ago, he went JFC for 24 hours. Followed me everywhere, 'JFC, JFC, JFC.' I had to bop him upside of the head with a piece of firewood so I could sleep. Had to hit that sucker *twice*. JFC for 24 fricking hours. It was some sick shit, Sheriff. You know how he gets when he go fitty."

Wallen and most of his deputies knew firsthand. Halusky would go off on some crazy rant and only time would bring him back. Shrinks had looked at him, social workers, school counselors, psychiatrists, neurologists.

"When Bugoo *got* fitty, Donny. He's dead now. What do you mean JFC?" This was a new element.

"Jesus Fucking Christ, JFC, it was all his own and I couldn't get him to stop or shut up so I threw coffee in his face, you know, how you stop a dog won't stop fucking your your prize bitch?"

"Did it stop him?"

"The firewood sent him night-night."

Moron. "Not *that* time," Sheriff Wallen said. "What happened today?"

"Bugoo jumped on me, started pounding."

"Your face isn't marked."

"That's on account I know all his moves, and he's kinda slow and telegraphs everything. I kept twisting and took his shots on my arms and back to start with, but he wouldn't stop yelling JFC or stop punching at me. He give me no choice, Sheriff, swear to god."

"What happened then? The fireplace poker?"

Olivanti lowered his voice and said, "I just done the one leg, Sheriff. I wanted to stop him, not cripple him. He was my pal."

"Did he stop?"

"Hell no, he was on top of me again and started trying to twist my head so he could break my neck. When he can't punch, he always goes for the head."

Wallen closed his eyes. This seemed so far to be self-defense, sort of. "So he wouldn't quit?"

"No way, ain't no quit in that boy. Crazy people are like that."

Wallen said, "There's quit in him now." He waited for further explanation but got something entirely off the subject.

"Two outs, two strikes, two runs down, two men on, bottom of the ninth. Know who was best ever at clearing the bases with a walk-off homer when it was like that?"

"Not a clue," the sheriff said.

The prisoner said, "Me neither, but Bugoo knew all sorts of shit like that. He seen almost every Tiger game was ever on the TV since he was ten, and he don't see baseball the way you and me see baseball."

Thanks to Olivanti, Bugoo wouldn't see baseball at all anymore, and Wallen hated the stupid game. It was like watching paint dry, or golf. "Donny, back to Bugoo?"

"Okay, right, Bugoo. So, he's got holt of my neck, but I bucked around and made me some space, which let me get my hand up to his face by his eye, and I told him, 'Bugoo, you batshit motherfucker, leave go or I'm gonna pluck out your fuckin' eyeball.'"

"He let up?'

Olivanti shook his head. "Hell no. Crazy people don't quit."

Donny was right about that, ergo the failure of tasers to stop some wigged-out citizens.

"What happened next?"

"Well, then I took out the eyeball and it got real messy, but that dang Bugoo wanted to keep fighting. Except right when he lost his eye, he let up maybe for a half-second, and I spun loose and told him to quit his shit, it was stupid and we needed to get his sorry ass up to the hospital to get his eyeball put back in. They can do that, right?"

Wallen said, "Not in this hospital, maybe Mayo Clinic or somewhere."

"Mayonaise got a clinic? No shit?"

Good grief. "Mayo is in Minnesota. I'm not a medical expert, Donny. I'm just telling you what I think. You guys were separated then, apart, right?"

"Not long. Bugoo's big and slow, but let him get in too close, and he's quick-fast as a dog on a possum's neck. He got hold of me again and this time I kept kicking on his bad leg, but all he did was hang on and hop on the good leg. He was growling and popping his teeth like a pissed-off sow bear and I knew he'd gone somewhere in his head he wasn't coming back from soon, so I got a chokehold on him and took the other eye out and head-butted that sumbitch, and *finally*, down he went."

"Dead?"

Olivetti looked incredulous. "Not from no head-butt. He got a head hard as a curling stone. He was still breathin'," the dead man's friend explained. "But then I looked at my friend and seen both his eyes gone and all that blood and I knew he was gonna never see no more baseball games and it made me real sad, and I was pissed he made me do this, and I thought, how can Bugoo have him a real life if he can't see no baseball? I thought, Hey! Bugoo be better off dead than a live blind man. Can't be no baseball man if you're blind, am I right?"

Seriously? "What happened to getting him to the hospital to have his eyes put back in?"

"I ain't gonna lie, Sheriff. I was wigged-out and pissed by then, and I knew that done was done and I told myself, 'Donny, this here is your best friend forever. What kind life he can have with no damn eyes? He'd be better off dead, Donny.' That's what I told myself, 'You got a duty to take care of your friend.'"

So much for self-defense. Now we're somewhere between Murder 1 and Murder 2. "*How* did you kill him?"

"Poker against his throat. Snapped his tradeo. Didn't take that long."

Tradeo was a local radio show used to sell junk people no longer wanted. The suspect meant trachea. "You're saying you killed him with the poker and now he's dead. What did you do next, did you try to revive him?"

"I cried is what I done, Sheriff. I cried hard and I ain't afraid to say it. My best friend was dead."

"Did you ever try to revive him, Donny?"

"Why? He was blind and dead and he was better off that way, but it makes me real sad."

"Dead because you didn't want him to go through life blind." A statement, not a question.

"Baseball," Olivanti said. "It was his *life*, dude. He didn't have no eyes no more. He never really had nothing *but* baseball. You remember when he won all that money on the TV?"

Wallen remembered. "Hundred and fifty grand as a contestant on a weekly national sports TV trivia quiz."

Olivanti scowled. "That was all so much bullshit. Them IRS pricks counted all them trips he made out to L.A. as pay and docked him big. When they got done with him, he barely made thirty grand. He hated them IRS pricks."

"Donny, did you write up a statement for Detective Herman?"

"Yes sir, back to the house. I wrote it best I could. I was kinda upset, and my spelling ain't so great, okay?"

—◆—

The sheriff's longtime spouse Val was an attorney in Houghton. She met her husband at their back door. "I just made a pot of fresh coffee. I heard you and your people had a trying day, Bugoo and Cuckoo?"

"Bugoo's dead."

"God almighty, what a shame. He was such a nice boy most of the time."

And insane, Wallen thought. Both boys were, and both of them had been walking around the community like time bombs looking for a place and time to explode. What the hell is wrong with us we let such people walk around without help?

"Accident?" his wife asked.

"Not exactly. We're still investigating, trying to nail down the facts."

"Donny's never been quite right," Val said. "He'll get off on mental grounds."

Maybe so, but with Halusky dead, the town now had one less nutwad on the street. Wallen stopped himself and sighed. Listen to you: nutwad? What happened to innocent until proven guilty? What is it about this place that makes for so many lethal goofballs? Heaven help us.

"I take it the boys were fighting again," Val said. "They seemed to be always at it, those two."

Wallen nodded.

"Fight over what?" she asked.

"JFC."

She stared at her husband. "What's that supposed to mean?"

"You don't want to know."

Honor Guard

NORMAL CRULLER, DEAD AND TOURING HEAVEN, WAS, AFTER THREE months, not exactly impressed. He'd grown up in the U.P., been assigned here by the Air Force, died here, and he'd be damned (so to speak) if Heaven didn't seem to be a dead ringer for the U.P., or vice versa. Death tended to leave a lot of the newly departed more than a little disoriented. Answers to life's questions after death? No answers, just lots more questions.

His bus ride ended in Houghton-Hancock, which in fact was two separate towns divided by a quarter mile of ice-cold shipping canal, but always referred to one place, conveniently hyphenated. It marked one as a foreigner if one said the name of one without the other, yin forever requiring the adjacency of yang in order to exist properly. It had been a long ride west from the Soo.

Vietnam was blood hot and the Houghton-Hancock bus depot was packed with students from Michigan Tech, thin, earnest-faced young men with black horn-rimmed glasses, acne scars, permanent condom contours in their wallets, and slide rules sheathed in stiff leather holsters, dangling from their belts like they were gunslinging desperadoes of old. They seemed a swaggering, desperately arrogant lot, strutting through the Greyhound Bus terminal chewing Snickers bars, looking ready to duel to the intellectual death with differential equations over no more a threat than a mere hundredth of a point in comparative G.P.A.

After twenty months in Southeast Asia (five tours), Norm couldn't stand the sight of such spoiled, self-assured, and safe boys. Muscle here was not measured by drive-on scales, as it was out west, but this was no less a competitive environment than military towns, where seas of testosterone flowed day and night. This was not even your effete liberal arts crowd; here they took succor from Pythagoras, Pascal, and the unquestioned absolutes of the isosceles triangle. By now, the day before Thanksgiving, the bus station's restrooms were filled with drunk and reeling revelers on their way to their homes in Flushing, Three Rivers, or Duluth. There were lots of Indian and/or Pakistani boys, Chinese and/or Japanese students, but it was largely only their white companions who seemed to be doing the holiday traveling, while students with the darker skins seemed to be tasked with holding down the ivory tower.

There were no buses to Copper Harbor this time of year, which seemed strange. Was this not Heaven, where tourist season theoretically was always to be in effect? Apparently not, and this seemed to be a significant difference between life and death. Norm tried to jot thoughts and observations in his notebook in which he was building a list for further consideration when he found time. Ten inches of fresh snow were already on the ground and more forecast. Snow in Heaven: another jot for the notebook. The streets were slick with new snow on black ice, the temperature panting in the high teens.

Standing on the south span of the Portage Ship Canal Lift Bridge, Norm got a quick preview of death by exposure and was considering abandoning a hitched ride to the tip of the Keweenaw Peninsula for a local hotel room. He dutifully wagged his thumb as traffic passed by in the snow and about an hour after his vague vigil began, a dented black hearse fishtailed to a stop next to the curb, the passenger window dropped, and he found himself staring at an unshaven cherubic face under a Cubs baseball cap. The face was smiling. A miniature plastic yellow, red, and green striped Vietnamese flag was affixed to the hearse's aerial.

"Hey man," the cherub greeted Norm through the window. "We got room if you don't mind riding with a stiff." Norm thought the man looked to be approximately the same age as the students at the bus terminal, but his eyes told another story, and he understood: It was the stunned, I-have-seen-the-shit, thousand-yard stare of a combat vet.

Norm tossed his gear behind the second seat and slid in. There was a coffin beside him on a carpeted platform. He introduced himself to the driver. "Normal Cruller."

"Cool, man. I'm called Stony," the driver said from up front. "The sorry piece of shit shotgun with me is the Minnow. And that's our main man Nooch in the pine beside you."

Both Stony and Minnow wore army uniforms that had seen better days.

"Body escort?" Norm asked.

"Fuckin' A," Stony said. "Pass a couple of brewskies forward and help yourself, man."

Norm saw no beer, and no cooler. He could see Stony watching him through the rearview mirror. The driver laughed. "Anything to keep worms out of remains can keep brewskies cold. Nooch has the beer."

Norm had no desire to dig into a coffin with remains. "Your friend a KIA?"

"There it is," Stoney said. "The three of us went to high school together up to Calumet, dropped out together, enlisted together, went through Basic and AIT together, and shipped to the Nam together. Triple-1, 17s, all airborne."

"Like the three Muscatelles," Minnow offered.

"Musketeers," Norm wanted to correct the man, but it was impolite to correct people and he was not certain of the proper etiquette in this situation.

"Not that Disney shit," Minnow complained. "Where's the beer, beer gunner?"

Norm was not eager to open the coffin. "You guys were with him then, your friend, what's his name?"

"The Nooch." Stony said. "He was one dumbass motherfucker."

Norm eased open the casket, felt around for ice, and found cans in the ice and pulled out three, passing two forward. He heard two can tops pop and Minnow passed a metal church key back.

Everyone sucked their beers. Stony said, "No fucking way we were with him, man. We started out together, but Nooch he took all that army shit like religion. We had us the good duty at Pleiku. Once in a while

Charlie lobbed some rockets, but we were deep in a CONEX tube reinforced by sandbags. Nothing got through that shit. We put in our year, had a howl of an R&R in Australia, and split. Motherfucker Nooch? He decides to re-up for a second tour. Can you believe that shit, *volunteered*?"

Norm felt Stony studying him through the rearview.

Stony said, "They shipped his ass into the boonies, out where the kill-your-ass serious shitephant lives. We don't know details but all they found of the Nooch was his head, man. It's in the box inside a bowling bag with ice."

Later, while groping for more beer, Cruller unzipped the bowling bag. The flesh was the color of sun-dried bone; the closed eyelids were yellowish and protruded like antique cue balls had been transplanted beneath them. Blond whiskers protruded from Nooch's chin. Norm touched the dead flesh and then his own. No difference except temperature. The corpse's eyelids fluttered and opened. A smile formed on its face.

"You lucky bastard," the head whispered.

"You're *talking*?" Norm asked. He felt himself sweating. Was the head talking or was he imagining all this shit?

"Why not?" the head asked. "You're dead and you're talking. Do me a favor?"

Norm nodded.

"Help me have a slug of brew, man. This head-only shit is seriously unhandy."

Norm tipped a can to the dead man's mouth. Nooch coughed, spat, and drank greedily until beer spilled out the corners of his mouth. "Been a long time," he said. "When you can get beer, you tend to take that shit for granted. Guess that holds true for a lot of things," Nooch lamented.

"Guess so," Norm said.

"How long you been dead?" Nooch asked.

"Three months."

"About the same for me, give or take. Took some time to find me and process me and I've been in transit since then, the whole time in bags and boxes and here I am scared shitless of the dark. This whole thing is like pretty weird. You ever drop acid?"

"Afraid not."

"It's a lot like this. You're here, you're there, you're kind of everywhere but nowhere."

"Your friends know how it is?"

"Stony and the Minnow?" He grinned. "Nah, I thought I'd save the surprise for the funeral. I'll wait until the church is filled and start yelling. That ought to scare the pants off of everyone and give them shit to talk about for years."

"That should do it," Norm agreed.

"Worst part," Nooch says, "is I don't know what comes next. Do you?"

"No. I've been trying to figure it out, but so far no dice."

"Bummer, man. How'd you get it?"

"Bail out. Broke my neck."

Nooch's eyes widened. "Pilot or Ranger?"

"Navigator."

"Nam?"

"Nope, about a hundred miles east of here."

Nooch said, "Guess it don't matter much where you are when the shit gets you, man. When it's your time, it's your time."

Norm gave the head in the bowling ball bag another slug of beer.

"Worst part is, I got no body. Blown the fuck up. Don't know what I'm going to do, being just a dead head, man."

"Tough," Norm said sympathetically.

"Hey man," Minnow called from up front. "What the hell's the hold up on the beer?"

"Sorry, I got distracted."

"Doing what, jawing with the stiff?"

"I gave him a beer."

The two up front started laughing with delight. "Far out, man." The Minnow said. "*That* is great!"

"Better close the lid," Nooch whispered. "Be cool, bro."

"You too." Norm quietly eased the casket lid into place after fishing out two more beers, which he passed forward. He told the two men, "Your friend back here says keep the noise down, he's trying to catch some Zs."

The two escorts howled. "That son of a bitch was always trying to catch some Zs."

A mile or so later the hearse reached a traffic light with a blinking red light tacked to a telephone pole with several two-by-fours. "I'll get out here," Norm said and opened the door.

"This ain't Copper Harbor," the Minnow say. "We ain't even close."

"This will do," Norm said. He tapped the casket once and got two taps in return. How Nooch managed that, he would never know. The thing is they were both dead and still found ways to communicate. Dead vets stick together no less than live ones.

Norm watched the hearse drive off. He wondered what had just happened. When he first died, he formulated a theory that where you fell would be your heaven, but now he wasn't sure this was right, and he wondered what would happen at Nooch's funeral. Who was he supposed to scare? Wasn't everybody here dead?

Kate's Bay

ANOTHER DAY BUTTONING UP IN HEAVEN AND A BITTERLY COLD NIGHT was settling in, cold, even for a dead man.

The sign by the Military Road read, "Village of Kate's Bay," no population number cited. The snow had stopped, stars were packing into the sky, and Normal Cruller looked up and found himself directly under Polaris, which, in his life as a navigator, had served as a significant minor diety.

Cruller was a large-boned, well-muscled man who always made for a seat with his back to a wall. He had been like this in life, too. Heaven had not changed him.

Kate's Bay consisted of a gas station with one very old pump, gas brand unknown; a boarded-up Dairie Kween; a grocery store that doubled as a post office; a two-story boarding hotel called Touhi's Hunt Club Inn; and, a tavern-restaurant with a weathered sign: "MerriLew's." There were lights on inside. It was the only building that looked open.

The village sat on a bleak, treeless hump of volcanic lava that stuck into Lake Superior, putting water on three sides of the village. There was a slight stiffening wind out of the northwest and Cruller found himself shivering, his jacket more suitable for an early tee time in Palm Springs than a wintry night in God's Kingdom.

Winter in Heaven? There were snowbanks along all the streets, some of them already four feet high, and he guessed they would get a lot higher before winter broke. Houghton-Hancock, thirty miles south, had picked up ten inches before he caught a ride north.

MerriLew's was paneled in knotty pine, the varnish yellowed to an early 1950s patina; the tables were small, draped with red-check oilcloths. There seemed to be no one in the place. Cruller sat down at the bar beside a heavy wall and rang a small bell that gave off a faint *ting*.

A voice behind the bar asked. "What'll it be, Mister?" Norm Cruller had learned that social interactions in Heaven trended toward genteel politeness.

"Screwdriver," Cruller told the voice. The voice came from the back of a deep shadow.

"Gin's on top," the voice said. "Juice is in the cooler below, and glasses where you find them."

"No gin in a screwdriver," Cruller said. "Vodka."

"Your drink, have it your way."

This was a strange wrinkle, even for Heaven. "You want me to make my own drink?"

"You can understand whatever you want," the voice said, "but if a screwdriver's what your heart's set on, you'll have to fix it yourself. Hard stuff's buck a shot; juice is on the house. Put your money in Mickey's right ear."

There was a large ceramic cookie jar on the end of the bar; Mickey Mouse's right ear was Missing In Action. "How do I get back there?" Cruller asked.

"That depends."

"On what?" He still couldn't pinpoint the location of the voice, which he decided was probably female, which in wine terms he'd describe as dry with hints of sandpaper. The voice had an otherworldly ring to it, which was a small surprise. So far in his months in Heaven, voices seemed pretty much the way they had sounded in life. There was no doubt a simple explanation, but no reference desk to consult.

"If you can jump, Mister, you can hop the top. If not, you can crawl under like the rest of us do. There's an opening to your left."

He saw how he could get under, but decided instead to vault over, which he did with a slightly off-balance landing. He found the cooler, opened it, and a small light came on. He glanced toward the voice and could see the outline of someone sitting. He tried not to stare. So far the customs and ways of Heaven seemed much like those in life, but he couldn't be sure, and he didn't want to offend if he could avoid it. Measured against an eternal clock, three months wasn't a long time to get adjusted to being dead.

Cruller made the screwdriver with two shots of unbranded vodka and put two curly dollar bills in the cookie jar, which was nearly devoid of greenbacks.

The voice said, "While you're up, Mister, make me a mai tai."

"How many kinds of rum do you have?"

"How many do you need?"

"Three would be nice."

"We've got one. I always make mai tais with one rum."

"Can't do that," Cruller told her. "I need three for a proper mai tai, two minimum."

"What *can* you make?" the voice asked.

"Is your rum light or dark?"

"Pale green bottle," the voice said.

"Got any fresh lemon?"

"Got what passes for fresh hereabouts. Fresh produce comes in sporadically, especially in winter. Lemons are in the cooler, but I never heard of no lemon in a mai tai."

"*Cuba Libre*," Cruller corrected her.

"Come again?"

"*Cuba Libre*, rum and Coke with a little lemon."

"I guess I had me a rum and Coke or two in my day," the voice said defensively. "But not with no lemon. I'd remember that."

"You'll like it," the improvising bartender said. Oddly enough he found himself wanting the voice to like his offering. He poured and mixed, added ice, a squeeze of lemon, and set the glass on the bar near the voice.

"Fetch it to me, Mister. I'm neither nimble nor nubile anymore."

He held the glass into the shadow, felt it being taken, heard sipping, followed by loud swallowing. "Right good," the voice said. "Now make me a Manhattan."

Once again he did as he was told, handed over the drink, and got another "Right good" in return.

"You drank *both* of those?" he asked.

"Drank the first, still sipping the second. This time I want me a rye and seven."

Cruller was astounded and confused by what was happening. "You want *another* drink?"

"To sip," the voice said. "Don't go getting some notion I'm a lush. Can you make the drink, or not? If you can't, stop wasting my damn time."

"I'm wasting *your* time?" Cruller didn't care for her tone.

She said sharply, "You let me be the judge of that. My time's my time, and I guess I know when it's being wasted."

The newcomer mixed the drink and over the next half-hour made six more. "Pretty damn good," the voice eventually declared. "Can't think of no more. Can you?"

"Ever had a Brave Bull?" he asked, feeling a surge of confidence. He had been an above-average navigator, and now he was proud to show off the bartending skills he had also learned from the Air Force.

"In bed, once . . . maybe," the voice said, and for the first time Cruller detected another sound, a sort of subtext, a sort of laugh twisted with a nasal snort, that might have been choking and not laughter at all. Impossible to say.

"I'll need tequila."

"Up top somewhere."

He found a clear bottle with a Mexican flag on the label. The green in the flag had faded to gray and the cap was too tight to open, maybe rusted shut. He held the bottle up to the light. "No worm," he told the voice.

"What worm?"

"In the tequila. What you've got here is mescal. Real tequila always has a worm on the bottom." Or was it the other way around? He tended to confuse the two when he was alive.

"Then it's not the real stuff," the voice noted unapologetically.

"It will have to do," Cruller said, seeing he was at a minor impasse.

"That's worth a point," the voice remarked.

"Meaning what?"

She countered. "What else goes in your Brave Bull?"

"Kahlúa."

"Far left, fat bottle."

Cruller wrenched the tequila cap, mixed the drink half and half, and gave it to the shadow, which made an unpleasant sound. "People *willingly* drink these?"

"Mainly to get drunk fast. Not for flavor or pleasure."

"*You* like 'em?"

"Hate 'em, but I don't drink much. Beer man mostly."

"Worth another point, what else you got in your trick bag?"

"Any cream around here?"

"Cream? This here's a tavern, not a malt shop."

"I need cream for a drink."

A faint buzzer stirred the stillness, two long bursts followed by a short one. "Dit-dit-dot," Cruller said.

"You you speak Morse?" the voice asked.

"Some," Cruller admitted.

"I'll add a point," the voice said, and this time he thought he could detect distinct, albeit slight, approval in the tone.

A woman walked into the bar. Norm heard her coming, her heels resonating like a single drumstick struck hard on a wooden floor. The newcomer was tall, and all woman, thirtyish, a lean five-seven with curly dark hair. She wore a long gray sweater with a gold link belt looped several times around. Bright red ski pants, black stiletto heels, four-inchers easily. Shiny gold scarf draped loosely around her neck and flipped with nonchalance over one shoulder, cowgirl style. She stepped to the other end of the bar and leaned over. Long eyelashes, black and curled, blue eye shadow. Thin, wide red lips.

"Take your eyes off that fella," the shadow voice cautioned. "He's working."

"Just looking," the newcomer said, and turned to the shadow.

"He needs some cream," the shadow voice said.

"He a stray, or what?" the new woman asked. She glanced at Cruller, raised an eyebrow, and departed, returning minutes later with a small glass bottle of cream from the Cowsit Lats Dairy. She set it on the bar without comment. The newcomer looked directly at Norm Cruller, gave him a tiny smile, a wink, a raised eyebrow, and departed.

In life, Norm would have read this as her interest in him, but this was Heaven, he was new, and he had no idea what the rules of such things were. Or if such things were even allowed, and he had no idea what the hell such signals meant, given his current surrounds.

"Don't even think about it," the shadow voice said. "She's off limits, understand? We got clear-cut rules here in Kate's Bay," she added.

He mixed Kahlúa and the cream, added two ice cubes, finger-stirred the mixture, and passed it to the shadow. He heard ice rattle, lips smacking.

Dit-dit-dot, the buzzer sounded again, twice the same signal, a calling code, maybe?

"Now what?" the voice wanted to know. The woman in the red ski pants reappeared. Norm thought she seemed a little annoyed and laboring to hide it.

"Try this," the shadow voice said.

The woman came under the bar and pressed slowly past Norm, pausing long enough for him to feel the firmness of her breasts against him. She went to the shadow's end of the bar and came back with the glass. The drink was half gone. She tasted it, shut her eyes, swirled it in her mouth like fine wine, swallowed.

"Nice," she said. "What's this called?"

"Kahlúa and cream," Norm said.

"Well?" the shadow demanded.

"Good, hey," the younger woman said, drained the drink, and handed the glass back to Norm. "How many points has he earned?" she asked the shadow voice.

"Ten on the standards, sixteen in all. A new record."

Red ski pants said, "Sixteen." Norm thought she sounded impressed.

"He's got the job. Yank the window sign."

"I never got around to putting it up," ski pants confessed. She reached down and squeezed Norm's leg, which made him jump slightly.

"You want the job or not?" the shadow voice asked.

"What job?"

"Barkeep," red ski pants said.

175

"What's it pay?" He didn't need a job right away. He had not exactly been living a high life and had some cash left from the life before he died. Moneywise he was in good shape, but harbored questions about why anyone would even need money in Heaven. The residence rules in Heaven seemed loose and unknown. There was no newcomers' group, no Welcome Wagon, and no orientation sessions for the newly deceased.

Shadow voice challenged, "You got other work?"

"Not at the moment," Norm said.

"Then what's it matter what this job pays?" Shadow voice asked. "Something's better than nothing, winter coming on and all."

He couldn't argue her logic and accepted the job of barkeep for MerriLew's.

"You can start tomorrow," the voice in the shadows said. "Your shift's one to five, an hour off to eat, and back on from six to one. We close at one a.m., earlier if we're not busy. You'll make the call on when. All tips are yours alone. What you do on your own time is your own business. Mona will show you to your room. Wage, tips, room, board, and you get to sleep in every morning. What you've got here, Mister, is what a lot of us call our own sweet corner of Heaven."

"Who am I working for?" he asked.

"Yourself," shadow voice said. "One always works for one's self."

"What's your name?" he asked.

"What's the outside sign say?"

He had to think for a while. "MerriLew?"

"I'm Kate," the voice said. "You've got to pay more attention."

The voice in the shadow was Kate. The lady in red ski pants was Mona, but how the women connected was unclear.

Having accepted employment, Norm was escorted by Mona across the road to Touhi's and guided him upstairs to a corner room. There were tall, thin windows on two sides and heavy black curtains. Norm dropped his backpack on a chair and stripped off his jacket. The tub in the bathroom was a huge, scarred white antique sitting on human-shaped feet. No showerhead.

Mona stood in the room, smiling while he explored. "Pretty nice, hey?" she said. "You'd pay serious money for this much space below the bridge."

Mackinac Bridge or the lift bridge between Houghton and Hancock? A bridge to Hell? It was hard to guess Mona's point of reference. "Been a long time since I've seen better," he told her. What he didn't tell her was that it would feel good to settle in one place for a while.

"You some flavor of traveling man?" she asked.

"Something like that." By some measures he suspected he had traveled farther than the boys who'd sailed around the moon.

"Anything else I can get for you?" Mona asked, her left eyebrow punctuating the question.

"Right now?"

She grinned, puckered her lips, blew a kiss at him, kicked off her shoes, peeled off her clothes, and stood naked before him, turning slowly to give him a full look. She had ample reason for pride.

Heaven, he thought, and reached for her, but she pushed his hands away. "You're not on the payroll until tomorrow," she whispered.

"What's that got to do with it?"

"Everything," she said, as quickly re-dressed and departed. He could hear her steps on the inn's uncarpeted wooden stairs, her body image burned into his mind.

―――

"Clear conscience," a voice said. Norm was more asleep than awake, but recognized the voice. It was Kate, his shadowy employer.

He rolled over and tried to see her, but it was still too dark. "You allergic to light?" he asked.

"We like to use first names here," she said. "I'm Kate."

"Kate," he repeated.

"Been watching you sleep," the woman said. "Can tell a lot about one by how a body sleeps, or don't."

"Is this part two of the interview process, Kate?"

"No, the job's yours. Kate's word is good and she says what she means and means what she says. After all, I am the daughter of the late and great Anna Clemenc."

The name meant nothing. "I thought work begins at one?"

"I felt a need to have the talk with you."

"The *talk*?"

"You're military," she said. "You like to talk?"

Former military seemed more accurate for a dead man. "Air Force," he admitted. "Depends on who I'm talking to and what we're talking about."

"You been to that Vietnam thing?"

"Thereabouts," he allowed.

"You find it pretty bad?"

"Bad enough." He sensed he couldn't take as much latitude with the facts with Kate as he had with others over the past ninety days in Heaven, better to keep it ambiguous.

"*You* don't know bad," Kate declared. "My mother and I knew bad. We *lived* it, and eventually it killed us."

This got his attention. Good, all of us are dead. Mona too? Finally some sense in all this. Norm wanted to sit up, and did halfway, but kept the covers at his waist. He had always slept nude, which according to his understanding of obscure demographics made him one of eight among American males. Before dying he had heard a sexual revolution was in the making, but apparently it hadn't reached most married beds. Did Mona sleep nude?

Kate said, "They called her Big Annie."

"Who?" Norm had a morning piss-erection and until he could void himself, it would persist.

"My mother Anna Clemenc? It's a proud Croatian name. Everyone knows Anna Clemenc. The Welsh, those uppity little Cousin Jacks, and their English masters, they ran the copper mines in these parts. Croats, Serbs, Slavs, drunken Irish, jabbering Italians, and morose Finns did the real mining and died doing it. Yessir, a lot of men died making copper," Kate said. "They dug it out pound by bloody pound. Pay was eighteen dollars a week for six days' work, ten-to-twelve-hour shifts. Superintendent where my father worked made eighty thousand dollars a year salary and got bonuses on top of that. It was abominable work for the men below ground who ran all the risk. Families couldn't be raised on eighteen dollars a week. It was a hard damn life."

Still groggy and distracted by his morning condition, Norm asked, "What about Babe Ruth?"

"That, loud mouthed fat-assed ballplayer? What *about* him?"

"He pulled down a hundred grand in 1929. Just for playing a boy's game."

"Salary or profit?" she asked.

"Salary, and what difference does it make?"

"Salary describes a working man, and profit tags a capitalist," she offered.

"That's bad?"

Kate chuckled. "You can bet that if they paid him that much, the man would probably be worth two or three times as much. Management always pays a man a lot less than he's worth."

Norm had some sympathy for Kate's view. He'd once had a squadron commander who refused to make takeoffs or landings, and only touched the steering column when the aircraft was level at cruise altitude and on full autopilot, thereby making his gesture entirely symbolic. This was the same man whose responsibilities included assuring that all squadron aircrews' performance was up to professional Strategic Air Command standards and signing off on all annual officer evaluations, called OERs, which directly affected an officer's future, like how high he might rise in rank or if he would rise at all.

The squadron C.O. eventually got orders to command an A-1E Sky-raider squadron in eastern Thailand. The man got drunk a week before he was to leave and wrapped his Lincoln Continental around an oak tree, killing him and his wife. Most of Norm's squadron mates shrugged and called it a chickenshit's chickenshit suicide.

Kate kept on, "Back in 1913 we had all we could take. It wasn't like now with a few die-hards trying to get through another winter. There were 95,000 people in the Keweenaw in those days and the whole damn world got copper off our sweat. In 1907 we got us a union, the Western Mine Workers, and when the mine operators started replacing two-man drill teams with killer one-man drills, the union called, 'Strike,' and by damn, that's what they did, even women and kids! The governor sent the whole damn state militia up here, 2,200 Detroit Bohunks with shotguns and Springfields. The mine owners hired their own special deputies they brought out here on trains from New York and Boston and armed them with cheap .38s. My mother walked every day at the head of the strikers' parades. She carried a silk American flag on an eight-foot-long pole, two inches in diameter. Most men couldn't even lift it, much less carry it, in the snow and wind. Anna Clemenc was powerful strong in heart, mind, and body," Kate said with great pride, her voice softening.

She went on, "Came a day when some militia boys tried to grab Big Annie's flag. One of them bastards poked a bayonet clean through her wrist, but missed the bones. My mother wrapped that flag around her like a blanket and told them bastards if they were going to take her flag, they'd have to ram their bayonets through the flag and her heart, not her arms. Wasn't long after that they arrested *her* for assault and battery. They arraigned her in Houghton and jailed her in Hancock. She did six months in the pokey with nothing but men to keep her company. My papa couldn't take it. He tried to take care of me, but took to drinking and finally lit out. When they released her, Mama brought me here to raise me. The union got busted, of course, and so too did my family. In the end, all we had left was Big Annie and me. She's my hero. They wrote a heap about her out East, called her the American Joan of Arc. Now everybody's forgotten us. True heroes don't last long in peoples' memories."

The idea of living with the descendant of an American St. Joan (via Croatia) was not unattractive. "You lived here all your life?" he asked her.

"On the floor below. Had me five husbands and they give me ten children, all girl babies, and all handsome. My husbands all died on me. Being a woman alone in these parts is a hard slog, but being a man is impossible. Now there's just Mona and me. The rest of the kids have run off. Mona, she's my baby, the cleverest of the flock."

Norm had the feeling she was trying to assess him. For what he could only guess, and right now he needed to take a leak, not jabber. But he said, "Grandchildren?"

"None yet that I know of because I wouldn't let my girls marry. It's too hard when you lose your man."

"Then there won't be any grandkids."

"There will be, there will be. Them girls all got the urge same as I had in the day. Women are born with it. Sooner or later it will happen. Won't matter who the fathers are because the only blood that matters comes direct from Anna Clemenc, through me. I'm Big Annie's daughter, her only one."

There was a certain single-mindedness to Kate, and Norm curiously thought of George Wallace. "Mona's your youngest?"

"Right at 35 now, which some claim is close to a woman's peak of lust. She does my books, keeps things organized around here. She's a real good girl, keeps to herself, thinks a lot, and talks little. Seems to take after me. But Mona don't seem to have the urge such as overwhelmed her sisters and mother. They all like to have burnt to a crisp with the carnal wants," Kate said. "But not my Mona. She's still as virgin as Mary Herself."

"Where are your other girls?"

"Here, there, everywhere. They come and they go. If you're here long enough you might meet some of them, or you might not. They're an erratic and unpredictable bunch, all of 'em but Mona. She's my baby."

"All your kids here in Heaven?" Norm asked.

"All born up here, but they've moved around some, mostly east and south."

It was coming dawn now, and Norm could finally see across the room. Kate was draped in black, a heavy veil over her head like an executioner's mask, a narrow slit for her eyes. A curtain of heavy black fabric hung over her body and didn't look a lot different than the curtains in his hotel room. She looked like a new statue awaiting ceremonial unveiling. Eventually she moved and Norm stared as she repaired to the hallway with a jerky motion he had never seen before. The movement was labored and suggested pain, albeit unvoiced. He heard a shushing of fabric and no sound of weight on the floor, almost as if she were weightless. Being weightless he could understand in Heaven, but feeling pain? Wasn't pain supposed to be banished here? Never much for the Bible, he seemed to vaguely remember something about tears, sorrow, and pain being gone after death, presumably meaning in Heaven.

Norm was on the verge of wetting himself. "Guess I'll get up," he said, hoping to move her along more quickly. He needed to use the toilet but couldn't bring himself to cross the room in his condition. Some people could waltz around in front of strangers in their all-together. He wasn't one of them, even in Heaven. When Kate was finally at the door, he made a dash for the bathroom, and as he made it to the door, she chirped quietly behind him, "Nice size."

⎯⚬⎯

Norm used the morning to explore Kate's Bay. The sky was the color of motor oil a thousand miles past a scheduled change. An occasional baby snow squall flitted across the village, leaving no major deposits.

The gas station was run on an honor system. The garage bay was empty and seemed to have been for a long time. Oil spots on the concrete were dry. Norm fiddled with the controls of the hydraulic lift but couldn't get it to move. No surprise there. Back in life he was known for a distinct lack of mechanical aptitude. When mechanical things didn't work, he kicked them, and sometimes (not often) they began to work again.

There was a fifty-foot-high pyramid of black-wall tires behind the service station, all of them blown out or thin-skinned. Just like the bar, there was a one-eared Mickey Mouse cookie jar on the counter in the gas station and a tarnished brass-key cash register. There was loose change in the cookie jar and a nest of cobwebs and lumps of ruddy turquoise dust.

Norm found Mona at the grocery. There was a post office sign over a counter at one end of the room and a bank of twenty-four wooden pigeonholes on a table behind her, each with its own number. There were no names, and all the slots were all empty.

Mona had a large crank-type adding machine on the counter in front of her. A tape spilled down like a white snake, and curled back from the floor. She was wearing a heavy black turtleneck under a tight black leather vest, black slacks, and knee-high leather boots with flat heels.

"Does everyone in Kate's Bay wear the color black?" he asked.

"Black's not a color," she quickly corrected him, "it's the absence of color." She pulled the lever on the adding machine and the tape snake rustled, jumped, and grew longer. "Always thought it odd what black seems to do to a man's libido," she remarked. "Nothing gets some men going faster than black. You sleep all right?" She looked up at him and smiled warmly.

"Like a dead man. Your mama came to see me this morning."

"I'm not surprised. Our Kate . . ." she said wistfully, "Well . . . she *loves* to talk. She tell you about Big Annie?"

Norm nodded. "The Keweenaw's Joan of Arc."

Mona smirked and depressed the lever again. While she talked she kept working. "Kate says of all her girls I look most like grandma Annie."

"She must have been a beautiful woman," Cruller said.

The corner of Mona's left eyebrow went up again. "You've got you the shameless nookie-line," she said. "Just the right timing, neither too fast and overeager, nor too slow and lackadaisical, and not at all pushy, but you don't hang back either. You had a lot of women, have you?"

He felt uneasy and changed the subject. "Kate says you run things around here."

Mona grimaced. "Nossir, what Kate told you was I do the bookkeeping and keep things organized. Kate would never say I run things. I don't. This is *her* town, her bay. Don't be fooled by what you think or see, Mister. Make no mistake: Kate's God in these parts."

"Last night she called this place Heaven. Now you're telling me she's God?"

"There you have it," Mona said. The tape snake chuffed again.

"That would make you an angel," Cruller said.

"Don't bother looking for my halo," she said. "I'm hired help, same as you."

"And Kate's management?"

Mona looked at him. "Best not to use that particular word around *her*." She glanced at her watch. "Two hours until you're officially on the payroll. That's when your chores start, but mine need doing now."

"Sorry, I was wondering if you have winter coats and jeans? My wardrobe's a little thin."

"You need things, just write a note and I'll see that you get what you want."

"Anything I want?"

"You betcha," she said with a wink. "We've got a few things, but our invento's down right now, winter coming, you know, fewer tourists?" She picked up a pencil and rubbed the eraser against her cheekbone. "What'll it be?"

Tourists in Heaven? Everyday this got more confusing. "Let me look around some. How do I pay?'

"We'll work it out," she said and went back to her machine.

Norm wandered. Most canned goods had yellowed labels. One wall rack held used Winchester rifles, all of them Model 94's of various vintages, their bluing tarnished. A glass case was filled with faded green boxes of Remington ammo. Six snow scoops were stacked against a wall, the top one's blade folded down like the flap of an envelope. Fishing lures, mostly unpainted brass spoons or spinners with treble hooks, hung from a wire stretched above the counter. There was a wooden barrel of work gloves and a sign: "Any Two 4 One Buck!" He tried several. They were all lefts. A wall shelf held dented quart tins of Genuine Rudyard Orchards Maple Syrup, next to red boxes of Ritz Crackers. He found a previously owned winter coat, and put the price tag by Mona, along with a note listing his pant and work shirt sizes.

"So," Mona said to his back "How many women *have* you had?"

Norm smiled and walked outside into a newly arrived baby snow squall.

At dinner Mona and Kate shared homemade potato soup to celebrate his first day on the job. Kate retold the story of Big Annie like it was a prayer or incantation, with no variations. Mona hurried back to her office where she was worrying herself sick over a three-dollar error she couldn't locate in her accounting.

With no customers, the first night on the job was uneventful. He closed the bar at ten sharp and trundled over to Touhi's to get some sleep.

Mona slipped into his room precisely at midnight, got him worked up by her presence and after a while, got up on the the bed, lifted her nighty, squatted over him, lowered herself down onto him, thrust hard one time, got up, hopped off the bed, and told him how "fantastic" it had been, assuring him their lovemaking would make her sleep, "real sweetly and soundly." Then she left the room.

Norm lay thinking. This was the second time a woman in Heaven used the one-stroke-only regimen, and he was beginning to wonder if this peculiar cultural phenomenon was indigenous to presumably the holiest place in the universe. It was seriously weird and not all that comforting. He'd seen death in Heaven, tears, sorrow, and all the many miseries in life, and it was unsettling. If he needed all that, shit he could have just stayed alive.

Next morning Kate was back in his room again, reciting the litany of Annie Clemenc, and a sort of routine began to suggest itself: Mona late at night, Kate before sunrise. Norm wondered if in not too many days or weeks he might prefer a visit from Big Annie herself, who sounded eminently more interesting and certainly more pragmatic than her only daughter.

—~—

Uncharacteristically warm winds hung over the area over the next month, melting a great bit of the village snowpack.

It was during this period that Mona came to his room one night after closing. This was normal, but this time she was not in a nightie and instead of indulging him in their heretofore-nightly single-stroke-poke ritual, she sat heavily on the end of his bed.

"The flow, itsa-no-go," she whispered.

"What?" Mona wasn't one to talk such gibberish.

She said, "No period, she does not flow, oh me, oh my, you and me, uh-oh, Kate's gonna kill us and both shall *die*."

"No worry," he said. "We're already dead."

Mona ignored him. "I simply can't imagine how this happened," she said. "We were *so* careful."

Ditto. There was pregnancy in Heaven? And it bordered on a miracle with steep up and downsides.

Kate had been quite precise about Mona's off-limits status, and though Mona had come to him quite willingly, and though there had never been more than a single stroke in a visit, Norm was certain that Kate would rule this a flagrant violation. It wasn't fair, but what was it? Heaven seemed to mirror life and life wasn't fair. After months in the afterlife, Norm had yet to see a single angel or anything of remotely supernatural origin. "Are you going to tell Kate?"

Mona smiled, kissed him tenderly, and departed without answering. Smiles and sweet kisses are poor answers and can be read positively or negatively, unless they reside in the countenance of a mafia don, in which case they are quite likely to be a subtle bon voyage.

Next morning and on time, Kate was back in his room droning on about Big Annie. For his part, Norm showed more than his usual interest. Mona was undoubtedly waiting for an opportune moment to break the bad news to her mama, and he did not want to get ahead of his sometime lover.

Norm had never been adept at resisting pain or delaying pleasure, and these traits persisted in Heaven. He'd once read an interesting book on animal behavior: Porcupines copulated daily; a ladybug's orgasm lasted six hours; queen bees killed their mates after fucking; salmon swam upstream to spawn but did not enjoy it. The book was poorly written. Did salmon not enjoy the upstream swim and the spawning? Wolverines did not like their own kind, which seemed to explain why there were so few of them. None of these facts were particularly interesting, but for reasons unknown to him, stayed with him like insidious earworms. He toyed with adding the following to the list: Species that limit copulation to a single stroke often die prematurely, and in great agony, not because of what they had, but from what they missed, and he would miss it, minimal though it was.

In Psych 101 at Land Grant U. Norm learned every human is unique. In General Communication Arts (GCA 100), Professor David K. Berlo taught students that meanings were in people, not in words; in Journalism School, the rule was that it did not matter one iota what people said as long as you spelled their names right, got what they said right, and stuck their words and statements between quotation marks.

He went into Mona's bedroom while she was working. He felt guilty but compelled. At one point during his stay he had scribbled several cards to pals and his former wife and sent them unsigned. He had no idea why he'd done this, then or now, but he had done it and regrets were for things not done, to wit with Mona, not those things actually done, to wit, also Mona. There was a very old, very large rolltop desk in her room. It had an immense number of small drawers with brass frames in which identifiers could be placed. None were. There were several yellowed envelopes in one drawer, and a live spider too, which struck him as unheavenly. The envelopes all bore a Chicago return address. The envelopes were bound by a pink string and when he turned the bundle over he found an unopened white envelope on the bottom. The return address was downstate in Michigan, his widow's hometown, but an unfamiliar address.

It took a moment to realize the envelope was addressed to him and written by his wife-in- life, Melanie. The bottom had been slit, an interesting and disturbing peek at Mona's ways. The note was dated a week before Thanksgiving, and read:

Hey Norm, I know this is you! Why are you doing this to us? Some creeps from OSI have been here several times. They're trying to find you and they are pissed. They're convinced you're yellow and on the run. I told them how you hit your head the night you jumped from the airplane and you haven't been right since. They said they'll find you eventually and the longer you run, the rougher it will be on you. They were not very nice to me and when I told them your military checks were messed up they said, 'That's your problem, lady.' Norm, you talked me into this stupid military thing and you know I've hated every minute. Will you please turn yourself in, or failing that, call Finance and fix the money thing? Please?

His former signed it "Love," which was just a word, and what actual meaning she had inside her was impossible to determine. Did being married to the woman four years qualify him for eternity in Heaven? Maybe. Mel had been one long pain in the ass. His whole life had been spent in places and with people generally not of his choosing. Democracy was often advertised as a place where you seemed to have a lot of choices, but were rarely allowed to make them.

Mona had pale gray stationery tucked neatly in one of the cubby-holes. He took a sheet and an envelope, found a pencil, and wrote.

Hey Mel, Sorry about the complications with Finance, but you've got to handle it on your own. I'm dead, remember? Sorry I talked you into the Air Force. Sorry, Sorry, So Sorry. Write if you get work or the urge for you-know-what. Love, Mr. Johnson.

Sex had always been wonderful with Melanie and she never ever complained about *that*. He addressed the note to her mother's address. She'd never be far from there. OSI in Heaven? Weird, yet he knew it was true and a face appeared in his mind and he cringed.

Norm wasn't angry with Mona, who was who she was and couldn't help rat-holing other peoples' mail; her grandmother couldn't stay out of other peoples' labor strikes either. It's wrong to apply personal standards to the actions of others. In some circumstances though, it's okay to apply your Johnson (said Johnson effect generally considered temporary).

He took his letter and returned the other things to their rightful places. He also wrote down all the animal facts he could remember and put the note in an envelope and wrote Mona's name on the front.

He considered leaving right then, but his conscience got the better of him. He could not bring himself to depart this safe harbor before looking in on Kate.

Norm found her in a room asleep in a wingback chair. He almost woke her up to say goodbye, but already knew more than he wanted to know about Big Annie.

Ambient light in the room was marginal, but enough to make things out. Curiosity was gnawing at him, a lifelong affliction. Kate's outer garment was heavy-duty duvetyn, the same dense fabric used in Hudson Bay blankets. The sight made him dizzy. Kate didn't exactly have legs; instead she had huge bulging lumps where legs should have been (or might still be), folds of discolored skin all over her. A filarial disease of some sort? This was not unknown in Southeast Asia. Avoid mosquitoes, he reminded himself. He lowered the black duvetyn and turned to her veil, which was like Muslim women wore. Kate had a thick, coarse black mustache, neatly trimmed. Interesting moles, though. Hundreds of them of all sizes, from BBs to Chiclets, all of them hanging down like black leeches and pygmy sleeping bats. Did the things rear up when she was awake or quiver like sea urchins? He would never know and sighed at the realization that you couldn't know everything, even in Heaven.

It took no time at all to pack. He used a pillowcase and knew by its fullness that he had prospered by his stay here. This had been a fun and fine respite, but in death as in life you needed to learn when it was time to make a change. Just as there are times when you couldn't know everything, there were just as many where you couldn't know anything for sure. Melanie might not understand what was afoot, but Norm did. OSI was the Office of Special Investigations and they were after him. He had been wrong. This was not Heaven, it was the antipode. Time to move on, and keep moving.

Sunny Italy

"You sure you want to do this today, Granpa?"

"Why would today be different?"

The boy hesitated, "Well, you've not been so steady on your feet the past few days."

"I haven't been steady on my feet for the past few decades, but that's not a point for debate. Do I catch fish?"

"You always do, but yesterday you looked . . . I don't know."

"Spit it out, boy." Grandson Tyrus was a good boy heading for a fine manhood and his daily companion all summer. The rest of the year it was a parade of friends and family, mostly daughters and granddaughters and their in-laws and coveys of shirttail cousins named for seasons of the year or cloying flowers. And patchouli, Jesus Christ, where did *that* crap come from? It was like being surrounded by bug-dope or Buddhist incense. The slightest sniff of that shit curled inside your head like a worm and ate your brain for hours. Rather sit in an outhouse all day than stand next to some fool with patchouli smeared on with a sponge.

Not much left in life to ask for. Would only ask whomever is in charge of this world and the next one (if there *was* a next one), that there be fewer women in summer. They tended to dilute the fishing experience, the sweet focus. Ty's a great companion, a partner and pal, and the boy's getting more than competent at tying flies, casting, reading the vagaries of river water. He has the sign of being the real thing, if the women will leave him be.

Funny how it was said that certain talents and aptitudes skipped generations, like an innate sense of direction or the ability to catch fish at will, or be a magnet for women. Carlo had the women, but the fishing? Hopeless in patience, but not a quitter. Just couldn't concentrate for long periods of time, his mind filled with the butterflies. Tried to give him the whole thing, but it wouldn't take. Fishing with flies is never entirely ours alone. We learn from others and pass it on. It's an obligation. The thing is that you fool yourself into thinking you've got it all, and then, pretty quick, you learn there's something important you don't know, which leads back to more didn't-know don't-knows, a vicious cycle. Not Carlo though. Nothing seemed to take with the boy. Could hunt, he could, but fishing? Clueless and hopeless. Not a lick of patience.

"You looked shaky," the boy finally managed.

Gubba Peraletti said, "Let me know how you do standing for hours in fifty-degree water when you're eighty-eight."

"Will you be around to hear me?" the boy asked with a smirk.

"Ty, my boy, I'll always hear you, and it won't matter what age either of us is."

Careful, he warned himself, you've been down this trail before. Don't think about those times and Carlo, it always gives you the *agita*. Stay here in the now and present with Ty. Enjoy what's now, you don't need old baggage. That stuff's all runway behind you and it's of no use to anyone. Bitterness about what a man doesn't have ruins the sweetness of what he has. You know better, but you're too damn stubborn. You don't like to let go and here it comes to show itself all over again, the damn replay that doesn't ever end, can't ever.

Kangas, the dough-faced lawyer with marshmallow fingers that never had a callus, schooled somewhere out East in blueblood land, had pranced back up here like some sort of educated god and weaseled his way to the top of the county draft board. Sick joke, that. What the hell did Kangas know about the military? Had what, a year of college-boy Rot-See, maybe two years? Never served a damn day. Ridiculous.

King Kangas, local ass-kissers called him back then, and me fresh out of the Air Force where I killed people in three wars. That sonovabitch Kangas played favorites, like a bishop hawking and auctioning indulgences, sometimes for cash, sometimes for favors.

Italian boys got no breaks from the draft board, not from Kangas. Certainly not Carlo, Jesus no, not our Carlo. I told Kangas, where's your brain? You know Carlo's head is in a fog, a dream world. He's fey.

"Gubba, Gubba, everyone in the county knows Carlo's the best man in the woods, better than much older and more experienced men. He'll do fine. You're being overprotective. Remember, you took your chances in Europe and Korea, and you made it out just fine."

True, if the word didn't include doubts, regrets, and lingering bitterness over almost every damn thing he'd done and seen. Kangas, you swollen mole, and where exactly did you take *your* chances for Uncle Sam? Never. And there he sat on his fat at a conference table deciding who would stay and who would go to die. Thumbs up, thumbs down, feeding the lions and beasts in the arena. Maybe the words were a hair different in recall, the sequence not crisply precise, but you got him good with a haymaker from his blind side and sent him sprawling across the floor, so shocked he couldn't even show anger.

Carlo did more than just fine, a pair of Silver Stars, one starting as a write-up for the Medal of Honor, later downgraded because the current brass preferred dead MOH winners. Silver Star, Bronze Star with a V for Valor, Purple Heart, all the usual fruit salad and gewgaws of the seriously bloodied. Carlo did great for three whole months, during which he became such a pain in the enemy's ass that they put a bounty on his head. Never heard this from Kangas, or even the Army. The word came from Carlo's company commander, a good kid who grew up in the Soo. Said he tried to get Carlo reassigned and out of the shit, recommended promoting him to get him into some REMF job, but this had gotten a no-can-do from upstairs. The brass at battalion and regiment were taken with the boy's prowess in hunting the enemy and wanted to keep pushing him for more, left him out in the deep shit, bare-assed beyond the pale, one letter said.

Kangas pushed his chair back as soon as you came through the door, but he couldn't get up fast enough and you gave it to him. People pulled you off him before you could kill the bastard.

"Granpa?"

"*What?*" The words and memories still stung like nettles. Pieces of Carlo come home in a box and bag. You had to fight the government and the mortician to see your own son, but you won, and right after that, you went over to King Kangas and beat hell out of him again. This time, he resigned his position "to spend more time with his family," which was abject bullshit. The asshole was a bachelor.

"You seem to daydream more than you fish," Ty said.

"Sometimes thinking is more a matter of remembering all the fish you've caught."

"You mean the good ones?"

"They're all good and I remember every fish, every place, every fly I used, even the time of day, and the weather at the time."

"Will I be like that?" Ty asked.

"Might be, and I sure hope so because remembering is almost always more pleasant than the actual events that made the memory. We don't remember pain, skeets, and buffalo gnats, brushes with bears, moose or poison ivy, getting lost, aches and pains, sweating like a whore in church, none of that stuff, only the good. I'm pretty sure this mental trick of forgetting was intended by our designer."

"God?"

"Never been able to pin it down so neatly. What I think is that some cosmic designer or force made us with a lot of damn flaws, and if we were a new car model, there'd be a quick and massive recall and two lifetimes of lawsuits, which nobody would win but big money."

You sued the US Government and Selective Service just to hassle Kangas for negligence and incompetence. Got the issue a lot of media coverage, even a story by Ed Bradley on *Sixty Minutes*, but the case got thrown out on a chickenshit technicality designed to protect government hind-ends. You lost Wife Number One after all the downstream shit that came with Carlo being killed in the war. Probably a net gain for her, all things considered. Married couples who lose kids rarely have what it takes to fight through the meaningless loss. You didn't. She didn't. We didn't.

"Do you think a lot about death, Gran'pa?"

"Probably less than it thinks about me."

"You want to go to Heaven?"

"Not if I can't smoke, drink, fish, hunt, and fart whenever and wherever I want to. You think Heaven will let a man fart out loud?"

"I'm not sure," fifteen-year-old Ty said. "I guess I never thought about it that way."

"What's your view of Heaven, Ty? You think it's peace, funeral music, sitting in a church pew 24/7? That sound like paradise to you, prayer book in your lap, pages rustling and everybody rattling rosary beads and such?"

"I don't know. Are you sure you're okay, Granpa? You look sort of chalky."

"Not enough sun. I'm fine. Go fish, we're burning daylight."

Enough mind-swimming in the murky past. Get to work. Fly rod under left armpit. Remove rubber tobacco packet from vest, nest pouch in vee of fishing vest front. Use right hand to take paper out of paper tin out of left vest pocket. Hold paper in left hand, sprinkle tobacco in a line in the paper with right hand, dribble some saliva on paper, roll with right hand, stick in mouth. Thumb a wooden match to life, light up the cigarette.

Damn, that tastes *good*. Doctor said one time you were in hospital with pneumonia, "Listen to me, Gubba, those damn cigarettes are turning your lungs black."

You said, "Listen, Doc, I spent two years sleeping in jet fuel where nothing grew, not even plants inside grow-labs. *That's* what turned my lungs black." The man laughed at you, released you from the hospital. Said "Go with God, Gubba," and you told him why the hell would you do that?

The old days in Sunny Italy, neighborhood of Tri-Mountain, not the country of. You picked dandelion heads for a quarter a bucket for Old Man Angeleli, shot robins and other songbirds with BB guns for the oldtimers to eat, brought them fresh wild brook trout from the Pilgrim, got paid in store-bought cigarettes and homemade ice-cold whisky Old Man Perlettini kept cooling in the pool beneath the wing dam in the headwaters of the Pilgrim. Based on all the work you done for all the old gents you knew exactly how many swallows you were entitled to and it was a matter of honor to never cheat.

Okay now, focus, what's the lake telling you today? Riser to the right, two o'clock, don't be in a hurry, let's see if it's got a rhythm. Does. Yessir. Gubba Magic No. 3, size 14, should do the trick, always has this time of year, why not this time? Bugs are almost always more predictable than people. All right, fish is rising up to a fly, opens its mouth, you can see the sharp white wink, how it takes the fly gently and settles down and backward. Then you lift the rod tip, feel the deep weight, set the hook, think, there, *got* you, my friend. No hurry, play it. You've got lots of time to land it.

Ty saw his grandfather suddenly lift his rod high to set the hook, saw the line go taut and start slicing water, and then his grandfather pitched forward face-first, like a tipped statue, and floated to the surface with air in his waders as the fly rod raced around him, as if it had taken on a life of its own. The boy ran toward the old man, trying to sort out all he was seeing, trying to remember to remain calm, no matter what, just the way Gubba had taught him, the way he'd want it.

Two Minutes Apart

"Wunno, Wunno, there's somebody in the deer blind!"

"That can't be, it's *our* property. Me and Twoey, *we* built them blinds."

"You built just the two and you shoulda built four, so me and Nelly could hunt same time as youse guys."

"You call what you do hunting? When's last time either of you even shot *at* a deer?"

"I don't like to kill them, I just like to watch them."

"Take your far-lookers instead of a rifle."

"Wouldn't be hunting without a gun. You need to get over here to the blind and fix this. I want to hunt."

"It's almost shooting hours, Jelly. I might miss a big buck here. What is it with you women? God almighty, youse got no sense of timing."

Jelly said, "Wasn't me who didn't build enough blinds, and it wasn't me put somebody else in a blind on our property. You want him hunting our deer, fine by me, but I came out here to hunt. You realize, I'm sure, that if you don't get this taken care of, it might be long, *long* time, before you get lucky again, bub. So, when you going to do something get this guy outten our blind?"

"Hell, Jelly, you *know* I'm way over in the Hurons, and it's almost shootin' hours and I can hear a deer just off my food plot, hon. Did you see who's in there?"

She said, "No, I did *not* see who, and no, I am *not* waltzing out in the open in front of some stranger with a rifle on the opening morning of deer season."

Husband Wunno countered, "Maybe we should let him stay there until I get my buck over here. If he pops one on our property from our blind, I'll confiscate it when I get there."

"Damn yout, Wunno."

"You're picking a helluva time for this stunt, Jelly."

"This is a damn *trespass*, not no stunt. You want me call the game warden?"

"Godammit, no way! Mighty Mouse Harris is damn prickly about bait, and we might be just a bit long on that stupid law." Wunno paused, sucked in a deep breath, added, "Jerry-Loser-Lewis, Jelly, okay, okay, I'm coming, and I'm coming fast, so just stay put, you hear me? I'll be there forty, fifty minutes max. Be primo shooting time when I get way the hell back there. Make sure this asshole doesn't shoot one of *our* bucks, hear?

"And just how do I do that?"

"Figure it out!" he said with a snarl.

"I'm no cop, Wunno."

"Thank god for small favors."

"You want your wife mixing it up with a stranger? What if he tries to rape me?"

"Jerry-Loser-Lewis, Jelly. Man goes hunting on opening day, his mind ain't on that other *stuff*. He ain't there to rape nobody, just to shoot one of our deer. Just stay the hell away from him, but if he leaves, follow him out to his wheels and write down the plate number."

"Just hurry, Wunno. I'm no Maxwell Smart."

"He was a TV guy, not real."

"Right, I'm not him."

—◦—

"My name's Jelly, Your Honor, that's with a 'y' not with a long 'e,' okay. You want to hear how I got that name, Jelly?"

Judge Heart said, "I'm sure it's a fascinating story, but not this morning for this proceeding. Just tell us what happened that day."

"Allrightyroo, I went out to hunt the hubby's blind on account he went to hunt another blind we got over to the west Hurons, hey. So

I head for his regular blind and there was a trespasser in it and that spooked me and I called Wunno, and he come flyin,' his chest all puffed up like a buck in the rut and filled with the blackest wind. Men, Your Honor, I swear I'll never understand you guys, no offense."

"He got there quickly, did he?"

"He come real fast, jumped out of his rig, never said a word to me, and run like a scalded dog right for the blind."

"Is the blind under discussion close to where you park?" the judge asked.

"I wouldn't call it close, no, cause if you park too close you leave the human stink and I guess that spooks the deer? It's maybe quarter mile. But we've never measured it."

"Were other vehicles parked near you?"

"No sir, just me and then Wunno when he come."

"Did you follow your husband?"

"Sure I followed, but he's a long, tall drink of water, and I couldn't keep up with them long legs of his and all that black wind he had up in his sails."

"Black wind?" the judge asked.

"Frosted, pissed, yanked off, so unhappy his face turns from black cherry-red to eight-ball black. I hate it when he gets that way. Scares me."

"Describe what you saw when you caught up," Judge Heart said.

The witness looked over to her lawyer. "I got to answer that, Little Harry?"

The lawyer sighed, "This isn't Perry Mason, just answer the judge, Jelly."

"What the heck am I paying you for if all you do is sit there with the drools?"

"Ms. Kokokovna," Judge Heart said sternly.

She looked up at the judge. "Your Honor, me being married and all, I'd feel better if you called me Mrs. instead of that feminazi Ms. junk."

"Mrs. it shall be," the judge said. "What exactly did you see when you got to the blind?"

"Little Harry?" she said.

"We've been over this," her attorney said. "Answer the judge, or take the fifth."

"We can drink in court?"

"Fifth *Amendment*, Jelly. It means you don't have to incriminate yourself."

"Is that even possible? I thought it took a man *and* a woman for incrimination, though I think I've heard talk of how they got some test tube stuff don't need either of them present for the deed to get done."

"Answer the question, Jelly. The judge has more cases to hear today and so too do I. This is just a preliminary hearing to gather facts, not the main bout."

"This is not boxing," Jelly said.

"It can feel like that at times," the judge allowed. "Please answer the question."

"Sure, Your Honor. I seen my Wunno putting some atomic whup-ass on the pumpkin."

"Pumpkin, refers to a hunter in a full blaze orange suit? Could you identify said pumpkin?" the judge asked.

"Couldn't see much until the stomping got done. Wunno, well you surely know about his temper, Judge, and it was like, completely out of control that morning in the woods. I've seen my hubby mad plenty of times, but this was a whole new side of the man. I thought if I yelled for him to stop, he'd either ignore me or start beating on me, and I'm not gonna lie, *that* did not appeal to me since it looked like Wunno was trying to kill the man and I'd never seen him like that mad before—though I seen him and his brother Twoey go at it a couple times when I thought they'd kill each other, but that was just brother stuff, you know? It didn't mean nothing."

"Your husband's temper is legendary?"

"And real, Your Honor, and of course we've all heard the Vietnam stories about how Wunno and Twoey slipped into enemy positions at night and cut Charlie throats."

The Judge asked, "Your husband told you that about Vietnam?"

"No, he ain't never said peep one about nothing to me."

"Did Twoey tell you?"

"You gotta understand, Your Honor, these boys're identical twins and tight-lipped on all things, you know? Wunno's the oldest, by two minutes, but other than that they're the same person. You see, we were up to the VFW for Wingy Wednesday and the twins had a few pops too many, which was okay on account I was designated driver and of course they started talking trash to each other and it got as quiet as church, and those boys they started telling about the things they done over to that war and I could see people turning white-sick. I'm not gonna lie, it upset me so much I didn't want to ride home with my own legal husband."

"Thank you for sharing all that," the judge said. "How long before you could see who Wunno was pummeling?"

"Well, it's funny, but I thought I heard this voice, soft as a sick bird, and it was saying 'I'm sorry, I'm sorry, this is just a terrible mistake, I swear, I'm so sorry and I won't do it again, so help me God.'"

The judge asked, "That's a quote? He said, 'So help me God?'"

"You bet, Your Honor. That is what I heard and that's when an itty-bitty voice somewheres inside my head said, 'Whoa, you might know this guy, Jelly.' But I couldn't be sure, Your Honor. I mean, by then the guy's voice was kind of garbled up bad by a mouthful of broken teeth and blood and such, but there was something in them words, how they got said that struck a funny note in my brain I guess, and I heard this voice saying, 'you know this man, Jelly, you do.' It was like the Fifth Angel in the Bible and that bottomless pit thing, you know, the locusts and three and a half days or whatever, and earthquakes killing seven thousand people, or eight? I never been much good with numbers."

"My Bible recall's never been so keen," Judge Heart said, "but I think you're referring to Revelation Two."

"Oh hell, Your Honor, all those Bibilical names are like thick winter stew in my head. If you say it was Revelation, that's by god good by me, it really is."

"And this somehow made the voice register?" the judge asked.

"Yes indeed. My mind was telling me, 'Hey Jelly we *know* this voice,' which by then, like I said, was barely a wet, spitty whisper, but what I heard the man say is just as I just told you, 'I'm sorry, I'm sorry, this is a terrible mistake,' and like that, see what I'm saying, Your Honor?"

The judge asked, "Whose voice was it, Mrs. K?"

"Well, I believed it was Father Paul of the Naked Heart Church."

"Correction, Your Honor, she means Sacred Heart," her lawyer corrected.

"Shut up, Little Harry. You know everybody calls it Naked Heart. There's a statue in the church with the heart of Jesus sticking out of his chest like somebody's trying to draw it up into a spaceship or whatever, or like them Asians do with fish in their markets. Wunno got some pictures of them fish when he was on R&R over to Hong Kong, which is kinda like China, and it sure looks the same, Your Honor."

"Father *Paul Heard*?" the judge asked.

"Yessir, that's what me and my brain decided."

"Did you try to call off your husband?" the judge asked.

"Was no point I could see, Wunno being caught up as he was in the blackest wind I ever seen on him. If I tried to step in, I figured I'd get the same thing the Father was getting."

"Your husband physically abuses you?" the judge asked.

"I guess he might think about it from time to time, but he's never laid hand nor glove on me in anger, Your Honor. See, I carry a five-shot .44 Colt and he knows I can use it and I'd send him to Hell if he smacked me . . . can I say Hell in court, Your Honor?"

"We'll allow it this once. Strike the offending word from the record, Mary Ruth," the judge instructed the court recorder, who nodded and smiled.

"At what point did you realize the victim was Father Paul?" the judge asked.

"Well, Your Honor, Wunno eventually run out of steam and the man he was beatin' on got up from the ground and tried to stagger away, but Wunno had beat him senselessly so all he could do was stumble like a rabid skunk and I went after him and got my arm around him and he said, 'Thank you, thank you, thank you, you saved my life,' and he began to cry. And then he started in again, 'Forgive me, forgive me, this is all a big mistake and I am so sorry, so sorry.' When I heard that and wiped some of the blood offen his face, well, Your Honor, I didn't know *what* to say."

"Because you realized the victim was Father Paul?"

"Not that. What made me sick to stomach was I remembered just how maybe I'd once give the priest permission to hunt the property and use the blind."

"But you called your husband to come get him out of the blind."

"I thought then it was some complete stranger was trespassing, not Father Paul, Your Honor. It was still pretty dark, opening morning. Could have been anybody and I didn't exactly remember telling Father Paul he could hunt there. Later, I kinda, sorta did, you know? Boy, did I feel stoopid. Can you imagine?"

"Mrs. K, you knew at this point that the victim was the priest?" the judge said.

"Your Honor, I don't like singling out Father Paul as no victim. Seems to me I'm as much a victim in this deal as he is. Life sure can get messy."

"How are *you* the victim?"

"Well, *a* victim, if not *the* victim, sure."

"Care to explain?"

"No, I just *feel* like I'm a victim is all."

"Did you, after discovering the man was Father Paul, inform your husband who it was or that you had given the man permission to hunt there?"

"Are you out of your ever-loving mind, Your Honor? Not on your darn life, and I apologize for the darn. Wunno is a jealous SOB and he ain't much a fan of priests or clerics of any brand or flavor. My sister Nelly and me, we never miss mass, but our husbands, the twins, they refuse to go, no matter what—you know . . . inducements we dangle before them, if you get my drift. And isn't it downright sickening that a woman has to resort to carnal trickery to get the hubby into the church where the whole wedded life thing got launched in the first place? It just doesn't seem right that a gal has to put out in order to get her hubby to the church to hear priests who have sworn off sex and such."

"Your quandary is abundantly clear, Mrs. K, but let me ask this for the record. Did you not tell your husband that you had given permission to the man that he had just beaten within a whisper of death?"

"I wouldn't put it that way," she said.

"Never imagined for a moment that you would," the judge came back. "How *would* you put it?"

"That's a fine shave you're making on the facts, Your Honor, because technically I can't give no permission. See, my name isn't on no deed or nothing for the camp nor for the Huron Mountains land neither. This is part of the prenup Wunno and me signed before we got hitched. He worked darn hard to earn enough to buy that property and build that camp and he didn't want it getting tied up in some messy divorce thingey. Being that my name isn't on the deed, I can't legally *give* permission to nobody to hunt there, and are you following me, Your Honor?"

"I'm doing my utmost. Do your husband and brother-in-law own said camp jointly?"

"I don't know, Your Honor, but if they do, I'm sure my sister had to sign a prenup just like me and Wunno done. The thing is, neither of them brothers is much on small talk such as who owns what, and so forth. Russian men ain't known as talkers."

The judge sucked in a deep breath. "When exactly did your husband learn that he had beat up the priest to whom you had given permission to hunt in the blind?"

"Like I said, Your Honor. The priest didn't have no *real* permission."

"Father Paul certainly must've *thought* he had permission."

"I know, I know. Boy that sure didn't turn out so well."

"The victim nearly died," the judge said.

"And *would* have, I didn't get him to the emergency room. I saved his life, thank you very much."

"On your way to the hospital, did the Father remind you that you had given him permission?"

"No, he didn't say nothing except he was sorry and all that stuff I already told."

"Have you *apologized* to Father Paul?"

"For *what?* I didn't do nothing wrong that I can see. This thing just didn't work out was all, besides I thought all this was settled, ya know?"

"Settled how?"

"What I'm paying you for, Little Harry?" the woman scolded her attorney. "Your Honor, a week after this misunfortunate event, my brother-in-law Twoey was out to his blind when this guy comes right up to him at first light and beats hell out of him. Sorry, I forgot about the hell word thing. You should see Twoey now. He looks a helluva lot worse than Father Paul ever did. My sis says she can't even stand to look at him and usually she's gaga about his looks, which between you and me I just don't see. He and his brother, my husband, are dead ringers, and to be honest neither of them's much to look at on their best day. Twoey was in hospital *two days longer* than Father Paul, see?"

"I'm sorry to say, Mrs. K, that I don't see, not at all. Perhaps you can enlighten us," the judge said.

"Happy to, Your Honor. The man who beat up my brother-in-law, Twoey, is the identical twin of Father Paul and his name's Father Raul, and I know priests swear off girlfriends and such, but you think God wants his boys on earth running around killing animals and putting whoop-ass on fellow human beings? I mean *really.*"

"I couldn't begin to say, Mrs. K. Your husband Wunno beat up Father Paul and Father Paul's twin brother, Father Raul, beat up your brother-in-law, and you're telling me this makes everything even-steven?"

"I don't know the legal term," she said. "You betcha."

"Just tell us what you think in whatever way is easiest for you.'

"Okay, Your Honor. Identical twin on one side beats up identical twin from the other side and then the identical twin of the first deal beats up on the other identical twin of the first deal, that's an eye for an eye and so forth, right?"

The judge turned to the sheriff and said, "Got any thoughts on all this, Ray-Ray?"

The sheriff, tugged at his gun belt, and slicked back his thick blond hair. "Even-steven works for me, Your Honor, though it also seems lacking in terms of pure justice, of which there isn't a whole lot of in these parts if you consider that Mrs. K, who caused these events in the first place, is getting off scot-free."

"Justice is always blind," the judge said, "and sometimes deaf and dumb as a rock when circumstances dictate. We're done here. I need a highball, and Mrs. K, the court orders you to inform your husband Wunno what happened and of your culpability in this matter."

"I don't know that word, Judge."

"Your guilt in this."

"Me? I'm not guilty, Your Honor. Was a *mistake* was all. You never made a mistake? I ain't legally guilty and that's what my lawyer told me when he took this case."

"I've made more than my share of mistakes," the judge said. "And you need to get a new lawyer."

"See, we all make mistakes, and I'll surely get me a new mouthpiece, Your Honor."

"Good," the judge said. "The court further orders that the sheriff accompany you when you inform your husband."

Mrs. K. snorted, and said, "My sister and me are identical twins too, judge, you listening? Did I tell you that, only she's two minutes older than me the way Wunno is two minutes older than Twoey, so you see how it is?"

"I do indeed," the judge said, rapped his gavel, looked over at the court recorder and said off-mike, "I think two highballs are in order, say two minutes apart?"

Moccasin Square Garden

(Ma-ki-zin Ga-ka-kish-in Gi-ti-gan)

ANOTHER ALL-DAY TRIBAL COUNCIL MEETING, THE USUAL WATCH-paint-dry eight-hour-yawn that left John Clash aching mentally and wishing to be anywhere but there. But Tribal Chairwoman Anna Redrocks insisted he attend all meetings unless he had an active case that couldn't be handled by his people. Most of this month had been grave-yard dead and he'd found no excuse to free himself.

The tribal police chief sat thinking, twenty years beyond 9/11 and his people were back to normal, arguing over trivial nothings. He tried his best to listen attentively to the verbal jousting and politicking from councilmen and tribal members and tried to shut it all out, but he couldn't bring himself to do it because he never knew when an odd com-ment might provide a clue or lead to a case or situation he'd encounter down the road. Most complaints the council heard concerned tribal family members, or the Great White Boogeyman. The meetings left him exhausted, disappointed, and a hair irritated. How was it that complaints always boiled down to "the other"? Not my family, it's the other family. Not the tribe, it's the damn whites around here. It was always other peo-ple (whites, Hispanics, Asians), never me or us. Everyone wanted to be the victim. It was discouraging, and understandable.

How could it be—after centuries of intermarriage and mutual history—that people in small communities still harbored suspicion and anger toward each other? He didn't understand it, and neither did either stupid side, but whenever someone was upset about some trivial event and couldn't blame a specific individual, the complaint always shifted to some white guy or some "hairy," and the whites were no better, yawping about "lazy, blood-sucking 'Nish.'" If opposites were said to make good mates in a marriage, why shouldn't that carry over into relations between races? People, ugh.

The whole thing in the tribe was exhausting. It had been this way all the time he was growing up. The "sides" then were red and white, and later in the army in Vietnam it had been black and white (and red) against yellow. In his early cop career in Detroit after Vietnam it seemed to come full circle, this time, white against red and white against black, and vice versa in all settings. Who could say who carried the weight for starting or maintaining the continual rub? He hated it. Only once in his life had he found another "other" who felt as he did. Just once.

Tonight he needed a respite from human pettiness and weakness, just him, his dog Copper, a good meal, maybe a little Cat Stevens music, a bottle or two of beer, early bedtime, and sweet, uninterrupted sleep.

He had just put on Cat and opened a can of Pickaxe Blond when the phone rang. "Clash," he answered.

The voice said, "Evening, Chief. I love it when I get to say that! Now hear this: Cap'n Redfeather is getting kicked tomorrow morning."

He had not heard this voice in years and at first didn't recognize it. "No way. Redfeather's got at least two years left."

"And now he don't," the voice said. "Ain't that some shit?" the man from the Michigan Corrections Department added. His informant had served in the Corps with him in Vietnam and had later joined Corrections and risen to a high position.

"Good behavior, no space, what's the reason?" the tribal police chief asked, groping for an explanation.

"Your boy's coming out with four teardrops, savvy? Gone live with his Mah-Mah."

Savvy? "You guys wouldn't release a man with even one tear and you're telling me Redfeather has four? He didn't have any when he went inside."

"*Git-hi mus-ko-maan*, white man," the contact said. "They got their own ways, eh."

There it was again, this time in Jacktown, the huge walled state prison in southern Michigan. Redfeather was coming back early. Trouble followed the man like a plague and had his whole life.

Clash finished his beer and punched in the Southern Prison of Southern Michigan number and got a voice, but before it could speak, Clash said, "Deputy Warden Deane, this is John Clash."

Deane said, "I assume you've heard Redfeather's coming out?"

"Just now, and I don't get it. What's going on? The judge made it clear at sentencing that we were to be notified if and when Redfeather was to be released, and by that I mean the tribe, my department, the county, everyone up here, including the victim, his family, as in all of us."

"State Corrections is not the jurist," the deputy warden said. "We're the warehouse. We follow orders and we have our own rules and ways."

"I'm told he's coming out with four teardrops."

The deputy warden groaned. "Inmates all got their tats, your blacks got theirs, your whites, your Hispanics, your tribal brothers, all their own tats, their own sign languages, their own jargons and vocabularies. Was a time when prison, like this country, was a melting pot, a homogenizer. Not that way anymore. Hasn't been for a long damn time. It's the Big House of Silos now, us against them, inside and out. Not sure why."

"Why is Redfeather being released early?"

"Simple truth," the deputy warden said, "the administration, the inmates, all of us are sick of his shit. He's all yours, and good luck with *that*." Clash heard the man laughing as he broke the connection.

Sick of his shit? What the hell does that *mean?* Clash stood staring at the phone as a sequence of events spilled through his mind, and he sat down to makes notes and a to-do list in his notebook as his dog Copper pawed him to get his attention or to distract him, the dog so smart it was impossible to separate serendipity from intent. He patted the lab's wide head. "I gotta go out again, boy, and just for tonight you can be my cop partner, but don't go embarrassing me, okay?"

The dog's heavy tail thumped once. This is your life, talking to a dog?

His to-do list was short. See Tribal Chairwoman Anna Redrocks and visit Redfeather's aging mother, who in her youth was known as an incorrigible good-time girl, but had transitioned into a highly respected tribal elder. In her youth they'd called her Ready Randi or R2 and she had always been headstrong and outspoken. Even now she was one of the few tribal members to use the spear of bluntness, to say things others either didn't know or were afraid to say, things they could not face or would not. Randi faced everything, save one, her son, who was coming out of prison early. Damn.

Her son, Captain Redfeather . . . stupid damn name which alone suggested the mother's view of her only child, who was no longer a kid. This had been Redfeather's second stint inside, the first time for comparatively minor offenses, the most recent one for attempted murder.

He needed to talk to Randi, find out if she'd gotten a call from Corrections about the early release. Damn state. You couldn't count on anyone below the bridge.

He also needed to talk to Houghton County Sheriff Nayar Sekhar. The sheriff was a good guy, a good partner, and over the years they had become friends. Maybe Nayar could talk to Redfeather's victim, Boobies Hoople (given name Parker), who had been born with prominent man-boobs that had gotten larger as he'd aged and now nobody called him anything but Boobies.

Why Redfeather had such enmity for Hoople remained a mystery. It certainly never came out during the trial or interviews. This being the Upper Peninsula, there were lots of theories, all made of hot air and bullshit. Tribals had their own theories and townies had theirs.

Bottom line, neither he nor Sekhar knew why the thing had happened. If Clash had to guess, he'd say something like "location." The two men had been at each other for years, and one night at the Bucket they apparently rubbed too close, and that was the tipping point for Redfeather, who damn near killed the other man. The events of the night were known, but the rest, the reasons? Nothing and who cared?

Clash knew he had to keep focused on the Cap'n, who was no doubt headed this way. Redfeather was a shit-magnet, a carrier, a violence vector who infected those around him. At the conclusion of the trial, Redfeather had pointed a finger at Hoople and said, "This ain't over."

Think practically, Clash. If Redfeather's kicked tomorrow, it won't be till midmorning. Jackson is what, 500–600 miles? That means he could be here as early as tomorrow night. Got to plan for that, meaning a twenty-four-hour planning window. Damn. Tonight's Thursday, tomorrow's Friday, and the bars will be full, especially the Bucket, which Tribals unendearingly called *Ma-ki-zin Ga-ka-kish-in Gi-ti-gan*, in English, Moccasin Square Garden.

First things first. He punched in a preset number. "Chairwoman, this is John Clash. Did you hear Captain Redfeather is being released from prison tomorrow morning?"

"Did the state notify *you*? I've heard nothing."

"No ma'am, I got it from another source, then confirmed it through the state, a deputy warden."

"And he's coming *here*?" the chairwoman asked.

"State says to his mother's, but that's unconfirmed."

"This does not please me," she said. "Nobody needs this," she added. "Randi does not need this."

"I'm going coordinate with Chief Sekhar."

"You trust that man? He's not one of us. He's *theirs*."

The same old shit, and right from the top. "He's not technically one of *them* either, Chairwoman."

"Why did Randi not say something today? She was at the meeting the whole time."

Clash wondered the same thing. "Maybe she doesn't know. I'll go see her tonight."

"I will not be happy if she knew and didn't share with us."

"She has no legal obligation to tell us."

"If you are about to entertain a ticking time bomb, the very least you can do is let your neighbors know."

The dog was batting at the back door. Clash let him in and the dog followed him to the bedroom where he sniffed his uniform, which Clash had tossed on the bed. If Joyce was still alive, she would never allow this, but she's not here and now I make all the calls on household routines. He scribbled in his notebook to pick up fresh uniforms from the laundry. His order had been ready last week, but he'd not gotten around to picking it up, and had neither the time nor the inclination.

As he made the note, he glanced at his late wife's photo and could sense her smile of satisfaction. "Happy?" he asked the photo.

Clash dressed quickly in his wrinkled uniform and looked at the dog. "Say bye to your mama, boy, we've got work to do." The dog woofed at the photo and followed his human partner through the house out to the tribal police vehicle. Clash considered driving his personal ride, a Ford F-150, but this was official business, which meant he had to be in uniform in the official vehicle.

Cap'n Redfeather coming home? What else is going to collide with us, he wondered. Asteroids? Wherever Redfeather went, shit happened, some of it, much of it, inexplicable, all of it bad. The chairwoman's right. We don't need this. I don't need this. Nobody needs this.

One thing Clash knew from his nineteen years as the tribe's police chief was that bad news tended to travel in schools, like fish in the big lake. The cop job had been good, with more highs than lows, but at sixty-five he wouldn't mind handing the whole damn mess over to someone else, someone with a good brain, common sense, younger eyes and legs, and a lot more energy.

He also knew that unfortunately, youth, legs, eyes, and energy were not enough. What the tribe needed was someone who could listen to people, someone with a solid education, real common sense, deep courage, and most importantly, someone with a latent mean streak they could pull out of the toolbox when it was needed.

Clash had six full-time officers and six auxiliary officers, and not one of them was what the tribe needed for a top cop. They were all good people and officers, all men and women he had personally selected, but not one of them had shown all the qualities needed to take over for him. Was he expecting too much of the younger officers? Maybe. Can't you let go, John? Maybe not.

Bottom line, he was a failure in not finding, hiring, and developing his own replacement, and this weighed on him.

Not that he had his own hair on fire when he started with the tribe. Cop work in Detroit had been one thing; the shift to the slower pace of the reservation and the tribe's politics another thing entirely, and difficult.

There was so much less action here, and so much more in the way of politics and behind-the-scenes negotiations. But he had matured, adapted, grew into the pace and the job, identified his own weaknesses, worked to eliminate them, tried to polish his skills. He had to learn to think long term, and his younger officers never seemed to think about improving, damn them.

Many of Clash's generation got drafted into the war in Southeast Asia. The kids now faced no draft and grew up with much more control over their own fate. Most of them were pretty good at taking direction and following orders and directives, but none of them seemed interested in taking any initiative, and now this asshole Redfeather was looming like a violent November gale. He needed to focus. This was not the time to contemplate retirement and succession and all that. He was the chief, and this was his job, and he needed to do it and stop thinking so damn much.

Clash let the dog jump into the truck and they headed out, and he immediately changed his mind about his to-do sequence. He'd talk to his colleague first, but not until he was parked out front with his lights out. Lights inside the sheriff's house were low, which gave him pause. He hated interrupting people in their private time. Nayar would be annoyed, but his wife Noor would no doubt go off the wall. One minute she'd be calm and friendly and the next minute she'd be ballistic, a kinetic, screaming, fist-waving bombshell. How did Nayar put up with *that*? Clash thought it would drive him crazy, but it wasn't his business. Joyce was bipolar before the disorder had a name and eventually killed herself, and he had no clue what was coming when she swallowed a .44, which was not a desperate plea for help, but a loud and emphatic good-fucking-bye. Who the hell was he to wonder about other relationships?

He got out of the truck with smartphone in hand, and hit the speed dial for his friend.

Sekhar answered gruffly. "Sheriff here, and this better be a goddamn emergency."

"Clash here, I'm parked in your driveway. We need to talk."

"Now?" Sekhar whispered. "Noor's in the, you know, mood? It's the first time in a month and you want to *talk . . . now*?"

Clash smiled. "Face-to-face. Redfeather's being released tomorrow."

"Well . . . shitfire. The State was supposed to notify me. Did they call you?"

"Nope, Indian telegraph, and I've verified it."

Clash's longtime nickname was "Sixsex" and Sekhar was called "Spawnbag." The first time they'd met, the day after Sekhar's election, they'd gone to Roy's Bakery on the canal west of Houghton and both ordered black coffee and cheddar cheese bagels. "Bagels for a dot and a feather," Sekhar quipped. Who knew? "Why do they call you Sixsex?" the new sheriff asked.

"My mom, I guess, a feather thing," Clash said. "What about you, Spawnbag?"

"My mother too. Dot thing." This had been their joke ever since the American Indian tribal police chief and Indian American Houghton County sheriff, the son of Indian immigrants who was now head of law enforcement for a rural, largely white county in the middle of the great white northern nowhere, had met.

Sekhar sighed. "Be out in a minute. If you hear shots, don't rush in. I'll already be dead and she'll shoot anything else that moves. You know how her temper is."

"Heard about it, haven't seen it."

"Lucky you."

"Real sorry about this, Nayar."

"Not as sorry as I am," the sheriff said.

Sekhar came outside in jeans and an open Hawaiian shirt, a cigarette in hand. "I hate you," he greeted his friend.

"Because I interrupted your bedroom plans?"

"That and the equipment your department has. Ford Raptors? Jesus Joseph. What's up with that?"

The tribal council kept its small police force equipped with all the latest technology and council members watched other tribes and regularly compared how their force stacked up. Clash loathed how much was done on appearances, not substance. The tribal equipment was far superior to any U.P. county's gear. This added to the historical white-red rub in the area.

There was no such rift between Clash and Sekhar. They joked about being the same creatures with different details, both of them were *wiisaakad*, mixed bloods. The sheriff's father was Mumbai-born, his mother a blonde Swedeling (her term) from Minnesota, who lived in India as a 3M executive's daughter and had fallen in love with the culture and many of the ways. Clash's mix was full-blood Anishnaabe father and blond mother from Santa Cruz, California. Two half-breeds as top cops of the county's two main tribes. Nayar was as brown as a coffee bean and looked like a born feather. Clash was towheaded and fair and looked like a wayward Viking. They were both outsiders. Both knew what they were doing. Sekhar had retired as a Michigan State Police lieutenant and had been easily elected sheriff. He was not just a colleague and friend, he was one hell of a cop with nerve, smarts, and good judgment. They each knew the other had his six, and if the shit began to fly, the other man would be right there.

Sekhar lit another cigarette. "That asshole Redfeather. Think he'll head for the Bucket?"

"That would be my first guess," Clash said. "That used to be Hoople's regular hangout, but my informant didn't mention the Bucket."

The sheriff said, "This won't be over until one of these worms is dead. Or somebody burns down that piece-of-shit bar. Moccasin Square Garden indeed. What a shithole. We'd better find Hoople or we'll have a small war brewing before we're ready. Why's Redfeather coming out early? He was supposed to have a minimum of ten."

Clash grinned, said quietly, "The state is sick of his shit."

Sekhar choked on smoke. "What the fuck does *that* mean? That's a legitimate legal release reason?" The sheriff had gotten a law degree from Cooley Law School while he had been stationed in East Lansing.

The sheriff added, "I think Hoople's living in Phillipsville with his girlfriend. She's Japanese, Suki, a schoolteacher who teaches computer technology at Calumet High. I can't understand how that moron rants against race-mixing between whites and Indians, but thinks Asian-White mixing is okay. What a dumbass. Cap'n's got to be what, forty-five now? And his mom's what, pushing ninety?"

"And still drives," Clash said. "Drives better than most of our young ones. I'm thinking if he comes directly home to mama, we'll have him back in lockup in less than forty-eight hours." The chief knew no leopard changed its spots.

"No bet," Sekhar said. "So what are we thinking on this?"

"I'll talk to his ma tonight, but I'm thinking both of us should visit Hoople. It's ten to twelve hours from Jackson to Baraga. Redfeather could be here early as tomorrow night.

"How's he *getting* here?" the sheriff asked.

"No idea, but the guy always seems to have a support system."

Sekhar rubbed his eyes. "Redfeather's kind always has help in the wings."

"What kind would that be?" Clash countered.

"Habitual scumbag kind."

Clash nodded. "We don't have much time."

Sekhar said, "Agreed, let's go see Hoople, get that out of the way. Maybe he's got a long trip planned, or something."

Clark chuckled. "I doubt he's ever been over First Bridge." In the Copper Country, First Bridge meant the Portage Lift Bridge between Houghton and Hancock, which connected the Keweenaw Peninsula to the larger Upper Peninsula. Technically and geographically the Keweenaw was an island and its inhabitants acted like it. When Keween-awians wanted to talk about the Mackinac Bridge, which connected the state's lower peninsula to the Upper Peninsulas, they called it Second Bridge, owing to the fact being that the lift bridge had been built decades before the bigger, more famous span.

"Okay, let me quick suit up and we'll go visit Hoople. We'll get a plan for tomorrow after we see Hoople and after you talk to Redfeather's mother."

"Tell Noor I'm sorry," Clash told his friend.

"Tell herself while I suit up."

"Me? I'm not coming inside. I'm not *that* sorry."

Sekhar grinned. "Smart man."

⌐ ⌐

Thirty minutes later they pulled up to a trailer at the end of a two-track that was across Fulton Creek from a place called the Walmart of Rocks. Every summer a tribe of wannabe, burned-out former hippies, calling themselves Eternal Life Through the Magic Power of Crystals, converged on the rock joint for a combination sales meeting and rainbow peoples' love and drug fest. Lots of tribals showed for the shindig, where they were welcomed on a wobbly premise that held that all natives had by birth alone some inside track to eternal life. Clash grimaced. It never occurred to such fools to look at reality.

Knocks on the trailer door brought no response. "Maybe he's dead," Sekhar said. "That would help."

Clash said, "Redfeather will find somebody. He has plenty of candidates to get after."

"Let's do a walk around," Sekhar suggested.

The cops found bony Hoople sitting naked and cross-legged on a massive cedar stump. His hands were palms-up on his knees, his mouth hanging slack and open, his eyes rolled back and the whites showing the color of bloody egg yolks.

"Yo, Earth to Hoop," Sekhar greeted the man, "Get your head in neutral, man, the law needs to talk to you."

The man mumbled, "I'm talking to the only law that matters."

"Well," Sekhar said, "if that's Redfeather on the other end of your line, you might want to ask him what time tomorrow he'll be here. You're going to do a lot better with cops on your six than some imaginary creature living in the sky above the woods."

Hoople opened his eyes. "Skeptic. I'm bonded to a spirit, not a creature, and I don't need no help from some guy thinks cows are sacred."

"I'm a Methodist, ass-wipe. My old man grew up Church of England in Bombay, now known as Mumbai, and my mom's a Lutheran from Brainerd, Minnesota."

"You don't look like no Methodist," Hoople said. "And none of that shit matters on account you still got the genes for holy cows. You can't help believing what you believe. We are all unwitting products of our gene pools. Me, it's an appreciation for the life beyond, and for you it's sacred cows and shit like that."

John Clash had heard enough nonsense. "Sit up and look at us, Hoople."

The man's eyes blinked and he whispered, "This better be good. If I don't get my deep meditation, I tend to have shallow days."

"Did you not hear the name Redfeather?" Sekhar asked.

"I heard just fine, but he can't get inside the meditating mind and what do I care, he's still got four years left in Jackson."

Interesting: Hoople had been keeping track.

Sekhar said, "Four years? Did you flunk arithmetic? Technically it's two more. Your math sucks."

"It's the brain damage he conferred on me is why," Hoople said.

"Conferred on you?" Clash said, "You've always been a moron, Hoop, but we don't hold it against you, even if it tends to get you in trouble, that and your unquenchable taste for the meth. What is it nowadays, Scooby Snacks or Shabu?"

These were local meth products. "Sir, I swear I quit all that shit cold chicken," Hoople said forcefully.

"Cold turkey," Sheriff Sekhar corrected the man.

"Whatever, let loose my junkage."

"Your girlfriend's idea you quit the shit?" Clash asked.

"She say no nookie for speed-boys. Man, she the Rolls Royce of pussy so I like, quit that shit cold chicken."

"Imagine that," Sekhar said. "This your trailer or hers?"

"Hers and mine, ours. She's like a schoolteacher and right over the creek from here is the corner for cosmetic divergence."

"Cosmic *convergence*," Sekhar corrected the man. "Are you not listening? You need to focus, Hoople. Redfeather will be here tomorrow."

"He, like, breakout?"

"No, he's being released early."

"Jesus, ain't you guys gonna do nothing? That motherfucker is coming here to get *me*. You *know* that."

"We don't know that," Sekhar said.

"Last thing he said in court, 'This ain't done,' man. I thought I had more time. This is not fair. You guys have to help me."

"You didn't know he was coming out?" Sekhar said.

Hoople squealed. "You guys aren't listening man. He's coming *here*."

"To live with his ma," the sheriff said.

"She's okay with that, have that crazy motherfucker in her house?"

Sekhar said, "He's one very small con, not a mob syndicate."

"You don't *understand*," Hoople told the men. "He'll kill me. He already tried once."

"He could've killed you eight years ago," Clash pointed out.

"He got tired was all, and some cops jumped his ass."

"He's eight years older than you. You think that's jacked up his energy and staying power?" Sekhar said.

"Them cons don't do nothing but pump iron, pop pills, and shit. They come out all ripped and ready."

"Hoop," Sekhar said. "The man is what, four-foot-eight. He's a runt. You got your ass kicked by a little fella, who's so uncoordinated he can hardly walk."

"Right! He ain't human, Redfeather ain't. He can *do* mind shit to people."

The tribal chief couldn't argue this. His feelings were similar and had been since Redfeather was a youngster and already a troublemaker. His mother, as great a woman as she was, would tolerate no criticism of her only child and protected him, no matter what the boy got into. "He's different," she'd say, "gifted in a very special way," which she never elaborated on.

Clash knew the kid had a gift for stirring shit and making violence materialize out of what appeared to be nothing. At times he wanted to think the man was evil, but he always turned away from this, because it was too philosophical. Cops were paid to deal with the real world and facts. What he knew was that whatever it was that was in Redfeather, it drew trouble and violence to him. Not that Redfeather was physically capable of much violence himself, but too often it happened when he was around.

One night at the Bucket, Redfeather had attacked Hoople with a hickory hammer handle. And the judge had given him ten years solid, no time off. He also told the court it was good for the community to be shed of such a bad influence, an albatross. Redfeather's mother had filed an appeal, but it had gone nowhere.

Sekhar said, "I could slip Hoople into the county lockup. We sometimes let military guys have beds when they're passing through and short on funds."

"My girl can come be with me, right?" Hoople asked immediately.

"You'll only be there a day or two," Sekhar told the man.

"Me and her don't like to be apart," Hoople said. "Like it hurts?"

Sekhar rolled his eyes, said, "*Really.*"

Hoople made a circle with his left thumb and forefinger and made poking motions with the forefinger of his right hand. "Every night, man— and every morning to get the day started right. That's what she says."

"*Twice a day?*" Sekhar said.

Hoople grinned. "I hate you even more," Sekhar whispered to his friend, then to Hoople, "Grab a gym bag, your dopp kit, and a change of clothes for a couple of days, and I'll check you into the Graybar Hotel."

"Dopp what?"

"Toiletries."

"Jail got toilets." Hoople said. "What's this hotel thing? I thought I was going to the county lockup."

Sekhar looked at Clash and shook his head. "Dumb as a brick and getting it twice a day. Go figure."

Hoople was soon back in the doorway. "Okay if I call Suki and let her know?"

The sheriff said, "No, and don't leave her a note either."

"She might move out on me."

"That would be to her credit, and at least you'll still be alive."

"Oh yeah," Hoople said and disappeared inside.

Sekhar said, "You'll talk to Redfeather's mother?"

"She's next on my list."

The man came outside wearing jeans and sandals.

Clash said before leaving the scene, "Tell us why Redfeather jumped you."

Hoople held out his hands. "That's the thing. See, *I* don't even *know.* Can I go to jail now, please? I don't like to stand outside."

⌒⌒

Randi Redfeather raised a thin white eyebrow when she saw Clash at her door. "Something wrong, Johnny?" She'd called him Johnny since he was a kid.

"Have you heard from Cap'n?"

"He writes to me once a month. I always hope for more, but it never changes. I should be thankful for that."

"When's the last time you got a letter?"

"Close to a month now."

"He mention plans when he gets released?"

The woman's face hardened. "What's this about, Johnny?"

"The state's releasing him tomorrow."

The woman stared past him, said, "Come in," and led him to the kitchen where she poured a cup of coffee for him from a full pot.

"He didn't tell you?" the chief asked.

She shook her head, said, "I hoped he'd go the full term and not get an early release. He never thinks about consequences. Everything is about now, this moment."

She said nothing more and turned away to brew a cup of tea for herself. This seemed to be a change in attitude from the man's longtime protector and defender.

She added over his shoulder, "He thinks he's normal and he somehow pushes people away. I know he's created a lot of trouble, Johnny, and it's often of his doing, but not always. Ever since he was a tyke, people went out of their way to rile him."

Clash thought Redfeather was born riled.

"How soon until he gets here?" she asked.

"Could be as early as tomorrow night, but we don't know. Did he ever talk about living with you when he got out?"

She ignored the question. "I'll have to make up his room. Clean his sheets, he likes clean sheets, you know, always has."

"I said he's coming to town, not necessarily to you and your house."

"You just asked if he'll be living with me when he gets out, Johnny. He doesn't have to ask me or even tell me. He's my boy. He's always stayed here with me. This is his home, our home."

Which no doubt contributed to the man's effect on others. Had the prison shrinks done anything with Redfeather? Would be interesting to know what they had seen, what they thought. "Do me a favor?" the police chief asked, and immediately added, "If he comes home, ask him to call me?" Clash left one of his cards on the table by his coffee cup.

"You know he don't like no police, Johnny, though he doesn't have nothing against you personally. It's your badge."

"I've got nothing personal against your son either. Please ask him to call me. I can save him a lot of trouble, sort of ease his reentry. Eight years is a long time to be away."

"Not around here," she said. "Memories are long."

Her son's included. "Thanks," he said and stood up.

"I'll try to get him to call, Johnny, but mostly he doesn't listen to his mother."

Mostly? Maybe she would tell him, maybe she wouldn't. He wouldn't count on it.

———

Friday night at the Bucket of Blood, its parking lot crammed with everything from baby Caddies to Hummers and all manner of pickup trucks from brand new to 40-plus years old.

Clash noticed a dozen or so motorcycles by the building, another contributing element to the Friday night fights. Bikers came to prove their mettle, as well as local toughs, battlers from a hundred miles away over into Wisconsin, and his people too, young men, out to show they were worthy warriors, which was about as dumb as it got. Real warriors joined the military, did their service, were honorably discharged, and duly honored by the tribe. You weren't a warrior until the tribe recognized you as such.

The Bucket had been in the same ancient building as long as Clash could remember, though he'd never been inside as a peace officer or as a patron. Not as a cop because the Blood was sixty miles from the Nish Rez and not as a customer because he hated bars.

The building was made from stone dating back to the copper's heyday mines and was low and dark like a bomb shelter. From what he'd heard, the floors inside were flat rock often awash with beer and puke, sometimes with blood in the mix. The place was a magnet for violence, everything from parking lot shootings to massive dustups inside. There was even a fenced-in area outside most regulars called the Blood Ring.

Sekhar sat quietly and after a long time said, "That one Thanksgiving my men arrested more than a hundred combatants here. Hell erupted over never-discovered reasons and blood flowed like it was coming out a garden hose. Couldn't count all the broken bones. Insurance paid the owner fifteen grand for damages, which was a joke. The whole damn place wasn't worth that. Always made me wonder if he'd put the crowd up to it. Wouldn't be the first time up here. Don't understand why some taverns never have trouble while places like this can't get away from it."

"Bucket of Blood," Clash reminded him.

"Yah, some nights that's no exaggeration," Sekhar said.

Tribal members had their own name for the place, Clash knew.

Why the hell did young fellows feel the need to fight over nothing to prove themselves? To whom? What dumbasses. Real warriors fought for reasons, fought with discipline and calm. Real fighting was about honor. Bar fights were about chaos and desperation, with most people fighting others they didn't know for reasons they couldn't explain and wouldn't understand if those reasons were tattooed on the backs of their fists.

There was an abandoned Catholic church directly across from the bar. Clash backed his department's unmarked Dodge van into the alley between the church and the old rectory. From there they had a pretty good view of the bar parking lot. Both men were in uniform. They had thermoses of coffee, knowing this could be a long night, no matter what went down. As the summer night thickened, the muggy air filled with skeets and blackflies.

"They got bugs like this in India?" Clash asked his friend as he brushed away buffalo gnats.

"Don't know. I've never been there."

"You're not curious about your homeland?"

"*This* is my homeland, asshole, same as yours."

Clash made sniffing sounds, as he smelled skunk weed faintly wafting. "The lads are lighting up early tonight," he said. "Most places they wait until it's good and dark. We've still got some twilight."

"They all probably have their Mickey Mouse Club cards, too." Mickey Mouse Club was local cop jargon for medical marijuana cards. "You think Redfeather will show tonight?" Sekhar asked.

Clash nodded. "My gut says yes. His mother said she'd have him call me, but I'm guessing she won't talk to him and even if she does, he won't listen to her. He never has. Our people think individuals need to own their own decisions, decide for themselves, accept the consequences, all that good stuff."

"You buy into that?"

"Maybe with adults, but not with kids. Their brains aren't ready to reasonably analyze anything before they act. Redfeather's mother always treated Captain like he was born an adult, which clearly he wasn't and isn't."

Sekhar rooted in his go bag, pulled out a battery-powered handheld radio. "Want one? I've got a pair."

It annoyed Clash that his people and the county's deputies and various city cops were not on the shared radio frequencies, but the tribal council ignored his pleas for communications compatibility and transparency, more evidence of "us and them" thinking.

"Thanks," Clash said, and took the handheld, turned it on and off, and clipped it to his duty belt.

Sekhar offered him a small battery-powered fan.

Clash shook his head. "Just rolls the air around, messes up ambient sound."

"I can't hear it," Sekhar said.

Clash said, "I can," and then he added, "Uh-oh. Is it my imagination or is the parking lot beginning to draw a crowd?"

"Definitely," Sekhar said. "Maybe it's too hot inside?"

The lawmen watched as the crowd grew, and more vehicles pulled into the lot. Nobody seemed to be moving inside. "Whatever 'it' is, it looks peaceful so far," Sekhar said.

Clash felt his hackles rippling with electricity. "So does spontaneous combustion just before ignition. Whatever it is, it's *inside*," Clash said, opening the van door.

"Front, back?" the sheriff asked, getting out. "You take the front. You'll never find the back way in. I know this place like a body part," Sekhar said and was gone before Clash could say anything.

The chief headed across the road to the bar, through the crowded parking lot, turning on all the professional cop switches he'd not yet toggled in his mind. He didn't hurry and he didn't dally and kept moving steadily, trying to stay alert for all threats. His mind played through his checklist: Be aware of who is around you, what they're doing, see threats early on. After so many years in uniform, most of this was automatic, but he never took it for granted.

Sekhar said the interior would be dark as a cave. And that a third to half of the crowd would be carrying concealed, a new feature of modern life, as if some Holy Spirit had commanded, Now Hear This, Mother-fuckers: Arm Thyselves. Too damn old and and still a cop, you need to have your head examined.

As he sliced through the crowd he heard more than one voice say, "Cops," as if where there was one there would be more, which was not far from the truth. Sekhar had deputies waiting to be called in from less than three miles away. The Keweenaw County sheriff had been briefed on what was up and had given his blessing for the tribal cop from Baraga County and the Houghton County sheriff to manage the situation.

Concealed weapons or not, the tribal police chief went inside, expecting to find a dark cavern, and instead found himself blinking and squinting at intense white light, the source of which he couldn't identify. What . . . the . . . hell? The light was so intense it was painful. He heard Sekhar yelling, "Somebody turn off those goddamn bright lights!"

A vaguely familiar voice somewhere to Clash's right side and ahead of him said, "Good luck finding the switch." Clash stopped where he was, shielded his eyes with his hand, and said, "Redfeather? Thought I'd get a phone call from you or your mother."

The man cackled. "The woman you think of as my old lady and I do not think alike, and she and I shall never reside together again."

The man's voice and hushed tone left Clash's nerve tips tingling and sparking. Need to get on my radio, have my people check his mother's house, just in case. With this man, anything was possible. "Corrections told us you were moving in with her."

"They say and do what's convenient for them," the man said.

Clash inched his way toward the voice and finally got close to the source of the sound, but not the light, which remained blinding.

"Where you at, John?" Sekhar called out.

"Here?" Clash answered.

"Got you, we're close."

Clash could sort of make out Redfeather, a backlit amorphous figure. Clash thought he saw a handgun on the table at his right side.

"Hasn't taken you long to fuck the dog, Cap'n," Clash said.

Redfeather looked down at the weapon. "Me?"

"You know the rules on felons with firearms."

"That's *not* mine."

"It looks to be in your possession."

"Optical delirium for law enforcement: Go ahead and check the prints. You won't find any of mine. What I need a pistol for?"

"You wiped it?"

"Listen up, Clash. I never touched it."

Clash didn't believe him. This was not how he envisioned this night going down. Redfeather was up to something, but apparently Boobies wasn't part of it. Damn.

Clash said into the light past the man, "You close, Nayar?"

"I can see him, but not you," Sekhar said. "We're blue-close, all three of us."

Blue-close was a code the two men worked out years before. It meant they would both have their holsters unsnapped, and be prepared to draw. Clash knew his partner would use his voice to maintain separation in case Redfeather grabbed the weapon and opened up.

Sekhar asked the man, "Why's everybody out in the parking lot?"

Redfeather said, "Not everybody. I'm right here."

"Just you?" Sekhar asked.

"It's always just me, right Chief?"

Clash kept trying to get a better look but the light was as intense as a solar flare up close. "True that, Cap'n, true that. Most of the time it's just you against the multitudes."

The man with the gun beside him said, "You talk fancy, John."

What was Redfeather up to? Clash felt his stomach tightening. Something very wrong here. Did Nayar see and feel it? "You were gone a long time, Cap'n."

"Not far enough and not long enough," the former convict said.

"They released you early," Clash said, trying to get closer to get some kind of a good visual. Everything was blurred by light.

"Feels pretty late to me," Redfeather said.

"You hoping to see Hoople again, finish it, I think is how you put it in the courtroom that day."

"I won't be seeing him where we're going," Redfeather said.

Where *we're* going? Bad, bad vibrations now, all senses on alert. Is Nayar feeling these vibes, sensing this?

"Seriously," Redfeather said. "Look at me, John. Do I look like I could inflict the kind of damage I was accused of? On Hoople? The man's twice my size."

"There were ten witnesses," Sekhar said. "You used a club."

Redfeather said, "An equalizer. They all hate me."

Sekhar said, "Hoople thinks you're back here to finish him off."

"The man's a moron."

"Want to tell us what that fracas was about?" the sheriff asked.

"Call it karma," Redfeather whispered.

"Why's the Bucket empty?" Sekhar asked again.

"Maybe the real show's outside and I'm just a sideshow, again."

Sekhar said, "John?"

"I'll check."

Sekhar stayed with Redfeather. Someone needed to go outside and figure out what was happening. Clash had earlier called his deputy, and asked her to check on Redfeather's mother. No call back yet. Why? The chief heard a fracas before it boiled inwards toward him, men and women alike all pounding on each other and pushing into the front section of the bar. This was beyond any experience he'd had, and he keyed his mike. "Looks like the war's outside, Nayar, moving inside."

"Copy," the sheriff said over the radio. "All units converge, full lights and music."

Clash heard sirens closing fast and soon deputies were spilling into the mix and he saw Houghton County uniforms, broke away, and headed back toward Redfeather and his partner. The bright light seemed to be dimming.

Clash heard his radio bonking, and hit the receive switch. "Chief, this is Jaimie. Randi Redfeather's dead, shot. M.E. is on the way, I've got things moving here."

The Chief whispered on his radio, "Copy, John. Messy outside?"

"Don't take much but some white gas and a red match to make a party," Redfeather said.

Clash could see the man now. He had gone to prison a lefty and now the pistol was on his right side, his left hand in his jacket pocket. Not a jacket, but a long-sleeve shirt. Over the waist, like a Filipino guayabera. Long sleeves in summer weather? His mother was dead, shot. Would ballistics on the weapon on the table match? Knew this was going to be trouble, but not like this.

Clash heard a crush of voices behind them, screaming, swearing, crying, hordes spilling into the bar like cattle into a killing chute. Why did he have *this* picture, he asked himself?

More light now, he could see Redfeather's face and saw that he was leering. "Know what they called me when I was a kid? Sideshow. Even the adults did."

Sekhar said, "John and I get called worse every day."

"You're adults and you're cops," Redfeather said. "I was this way. In prison they called me Toulouse and it wasn't no put-down. But Sideshow? Hey kid, when's your old lady selling you to the Ringling Brothers. Captain the freak, Cap'n Sideshow."

"Not everyone was that way," Clash told the man.

"That is true, John. You always defended me, but when you weren't around they really gave it to me, my own brothers, my own tribe, white boys, teachers, elders, everybody. I couldn't fight. Look at me. I learned how to manipulate, create situations to leave others bloody and hurt."

"Until Hoople," Clash said.

"My first and only violent act, but my lawyer was lazy and the judge threw everything at me. Bastard even called me Sideshow under his breath."

Clash said, "I'm real sorry, Cap'n. We can't undo the past, but you're free now and you're healthy. You have some choices and a new chance."

Redfeather cackled. "The prison medics said my state of mental health is questionable. How's that for a detailed medical diagnosis?"

"They let you go," Sekhar pointed out.

"They didn't want it to go down on their watch," Redfeather said quietly.

It? Damn pronouns. Clash felt his heart bucking. Focus. He watched the seated man light a cigarette. Saw him put it in his mouth right-handed and light it right-handed, the left hand never left that pocket. Why?

"You were left-handed when you went inside," Clash pointed out.

"Got knocked down playing handball. Docs wanted to put it in a cast, but I told them fuck off, I can use a pocket."

Plausible? Clash asked himself. "When did this happen?"

"Week or two back," Redfeather said.

Clash stiffened. Nobody learned to use the other hand the way Redfeather was using his right, not in one or two weeks, not even in one month.

More people were pushing into the bar, despite more deputies arriving and trying to push the crowd outside and keep them out there.

Redfeather grinned, raised his right hand, and shook his stubby fingers. "Let them all in for the finale! The thing is," Redfeather said, "I've learned to appreciate the top mob guys whose main skills are organizing. It's a lot easier when you've got yourself organized, planned things down to the last detail."

Clash flinched. What the hell is he talking about?

"No wonder the world is so fucked up," the parolee said. "But if you understand, you can get everybody's attention and suddenly the sideshow becomes the main attraction, your show, all yours."

Clash heard four muffled explosions timed almost the same, heard a din as more screaming people pushed into the bar.

Redfeather was leering. "Sinatra called it Mother Audience."

Good god, Clash thought. *Good God.*

———

Late the next afternoon, it was just Clash and Sekhar in the tiny Keweenaw County Jail in Eagle River. The two men were exhausted and wrung out. Prosecuting attorneys from three counties, four different judges and magistrates, the county medical examiner, a Houghton County homicide detective, two state troopers from the Calumet Post, a state police homicide dick out of Negaunee, several Homeland Security agents, two FBI guys from Marquette. It seemed everybody wanted a piece of this, all with questions, most of them repetitive.

"When did you figure it out?" Sekhar asked his friend.

"He was experienced with his right hand and I knew he had been a leftie all his life. You?"

"There was a TV on in the bar, no sound, but I saw this big screen picture of a suicide bomber in his vest and when I saw his clothes, I thought that profile looks familiar, and when I looked hard at Redfeather, I knew."

Sekhar said, "You ever consider he might have a deadman's switch?

"Maybe passed through my mind just before I pulled the trigger," Clash said.

They had fired at the same time, both at the man's head. The bar, which had been in a melee, came to a sudden but momentary halt, followed by an all-out panic to get back outside. There were multiple injuries, numbers still not tallied, but only one dead, the right one.

While deputies tried to deal with the crowd, Clash and Sekhar had checked Redfeather, found the vest under his shirt, and a switch in the pocket where his left hand had been.

"You see him make a move?" Sekhar asked.

"No, I just knew, you?"

Sekhar nodded. "We spend too damn much time together, John. We think alike, react alike. Next thing you know, our periods will synchronize." Sekhar offered his friend a cigarette.

Clash took it, lit up, inhaled and exhaled forcefully. "Dot."

Sekhar took back the smoke, smiled, and took a hit. "Feather."

Clash took another puff. "Bovine worshipper."

Sekhar took his turn, said, "Ki Yi."

"What the fuck is Ki Yi?" Clash asked.

Sekhar said deadpan. "Like when you and your red brothers whoop and pound drums and yell, *Ki* yi yi, *Ki* yi yi, *Ki* yi yi."

"I need to retire," Clash said.

"And do what, sell Indian souvenirs?"

"Not shoot people first, then learn to Ky Yi."

"You wouldn't last a week."

"Probably right. What's Allah's take on all this shit?"

"Ask a Pakistani," Sekhar said. "Our guy is Krishna."

Clash had never before killed anyone in the line of police duty. Neither had his friend Nayar.

Sekhar said quietly, "We stopped the unspeakable last night, John."

Clash said, "Yah." The word "sideshow" was stuck in a loop in his brain.

The sheriff said, "The Feds don't want us together until the investigation's complete."

"I don't answer to Feds," Clash said. He'd nearly said, your Feds, but caught himself. The tribe was a sovereign nation, its own Fed. Nayar was part of the other side. Damn.

Just One More Plate at the Table

Udo Anchoring wasn't the most polished apple in the basket, but he was her apple and for Persis that was enough. Best of all, he was as malleable as raw copper plucked directly from a vein in the earth's muscle. On the downside, malleable people tended to be shaped and motivated by whoever talked to them last, but Persis understood this about her hubby and so far she had been able to compensate. From time to time he would throw a challenge at her that forced her to think deep and hard for a creative solution.

She understood him better than he understood himself, and she had since they first met ten years ago. It had been a whirlwind courtship and a simple no-church wedding (why waste the the money?). He'd gone along with whatever she suggested, Udo being at heart the sort of man who abhorred controversy, conflict, and harsh words. He wasn't comfortable with people who talked a lot or used more than a few simple words. The fewer syllables the better. Complicated words and talkers irritated, intimidated, or confused him, and Udo hated anything that made life anything other than straightforward no-bumps simple.

If not comfortable with word rivers, Persis knew Udo was, nevertheless, a patient and attentive listener, and like a poor poker player, which he was, he had not just one, but a plethora of gestures and facial expressions that were blatant tells. She patiently learned to read them, and she used the input to make slight course corrections in order to hold his interest and focus.

If she had a concern, it was Udo's pal, that scallywag Cousin Jack Rhys, who, unlike her husband, lacked inky Cornwallian seriousness and focus. Instead, Rhys Trepolpen had an inexplicable bent toward dissipation, with women and whiskey topping the list, and a sort of woodsy wanderlust that frequently pushed him out to what he called his "Camp of Kings," out near the tip of the Keweenaw at the location of the old mining town called Wyoming, in its notorious day better known by its other name, Helltown. Rhys's Camp of Kings had little more sophistication than a little boy's ramshackle fort cluttered with toys. That goofy Bill Clinton might be in the White House now, and the economy starting to boil after being cold so long, but she sensed trouble brewing on the home front. Fast Willie could talk, but there weren't enough words to push companies to reopen copper mines shut down for almost a hundred years. There was also no way the Prez could handle her problem, which left it up to her.

What sometimes rubbed at her was Udo's strong attraction to his chum's place. So far it had not become an issue, in great part because she was able to replace his interest with something better, which focused on the bedroom, an activity her Udo could never refuse and which he enjoyed immensely, not that he would ever say so out loud because, well . . . talking "all *that* stuff" embarrassed him. Talking aside, he loved the doing, that she knew.

If there was a disappointment, it was their failure to have children. Persis wanted kids, wanted them desperately, but as the years unfolded, the analytical side of her suggested that if all her attention was taken up by children, Udo might easily be led in directions harmful to their marriage and she certainly didn't want that. In the end, she decided that having no children was a fair blessing splintered off the law of unintended consequences.

No, her Udo was a good, solid man, and she was satisfied. She knew that as long as she kept her eye on her man, their marriage would continue to be blessed, if not by children and grandchildren, then by a relationship that would keep growing stronger over the years. She was almost to the point where she could count on Udo, but she was also a realist and knew that even the most experienced sailor had to keep an eye peeled for bad weather and other threats. It wasn't that difficult. One simply had to keep an eye on the water ahead and make gentle corrections to prevent being forced into one huge, risky adjustment to save the ship. Her dad had been a Great Lakes master and had taught her, his only daughter, as if she were a master-in-training. "Make no mistake, Pers, a good captain's got to be a despot, benevolent if practicable, but not one of those squishy democratic let-the-group-decide fools. One person makes the decisions for a ship, or a family."

Her late dad had been the smartest, most stable and reliable man she had ever known.

"You decide everything for our family, Daddy?"

He had grinned at that. "Your mother captains the homeship, Pers, but she makes people think it's me in charge because that's what people expect."

"You like her being the captain at home?" she asked her father.

"It's not a matter of like or dislike, hon. Some are born to be captains. Most aren't. When you're born to it, you don't think in terms of like and dislike, you just get on with doing what you were born to do. And every place, be it a ship or a home, needs the right person at the helm."

She'd always felt she would have made a good ship's captain, but that part of life wasn't yet ready for women.

In the Mr. and Mrs. Udo Anchoring household, Pers was the captain, and this morning she saw dangerous shoals ahead. Udo was out to boys' camp with Rhys and they would be back today and she knew she had to be ready for them.

Three days ago, on his way out the door, Udo said matter-of-factly, "Rhys's little house in town, she burned down to ground and now he lives for whole summer out camp, but he can't do that come winter, eh. Says he got the real good insurances on little house burned down, so instead of he spend all that money to build little new house, he says to me, 'How about I build you and Pers an extra room on your house and I pay for it, live there, split taxes, food, and such, half and each.' Seems fair to me. What do you think, Pers?"

Half and each indeed. "Udo honey, I need some time to think through such an offer," she told her husband. "Is Rhys expecting me to be his housekeeper and cook?"

"Well I heard him say about food, but he didn't say none of the rest of that what you just said, but it's just one more plate at the table, right?"

Had Adam been as clueless in the Garden of Eden? No doubt. Mother use to say, "Pers, boys will go through life in their own dream lives if we girls don't rudely jar them awake from time to time."

"How will I know when it's one of those times, Mother?"

Her mother laughed and hugged her. "Don't worry about that, Pers. You'll know."

Mother was right. Times for action always made themselves dramatically clear. The question was how much jarring was needed for a particular situation. I'm not your mother, Udo, she told herself. Nor do I intend to be.

The boys, who said they'd be back from the woods by noon, didn't show up until a quarter to six. Both drove pickups loaded with junk, presumably Rhys Trepolpen's earthly possessions rescued from the little-house-in-town fire. What destination they had in mind was clear.

When the men came in, she gave them each a bottle of Pickaxe Blond from the fridge and told them to wash up, supper would be served at six sharp. Persis Anchoring rested her hand on Rhys's shoulder and felt him recoil. "I've given your extra room proposal serious consideration, Rhys. Shall we talk about it after supper, as adults?"

She saw the two men glance at each other. Rhys answered with a shrug and a nod, but avoided eye contact. Men were such pathetic creatures, deer caught in headlights and held stupefied by anything they didn't understand or control. Good. She had not stretched the truth. She had indeed thought long and hard on this room business, even wrote up an extensive for and against list, and after considerable mental and emotional turmoil her path was clear and all that remained was to apply her creativity to the appropriate jolt of reality for the boys.

Part of her didn't want to harm their friendship, but another part of her was telling her that if Udo continued to run with Rhys, her husband was sure to travel paths she would either have to ignore or steer him away. If Rhys had to go, that would be a shame for Udo, a real shame, but bottom line, Rhys needed to find a new BFF.

She felt no rancor, only clamped-jaw resolve to do what had to be done. Women were somehow born knowing life was hard, and Mother always said it wouldn't hurt for men to know some of the same. The issue in her mind was one of degree. It took a pretty good rap on the knuckles to get the attention of some men, hubby Udo included.

The pals came back from washing up and sat down to their second beers. She said, "Enjoy your libations, boys. I have to freshen up for dinner."

As she left the kitchen she heard Rhys ask, "What's she mean, freshen up?" No answer came from Udo.

Persis had at one time seriously considered a career in theater. She had a great memory for lines and an innate sense of timing. Tonight's lines would be her own and she had been weighing each as carefully as a director planning a live show.

By the time the pals had leisurely downed two cans each of Pickaxe Blonde, Persis made her entry, earning a gasp from her hubby, and Rhys's mouth hung open, a classic cash register response.

"Pers," her husband said with great difficulty, "What . . .?"

She cut him off. "You wonder why I'm dressed like this? I figure if we're to be housemates, we should take an honest open look at how it will be, right?"

"B-b-but," her husband stammered, "You're *naked*, Pers."

"Nonsense, Udo. I have on an apron."

"T-t-that's *all*," Udo said.

"Clothes, naked, what's the difference among intimate housemates? We've only one bathroom Udo, so Rhys had better get used to looking at me the way God made me." She turned and looked directly at her husband. "Your friend's offer to pay for the extra room, and half our food and taxes, is generous indeed, but his presence here changes everything. Our home, our private residency, will become more public, and Rhys here will play a role somewhere between a permanently visiting friend and an adjunct family member. You know, like a second husband. I'm thinking, either way, certain obligations are inferred."

"Y-y-you've g-got *no* clothes on," Udo repeated.

"I have to admit, I think I like how this prospect feels. If Rhys lives with us, he will surely see me disrobed—and vice versa—so why not get past that right now? You boys should feel free to disrobe so we can all see each other for who we are."

"I'm staying just the way I am," Udo declared.

Persis watched Rhys look to Udo, who made a less-than-convincing nod, and mumbled, "Me too, I'm good just how I am."

She smiled. "I think your monetary proposal is more than fair, Rhys, and I feel compelled to match your offer on the social side of this arrangement, and by this I refer specifically to what is sometimes called conjugal relations. The dictionary defines this as relating to marriage, but so many people now are divorced, or playing house, or just plain sleeping around without marrying, that it seems marriage has lost much of its meaning. Rather than allow ourselves to stumble blindly into some sort of social aberration, I think what we will be doing won't even be unusual by modern standards."

"What the hell's *g-got into* you?" Udo asked his wife.

She touched her husband's shoulder. "Not a thing yet, honey. I feel empowered, even free. Every woman fantasizes about having two lovers."

Rhys's eyes were bulging. "I never mentioned nothing about this . . ." he said. "Just some taxes and grub and such."

"I didn't mean to imply you did, Rhys. This is entirely *my* idea. We can sleep three to a bed and take turns, or sleep in separate rooms and you boys can take turns, but here's my deal-breaker, and it's the only one. I choose who I sleep with and when on any given day, and you fellas will have no choice but to comply."

Rhys looked at his pal. "Is the wife off her bloody rocker?"

"She ain't like this normally, Rhys. W-what you mean *the* wife? She ain't the family truck. My wife—she's not usually like this, tell him Pers."

"I am not in the least bit crazy and certainly not off my rocker. What I am, after ten years of marriage, is horny and curious." Here she paused before adding, "Now I could just go behind your back, Udo honey, and do stuff with Rhys, but I love you and that would hurt you. It wouldn't mean anything but a wee bit of fun. But I can't do that to my honey. This way there's no secret. I'll say I want to sleep with Rhys tonight and that will make everything fine and entirely on the up-and-up. Do you see how gloriously simple and straightforward this is?" She saw that she had Rhys's full attention.

"I ain't sayin' yes," Rhys said, "but I ain't saying no. What do you think, Udo?"

"Why're you doing this, Per?"

His wife said, "I'm just trying to be fair and to anticipate questions and potential misunderstandings, which in relationships often boil down to money and sexual incompatibility."

"We ain't inuncompalpible," Udo countered.

Pers said, "No, no, we're just fine hon, you and me, but I think I'd better take Rhys upstairs after dinner and find out if he and I are compatible. If not, then the deal will be off. You can watch if you want, hon."

Udo jerked his friend to his feet and pushed him toward the door. "No room, no nothing, stay the hell away from me, and stay the hell away from my home and my wife."

"Dammit, Udo, this wasn't my idea her takin' offen her duds," Rhys tried to argue over his shoulder.

"Maybe not, but I didn't hear you objecting to sleeping with my wife, and don't think I didn't see the look in your damn eyes neither."

"Hell yes, I looked at her," Rhys said. "I got warm blood, don't I? She *wanted* me to look."

Udo punched the man in the nose, pushed him outside, and slammed the door. When he got back to the small dining room table, Pers was dressed in her regular clothes and putting supper on their plates.

Udo was silent as they ate and eventually said, "I don't understand."

Pers patted her husband's hand and smiled. "You know how we women can be."

Judge on a Copper Boulder

DANNY POVOLSTIK WAS FORLORN, HIS SHOULDERS SLUMPED, AND SO primed for tears he had to stop walking and wait to get his emotions under control. This couldn't be happening, but it was and here he was about to *cry*. Povolstik men didn't cry. No way, not ever. The old man would kill him for the tears and the ticket.

This whole thing was so stupid, so embarrassing. Had his driver's license not two full days and got a ticket! Way to go, dope-ass. Worse, it was from a cop driving an old-man sedan with no gumball, the paint so dull and gray and faded you couldn't make out the damn shields on the side doors. Not fair! Lake Linden Police Department. What the hell was that, an old fat guy with an equally old ride? He had roared up on him like Danny was a lame turtle, swerved in front of him, and cut him off, just like that, bing-bang, no cop, cop. Wah!

"License and registration," the cop said firmly.

"Aren't you supposed to turn on your gumball when you pull over somebody?"

"You have you a case of red ass over your own incompetent performance, kid. Way to go, telling me how to do *my* job, when you obviously can't do *yours*? Congratulations. That's rich. Okay, you want *Dragnet*, just the facts, hotshot? Here's a fact: The light ain't never worked right since some bright bulb bought this used Plymouth albatross offen the Marquette County Sheriff's Department. You got a complaint, take your shit to Marquette, but first stop whining like a little girl, and cough up your license and registration, sonny. It's cold out here."

Minutes of silence passed while the cop wrote the ticket for speeding, five over. Geez, talk about chintzy. The old cop pushed the ticket through the window. "You've got to appear before the J.P. in Calumet, the time and date's on the bottom. You don't show, we'll issue a bench warrant for your arrest."

"Can I do this by phone and mail?"

"No, you have to go before the J.P., end of discussion. Just sign where I put the 'x' on the bottom and I'll give you your copy."

Danny read the ticket. "This says the appearance date is a Monday. I have school that day."

"Doubles your challenge, a ticket *and* school, oh my. Get the hell on your way, sonny, and stop acting like that asshole Fireball Roberts."

Fireball who? Povolstik stared at the carbon smudges on his hands and wondered if anything would take it off. Maybe he'd have to resort to the awful Fels Naptha Mom was such a believer in. He hated that smell.

The cop's parting words after the Fireball remark were: "Pay that ticket, Danny-boy, or I shall take great pleasure in calling over to my brother officers in south Houghton County and sending them a warrant under which they will happily haul your young butt unceremoniously, but quite memorably, to the county clink. Snatch you right out of class, if need be. Might arrest your parents too. You got parents?"

"I got parents. You can't do that."

The cop held up his big hands. "I can't? This is your first ticket and I've written like thousands and *you're* telling me what *I* can't do?"

A ticket for five miles per hour over? It wasn't like he'd murdered someone. Did murderers actually get ticketed? Had to tell himself to stop his mind wandering, keep his attention on the problem, let murderers take care of themselves. A ticket? A ticket! And if the old man finds out! Too terrible to think about. Two days with his license and he gets a ticket from a fat old town cop? What's the address on the ticket? Check it again, stop acting like a baby. He skipped school to be here in Calumet, now he needed to do what he had to do to make all this go away.

The old man wouldn't bat an eye at his missing school. He thinks school's a waste of time, "Dat hull damn skull t'ing," he called it. "Boy, he hits four an' ten year he belong down mine, same like 'is uncles and cousins."

Focus, Danny. This address matched the one on his ticket. Next door there was a tobacconist, and the sign overhead read, EVERMAN'S ROCK SHOP. What the heck? Rock shop? Keep looking. Oh yeah, there was small white sign: WILLIAM A. O'DAY EVERMAN, JUSTICE OF THE PEACE. Just great. O'Day Everman? Shit. He was so screwed, could feel it. Wake up! Screwed isn't dead. But if the old man finds out about this, you will be dead, or wishing you was. Take care of this now, figure it out, handle it.

Tried the handle, and it worked, push the door in, or pull it out? The door was huge and heavy as iron, high as the town's monstrous soot-covered snowbanks. He peeked tentatively inside. Told himself to grow balls.

"Close the damn door," a voice thundered. "Costs money to heat this dinosaur."

Danny closed the heavy door and felt a wall of heat and smells engulf him. Place smelled like Uncle Johann's Tri-Mountain barbershop, sweaty male bodies, wet wools, melting slush, tobacco, wintergreen, cheap aftershave, shiny Brilliantined and Brylcreemed hair, and something like full-up outhouse. A radio was blaring with a program called Tradio. Mom and her girlfriends loved that show, which let area neighbors sell, trade, and barter stuff over the radio.

"Come in, come in, young man, and state your business."

"I'm supposed to pay a ticket?" the boy ventured.

"Boys!" the voice roared, "Turn down that bloody radio, I've got a case to adjudicate! Come closer young man, so I can have a look at you."

Us adjudicate? What's this, then? Danny entered the room and saw a short, rotund man with wild white hair tipped corn-yellow and skin pink as a Florida flamingo. The man wore a yellow plaid shirt and black trousers. He had red slippers on his tiny feet, and no socks. The man stepped around a table to a three-foot-high flat-topped boulder, and sat down. Danny could see the boulder was pure float copper. How it had gotten here was impossible to know. His old man talked about such boulders he'd seen deep in the earth and what a pain in the ass they were to deal with down there. There was a four-foot wooden wall in front of the copper and another sign, WILLIAM O. EVERMAN, JUSTICE OF THE PEACE.

After three or four tries, the man finally wedged a gold-rimmed monocle into his right eye socket, held out a pudgy left hand, and wiggled his fingers. "Let's have a look that ticket, young man."

The J.P. studied the ticket and grunted several times. "Haven't even got my copy yet. Did the officer happen to give you my copy, and ask you to bring it to me today?"

"No sir."

"No sir, *Your Honor*," the J.P. said.

"No sir, Your Honor, he didn't give me your copy."

"Attaboy, that's much better. You know what etymology is?"

"Bug study?"

J.P. Everman guffawed. "Good try. That's a good one. Boys, did you hear this young fella? Etymology he confuses with entomology, a common problem, I'm thinking. We got a new President wants us to fly into space with the damn Russians, but this country is mired in anti-intellectualism, sees science as something only peculiar people do. Hell, was a Yooper from Ishpeming helped make the bomb that won the Big War!"

The men gathered in the J.P.'s room all laughed and nodded agreement. They smelled to Danny Povolstik like unwashed wet dogs. Why was the J.P. hanging out with this raggedy crowd?

"For your edification, young man, etymology is a word that comes down to us from a whole slew of ancient lingos, and boils down to origin or truth, as in what comes first. Your daddy and you have the birds and bees talk yet?"

"No, Your Honor."

"But you think you know about sex?"

"I suppose, Your Honor." *God*, what *is* this?

"What no doubt you surmise is undoubtedly largely correct," Everman said, and looked at the traffic ticket. "Sweet sixteen, just, and I bet you have many the occasion to dwell on the delicious mysteries of the girls, am I right? Of course I'm right. All normal people think some on such things, even these old reprobates over there by the radio. Right boys? Am I right, of course I'm right!" All the men nodded but continued to lean toward the radio, which they had turned down, but not all that far. Danny could hear snippets, which made focusing on the judge difficult.

Everman continued, "You may find it hard to believe this, son, but this old relic of a J.P. was once sixteen. The word 'suppose' comes from thirteenth-century French, which took the place of its Latin forerunners *supponere* and *poner*, past participle positive. It boils down in plain twentieth-century English to assuming something we take to be true. Povolstik, am I saying your name correctly, young man?"

"Yes sir, Your Honor."

"I assume that you assume that this is the place where one pleads guilty or not guilty and pays a fine if the pleading is the former."

The J.P. was confusing him and seemed to be enjoying himself.

"This is the address on the ticket, Your Honor."

Everman smiled. "Indeed it is, but how am I supposed to adjudicate said ticket if I don't have my *own* copy, as required by law?"

The boy shook his head, had no answer, his voice failing him.

"This being Monday, I assume you're supposed to be in school today, and because I see no parents in tow, I assume you skipped and they are unaware of this fact?"

"Yes, Your Honor."

"Came here to court, instead of to school where at your age the law says you've got to be. There, *not* here."

"I'm here, yes, Your Honor, to pay the ticket."

"Had your license two days and already got yourself a ticket?"

"Yes, Your Honor." So embarrassing. How did I let this *happen*?

"Your folks know about this ticket?"

"They don't, Your Honor."

"You're skipping school, I suppose, you hear how I just used that word?"

"Yes, Your Honor."

"What school are you playing hookey from?"

"Painesdale, Your Honor."

"Southern boy, hey?"

"Your Honor?"

"That was a joke, Mr. Povolstik. Painesdale is in south Houghton County."

"There're places further south, Your Honor."

The J.P. nodded. "Geographic point well taken, my boy, and so there are. I withdraw the quip and solemnly swear to never employ it again—at least with you. Here's what we're going to do, Mr. Povolstik. I will telephone the arresting officer and hear his report orally. Meet with your approval?"

This guy is *loopy.* "You're the boss, Your Honor."

"Doggone right I am. Your conclusion shows high intelligence or solid common sense, which often do not cohabitate, and yet are erroneously and commonly conflated to be twins, which is to say they recognize the reality of one's circumstances. Look around this room and see for yourself. Every man-jack here has stood where you stand today. *No centus nota faci sunt,* you a Latin man, are you, Mr. Povolstik?"

Latin? "No sir, no Latin."

"Pity. It means the guilty become the familiar."

Can't he just get this over? "Thank you, Your Honor." What the hell was wrong with this man? *And* them. If they all had legal problems why were they hanging out here? Then a horrible thought, what if he sentences me to hang out with them?

"Just for the record, there's no John Dillingers in this crowd of miscreants, just fusty old prospectors a couple centuries too late for the kind of life they think they were meant to live. Not their fault. Call it the ever-fickle finger of fate, one of our creator's insipid jests. They come here every day to commiserate over the state of the world and I don't suppose a strapping lad like you would find such gatherings adequately pregnant to titillate your fecund sixteen-year-old mind. What year are you at Painesdale, home of the Jets?"

"Sophomore, Your Honor."

"Good, you've got your whole school career yet ahead. What kind of grades?"

"Mostly Bs, a few As and a C or two."

"C in what?"

"Typing, Your Honor."

The jurist nodded. "A much overrated skill given the utility, low cost, and simple technology of graphite in Number Two wooden pencils. Just stand right there and let me call Officer Clarke, did he tell you his name?"

"No, Your Honor."

"Did said officer treat you professionally and politely? I abhor public servants who disrespect the public, which pays their salaries."

"He called me Danny-Boy and Hotshot, Your Honor."

"Not asshole?"

"No, Your Honor, not that word."

"Good sign this. Officer Clarke favors that word for most souls he pulls over. That he didn't use it on you suggests he saw something promising, which I can say is a rare event for Officer Clarke. You may stand at ease, son. We're making progress here. May not feel that way to one standing before the bench of judgment, but I give you my word we are moving right along."

Felt sweat, told himself it was the heat in his head, knew it was nothing to do with the temperature in the room. He tried to block out the judge's phone conversation and listen to the radio.

The J.P. possessed the sort of voice one could not easily ignore. "Officer Clarke, J.P. Everman here. I've got a young fella before me with a ticket you issued. The system hasn't gotten the paperwork to me yet, so I thought I'd give you a ring. Name's Povolstik, just turned sixteen when you had your encounter. Want to tell me what happened?"

Danny heard someone on the radio wanting to trade a single-shot Sears .410 shotgun for long-ear snowshoes.

"What's that?" Everman said. "He did, eh? Hmm. Isn't that something? It *was*? You don't say. Well, thank you Officer, be safe out there among our local lawless hordes and downstate summer marauders."

The J.P. hung up and looked down. "You've been charged with exceeding the posted speed limit by five miles per hour, how do you plead, guilty or not guilty?"

"I didn't exceed it by *that* much, Your Honor."

Everman chuckled. "You confess with your own vocabulary. A speed limit is like pregnancy, young man. You either are, or you are not. Clarke's a stickler, I'll grant you that, but he's also fair and possesses good common sense, something I can't say about many other peace officers hearabouts."

The judge grinned. "Here's the skinny, Mr. Povolstik. Officer Clarke could have thumped you with careless or reckless driving. Had he gone down that route, you could have kissed your spanking new license bye-bye for a long, long time. But he gave you a break, son, a big break. What he observed was you trying to hot rod down Lake Linden's main drag but there was so dang much ice you couldn't get up any traction or serious speed, and there was almost no traffic at the time, so he calculated you didn't represent a significant threat to life and limb, and as it should be, except your own. What you did was stupid and ill-conceived for sure, but not overly threatening to the community's well-being. Guilty or not guilty?"

"Guilty, Your Honor." Please, let this be done.

"Good, here's how this will proceed. I'm accepting your plea of guilty and I'm fining you sixteen dollars, coin of the realm. You got that much cash?"

"I have only got twelve bucks, uh dollars, and change, Your Honor."

"Okay, you can keep the change, son, and we'll call it a done deal at twelve bucks even, and I expect you to get over to Lake Linden and thank Officer Clarke for giving you a break. How cold is it outside?" Everman asked the crowd by the radio.

"Centigrade or Fahrenheit?" one of the men countered.

"This nation is a pure Fahrenheit nation, what's the temp?"

"Minus 19," someone said.

The J.P. looked at the young man before him. "That's real brisk, a long haul from freezing, and it's a long way back to Painesdale. You can put off the visit with Clarke until conditions improve. Here we are in February's slime. The Roman calendar maker could've dropped this month all together, but cold as it might be this day, we also know that there will come a day bearing spring like a gift from the God of mercy. Cold as it is, Mr. Povolstik, might you have a libation before you shove off?"

"Libation, your Honor?"

"A swig, a snort, a drink of something to warm your innards and entrails, what some hunters and butchers call 'lights.'"

This man was nuts. "I can't drink and drive, Your Honor, and I'm too young to drink at all."

Everman sighed. "Court's adjourned. You can call me Bill when court's not in session, Danny, same as those odiferous knuckledraggers leaning on the radio. We are not talking hardass whiskey, son, just some homemade chokecherry wine made by yours truly with low concentrations of alcohol, but guaranteed to give you a surge of heat. What say you?"

Nothing about this felt real. "I guess . . . Bill. If you say it's okay?"

"I do and it is. Boys, turn up that blasted radio. Anybody made a trade for that four-ten yet? I've got more snowshoes in my barn than most snowshoe factories and a grandson that scattergun might just fit."

"Ain't been no trade made yet, Bill. It's Sears and they ain't worth much."

Everman retorted, "Nonsense, you old horses. A boy's first gun is like his first woman. He don't forget her ever." The J.P. turned to Danny. "You remember your first love-making, your introductory nookie, Danny."

The boy took the glass of wine and kept drinking as he turned red, hoping the men would think it was the wine. Love-making? He had to get the hell out of this place.

Bill said, "Good, good, I wrote down the number of that fella with the shotgun. One of you numbskulls please call the number and make the deal."

The judge looked over at Danny, "I'm the shadow bank on this deal. Can't have our state's duly sworn J.P.s out on the public radio airways as a common trader, can we? Pour this boy another jigger of Bill's Special Sauce."

The boy swallowed the fire in a gulp, handed the jigger back to a man with a red beard with some singed whiskers, and tried to thank the J.P., who was beginning a lecture on the .410 caliber and how he'd once owned one inlaid with agates dug from basalt beds on the north side of Brockway Mountain.

Just as Danny reached the door, Everman yelled at him, "Don't worry about your folks finding out about this from me, Danny-boy. But you might think on how much better it might be if they heard if from you. I can promise you I won't let it slip, but these onetime law-breaking ne'er-do-wells and scofflaws here I cannot and shall not vouch for."

Danny Povolstik stepped outside onto Fifth Street and into the February cold. He heard a cranky voice shouting for him to "Close the damn door." He stuck his hands in his pockets. Really, apologize to the cop for a 12-dollar ticket? What was the J.P.'s *problem*?? And what about one of those other men telling his parents? What were the odds? All odds other than "no chance" were equally bad. Damn. No choice but to go see Officer Clarke, apologize, and take it one step at a time after that. The old man was always lecturing about this or that. "There's bosses and there's the rest of us." Maybe the old man was right for once. The J.P. sure felt like a boss, and so too did the cop, both of whom also showed some common sense and mercy, both qualities in the old man's mind not being traits of real bosses, who to him had to be more like Hitler and Stalin, not the new president. Maybe the old man didn't know what he was talking about. He needed to stop thinking, see the cop, and go home. It had been the happiest day of his life to get his new license. Now he wondered if it was about to become a lifelong burden.

Food Aversion

IT WAS 1960, THE YEAR AFTER YOUNG QUEEN ELIZABETH VISITED town, and the old man, having miraculously finagled a job with Algoma Steel on the Soo Canada side, moved the family across the St. Mary's River to be closer to the mill and work. One year on, Ivan Gamerov was still trying to figure out what the hell a Canadian was, and in that vein he was at the moment suspiciously eyeing the red plate heaped with chunks of eel in goopy green sauce and wondering if he could choke down such crap. Eel! Good God! People across the river in Soo, Michigan, didn't eat eels. What the hell was wrong with these people? All the while he was looking and weighing, he saw his friend Marcel La Tendresse making like a conveyor belt, pushing down the disgusting meat as quickly as he could stuff his mouth.

Nobody dared speak when the La Tendresse clan ate and this gave Ivan pause to ponder if living on John Street was like a separate planet where all species were thrown together as neighbors, not in the same neighborhood, but each in their own: Poles, Ukes, Frenchies, Krauts, Czechs, Croats and Serbs, Hungarians, Slovenians, some oddball, belligerent Greeks, even a few dozen Chinese, all pressed into their own two-square-block rows of wood houses, seven or eight blocks from the entrance to the steel plant, each neighborhood a crocodile of rented company houses, all them eating different foods, which made Ivan wonder what really defined Canadians.

Italians, Finns, and Canadian English did not live on John Street or anywhere near. All three of these races (the preferred word in the Sault then) preferred their own company and languages. The English, of course, ran Soo Canada and lived in those parts of town not open to anyone but the historical English toffs, here meaning the ruling business class, not those with royal blood, who were in the very different and much higher British ruling class.

Ivan and his friend Marcel, both were nearing fifteen, and had been neighbors for the past year and classmates at St. Joseph's Collegiate. The two boys had hit it off from the beginning, but Ivan drew a line when it came to eating eels with his French friend. Eels weren't even the worst of what passed for food in the La Tendresse household: frogs, figs, animal guts, creamy slop. Good gravy! Ivan sat quietly, trying his best to summon up the intestinal fortitude to gag down at least one eel chunk without giving it a round trip. He prayed to God for a miracle, for God to find a way to extricate him from such awful circumstances. *Eel? Please, God, not this!* What French maniac had been first to eat such junk? And why?

A knock on the front door interrupted the midday meal and moments later Algoma Central Railroad engineer Firkus James stood at the table in front of Marcel's father, Bastien La Tendresse, himself an Algoma line engineer and longtime colleague of the Croat Stimach.

"Keely Biggler, he tells me he run down the Fourteen this morning, seen your camp, Bas. He say it look like the bear gotten in there. Was okay yesterday when I seen, but door she torn off today, so fresh this break-in is, eh."

Mr. La Tendresse was an unexcitable man. Sometimes with his thick eyelids it was difficult to tell if he was even awake. Marcel's father, having heard the news, sat there blinking like a lizard on a sunny rock.

Ivan waited for his friend's father to say something, but couldn't restrain himself. "Mister La Tendresse, *s'il vous plait*, I think Marcel and me could ride the Fourteen up and take care of that bear for you."

James immediately smiled, "Sounds good idea, Bas. I've got this afternoon's run. The boys want, they can jump in the baggage car and we'll drop them."

"We can do this," Ivan said, wishing his friend would say something positive on the bandwagon. Why he'd said anything would never be clear to him, but he had.

"*You* two *kids?*" Bastien La Tendresse said, grinning and eyeing the boys. "You take on the *cambrioleur?*"

Marcel looked over at his friend and translated. "He means burglar." He then turned to his father. "We've got the Enfield, Papa."

"You've never shot a bear," Marcel's father said to his son. "Never even hunted."

"I've shot bears," Ivan volunteered. His father Andrey had his five brothers in the bush with him from the time the boys were five. Until they were sixteen, they were bipedal pack animals, observers, and cheap child labor. No one was allowed to shoot a large animal until they were seventeen, which meant Ivan had more than two years remaining in his apprenticeship.

But he had seen his old man and four brothers shoot many bears and deer in Michigan, as well as a wolf, a lynx, and several moose on annual hunting trips to Lake Matinda, east of town. The old man had never said so, but Ivan guessed his father wanted to live closer to good hunting as much as the new job. Seeing the old man kill such things and doing it himself didn't seem all that much of a jump. He'd shot rifles and shotguns his whole life. "We can take care of this," the boy said, "Marcel and me. Tonight."

The cabin was less than one hundred yards from the Algoma line tracks, the Fourteen Route, which was what it was called no matter whether the train ran north or south. Ivan couldn't fathom why Marcel's father had built so close to the tracks. His old man would never tolerate being so close to other people. If a destination wasn't a two or three-hour hike one way it was too close for the old man.

As reported by the railroader, the front door had been rent from massive wood-and-iron-plate hinges. The cabin was one large room with a fieldstone fireplace. Cabinets had been ripped from the walls and all but two or three cans crushed, ripped, and bent. There was scat everywhere, huge formless piles of black shit sprinkled with twinkling dots that were probably high bush cranberries. There were four bunks, two each along the walls and in the middle of the room, a hand-hewn white cedar table, a pile of firewood, kindling in a Diamond Explosives wooden box, and a black Kalamazoo Foundry iron stove on a stone hearth.

"You sure we can do this?" Marcel asked as they examined the damage.

"It'll be easy. You'll be up on one bunk with the torch, and I'll be up on the other side of the room with the Enfield."

Torch was Canadian for flashlight and Ivan had no idea why, but he kind of liked the word. "You always smell a bear before you see one up close. We'll let it get inside with us, and then I'll say your name, you'll light the bear, and I'll shoot it, you'll see."

"It's my family's rifle," Marcel told his friend. "I should shoot."

"How many bear you shot before?" Ivan countered.

Marcel shook his head sheepishly and Ivan said confidently, "When I see the bear, you shine it, and I'll shoot it. The adults are counting on us."

"Seems too simple. You sure that's all there is to it?"

"It's a bear, not a dragon."

"Why do you think the bear broke in?" Marcel asked.

"Judging by claw marks outside on the doorjamb, I think he's wanting to claim this place for his winter sleep."

"Where did he go, then?" Marcel said. Then, "*Merde*, my mama see this mess and she go *Fou comme un rat de merde*."

Ivan complained, "Don't be throwing your froggy French at me and I won't speak no Russky at you. We agreed to this way back when we first become friends. What's that mean, anyway?"

"I said this make mama crazy as a shithouse rat."

Ivan cocked an eyebrow. "You think shithouse rats are crazier than other kinds of rats?"

"It's just a saying, okay? Rats are rats. But we've got to clean this up real good. Mama can't ever see this."

"Your old man lets your mother come to hunting camp?"

"*Mais, oui*, your mama she don't come out to your camp?"

"Andrey won't let no women near any hunting camp, nevermind *his* camp. Says it's not a proper place for women, especially mothers. 'Bad luck,' he says."

"My mother would never accept that. You Russians are different."

"We're Americans, not Russians. Soon as we left Russia, we weren't Russians any more."

"But you are still Americans here in Canada *n'est ce pas*? Shouldn't you be Canadians now?"

"No, because this is how you Canadians do things. Look at your family. You're French, not Canadian."

"We have two languages in Canada, English and French, both equal."

Ivan changed the subject. "The bear left the cabin messed up, and we have to leave it like this until we kill the damn thing. If he comes and sees it's all changed, he'll spook away."

"Won't he smell us first?" Marcel asked.

"There's human body stink all over this place already, and that didn't keep him out. Besides, we'll be up on the bunks and he won't be able to get as good a sniff. He won't expect nobody on top a bunk bed. Bears don't look up."

"You don't *know* that," Marcel said.

"Hell I don't."

"We do this thing in the dark?"

"Well, I doubt he'll march back in the daylight. He's probably off taking him a nap right now. Bears are night critters, like the sporting ladies down to the Royal Beaver Club on Queen Street."

"You never seen those ladies at that club."

"I've got brothers and they have," and probably the old man had too, but neither the brothers nor their father ever said anything.

"This doesn't sound easy and it doesn't sound safe. You also don't know if this is a male or a mother bear with cubs."

"Did you not see the tracks outside? This is one adult bear and boy or girl don't matter either way. Burglar's a burglar. We have the Enfield and the bear don't. You afraid of the dark?" Ivan asked his friend.

"A little I guess, sometimes, but only if there's a bear in my room."

"We've got the torch and that will light it up in here like it's midday."

"Maybe we ought leave this to adults," Marcel suggested.

"Sissy," Ivan said, and the boys wrestled until they were laughing.

—◦—

Mrs. La Tendresse had tried to send cold eel with them, several fresh-baked baguettes, and some stinky cheese, but seeing this Ivan quick-fast ran home and his mother helped him pile peanut butter and sliced sweet onions on thick slices of fresh Russian black bread, which would be good enough for Ivan. Besides, he worried that the smell of eel might get the bear all worked up. Why this would be so, he wasn't sure, but he knew from somewhere that bears liked fish guts and eels were sort of fish, right? His father Andrey told his boys that bears couldn't see for beans, and that the worst bear's nose was still thousands of times better than the best human's eyes.

Early winter nights in the north came in fast, almost like a switch got thrown.

They ate outside the cabin and as it darkened they reluctantly moved inside, crawled up onto their bunks, and tried to settle in for the wait. Without a fire and with the wrecked door hanging open, it was cold in the cabin.

"We need to test the torch," Ivan told his friend.

"It works. I checked it on the train."

"I didn't see you check it on the train."

"You were taking a pee."

Ivan found himself dozing off until a nasty whiff of bear jerked him awake. Was Marcel awake? No light inside, no way to see him, the bear, or anything. No moon outside, no stars, black. The bear reeked of rotting flesh and god only knew what else. He could not only smell the animal, he could hear it sniffing as it eased its way inside, quietly pushing past the hanging door.

Ivan slowly and quietly thumbed the safety forward to off. There was already a round ready to go and nine more behind it. The short magazine Lee Enfield MCV weighed eight pounds, but it was just short of four feet long and Ivan wished he had practiced swinging it at a target in darkness. Worse, only now did he remember the rifle had a peep sight and how the hell was that going to work in all the dark? He decided it would not matter if Marcel did his job and lit the animal, which should be easy enough.

The time seemed interminable but finally Ivan smelled and heard the bear between the two bunks. He swallowed hard and gave the signal for light: "Marcel."

At the sound of the voice, can debris skittered around and the bear coughed a couple of times. The smell seemed greater every second. Ivan again said, "*Marcel.*" What the hell was he doing over there?

No response. Louder yet, "*Marcel, bear.*"

Still Nothing. Ivan realized it was directly below his bunk. Sweet Jesus! "Goddamn you, Marcel, light this damn bear right now or I come over there and kick your ass good."

Ivan tried to line up the bear in the peep sight but couldn't see anything. It was worthless in the darkness, and Ivan yelled "*Bear!*" even louder and this time the light came on, but swung directly up to Ivan's face, lighting him like a statue on a pedestal, and blinding him. He instinctively ducked so the bear wouldn't see him.

"The bear is there, Ivan, shoot that bear, *shoot him!*"

"Get the light on the bear! Not on me!"

The light danced around the room. "Where the bear goes, I don't see no bear now."

"Marcel, slow down, take a deep breath, exhale slowly, move the light slowly."

"*Merde.* How big this bear he is?"

"You didn't' see it?"

"Just saw glimpse, eh."

"It's big."

"How big big?"

"Four hundred pounds maybe, shut up, put the light down between us, and listen."

"How many kilos, four hundred pounds? I think maybe I shit my pants."

"That's the bear, not you."

Next thing Ivan knew he had Marcel on the top bunk with him and his friend was shaking. "*Putain, putain!* You separate us in *my* family cabin, and just you got *my* family's rifle."

"Jesus, Marcel get back to your bunk, we ain't done here."

Marcel refused to return to the other bunk. "I'm afraid, Ivan. Why we can't we stay together? Why you do this like this? I stay here, no discussion. My cabin, my rules."

Ivan heard the animal again. It should have been long gone by now. Marcel must have walked right by it. "Stop whining, and pull yourself together, you've got to light up the bear."

Nothing happened. "Give *me* the goddamn light," Ivan demanded. Marcel had a death grip on the flashlight. Ivan wrenched it away only after a brief, violent struggle. He shone the beam around. No bear. "Damn, he's gone and he won't come back tonight. You blew it."

"Is *your* fault, you don't say 'bear' first off. Your voice too soft, I don't think I hear my name."

"You moron, you were asleep, weren't you?"

"I don't like you. Okay, maybe a little sleep, I don't know, you know, spoon-drop, eh?" Adults in Marcel's family would sit in soft chairs with a spoon on the back of a hand, and when they fell asleep, the spoon would drop to the floor, wake them up, and the short nap would be over. Spoon-dropper. Crazy French!

Marcel said "Now *I* need real sleep."

Ivan was tired, hungry, and not a little unsteady. The bear had been not four feet from him. "You need to operate the light when the bear comes back."

"You just said it won't be back tonight."

"I know what I said, and it's probably true, but you can't never tell with bears. They're unpredictable as Chinamen."

"I want sleep. You say bear gone. We go look, come morning. Marcel is tired and *maintenant je vais dormir.*"

"You're going to *sleep?*"

"*Oui.*"

Ivan sighed and checked that the safety was back on. No watch. How long was the night going to be, and worse, how much colder would it get? This adventure had looked a lot simpler sitting at the table in the La Tendresse's house this morning.

Morning came, *finally*. Ivan had dozed off, but remained intermittently awake if not fully alert. Marcel seemed to sleep soundly and rarely stirred. "Hungry," Marcel said as soon as he awoke, smacking his lips to get rid of night cotton.

Ivan said sternly, "We'll eat *after* we take care of the bear."

"He could be miles away. How you think we find him?"

"He won't be far. He wants this place for winter."

"Maybe we let him have it."

"And have the adults laugh at us? No, we're gonna get this bugger."

"But it ain't hurt nobody."

"You said yourself the damage alone would make your mama batshit crazy. Once a bear gets into a place, it will keep coming back."

"How you know that?"

"I hear my papa and my brothers talk. It can't be far away."

"What we do, say 'hey bear, you go away now?'"

"We're not going to talk to it, we're gonna kill it."

"Again, it ain't hurt nobody."

Ivan said, "And it ain't dead yet neither. Only safe bear is a dead bear."

"Seems cruel we kill him just because he wants to eat and sleep. What if somebody wants kill us because we want eat?"

"Jesus, Marcel, a bear's not a person. *It's a bear.*"

"Indians think bears got person inside them."

"Good, we'll shoot this thing, skin it, and find out if the Indians are full of crap."

"Indians know about bears, Ojibwe have clan called bear."

"Chicago's got bears too and most football fans down there wouldn't recognize a real bear from a bull."

"This is not a joke," Marcel said. "We're Catholic and we believe we eat the body and blood of Our Lord Jesus Christ at mass."

"That stuff's what they call symbolic, and what the hell does that have to do with this bear?" Body and blood of Jesus? No wonder his friend ate eel.

"Not symbol, *real*. Father Stan says so, the miracle of transubstantiation."

They were wasting time and Ivan was getting annoyed. "Marcel. This isn't mass and it ain't got nothing to do with Jesus. It's a damn bear we told your old man we'd take care of."

"We can't do it," Marcel said, "kids like us."

Ivan slid off the bed and ordered his friend down.

"I like it up here."

"I've got the Enfield and if I leave, and that bear comes back, what are you going to do?"

Marcel was suddenly beside him.

They went outside. The air looked and smelled like snow coming. Heavy September frost. Fresh tracks in soft dirt and mud by the cabin. "This is him," Ivan said.

"You don't know that. Could be two bears."

"If you'd've done the light right last night when we needed it, we'd know. In fact we'd be getting ready to catch the train by now. But you turned chicken and now we've got to go *find* the thing."

"We don't have to get that close," Marcel said. "We've got the rifle."

"We won't have to get too close *if* the bear cooperates." They tended toward unpredictably.

"All this makes me feel . . . funny," Marcel complained.

Ivan looked at his friend. "*Funny?*"

"The cabin is so dirty."

"You feel funny because the cabin is dirty?"

"You know my mama, a place for everything, everything in its place, you know?"

Ivan smiled. His mama? "That's good, Marcel, hold on to that. We're going to put the bear in its place—for your mama's sake. Then we'll clean the cabin."

"We should clean it now."

"We're not cleaning anything until the bear is dead. There's no point until then."

"I'm not liking this. We should go flag the Fourteen, head for home, tell the adults."

"We *promised* your father we'd do this for him."

"Mama will intercede with Papa. It will be okay, you'll see. They'll laugh, say it's okay, they're just kids."

Just kids? Ivan said, "We came to kill a bear and I intend to see it through."

"It's too dangerous," Marcel said. "I'll pray to St. Hubert and St Eustace."

"The church and its saints have their noses in enough stuff. We don't need their help. Of course it's dangerous. That's what makes it fun." Unlike eating eel the color of green tomatoes.

"It's hardly dawn," Marcel said, looking around.

"We want to find the bear before it beds down for the day."

"What time is that?"

"Bears don't wear watches, Marcel. They're animals."

"How you know these things, Ivan?"

"We're wasting time."

"But I'm *hungry*."

In addition to the Russian bread sandwiches from last night, Ivan and his mother had made six trapper sandwiches for each boy, which Ivan had in his pack in the spruces where he had hoisted it yesterday. The sandwiches were made of peanut butter, jelly, honey, and uncooked oatmeal all bashed and mashed together into a thick substance they slathered onto homemade rye with spoons. The sandwiches would keep for a long time. They were packed with calories and protein. "Get your pack down and have a sandwich."

"I mean *hot* food, eggs, bacon, toast, *pomme de terre*. It's time for *petit dejeuner*," Marcel whined.

"We're in the bush. There's no hot food out here until this bear is dead."

"You're not any fun. This was supposed to be an adventure."

Ivan told his friend, "Adventure in the bush does not include a full stomach."

"What if we only wound that bear?"

We? "I don't miss what I shoot at," Ivan said confidently, tiring of his friend's foot-dragging.

Ivan walked about twenty yards and said, "I've got the track."

"Who taught you how to do this?"

"My old man taught all of his boys."

"Is there a book or something?"

Marcel liked to learn from books. Ivan didn't. "The book's in his head, not on paper. It's experience. He doesn't read English so good." Or Russian, for that matter.

The bear's tracks were easy enough to follow, the ground mostly rocky and fairly barren but with patches of dirt and some mud. The track angled along a scrub oak ridge to where the ridge dipped into an endless black spruce swamp, creating an isthmus between small lakes. It took them an hour to reach the place. Ivan's legs were soaked to the knees by wet grasses and frost. He had binoculars around his neck, but preferred his own eyes.

Behind him, Marcel was muttering, "I'm tired. That sandwich was terrible."

"It's not as bad as eel."

"Eel is royal food."

"You're *not* royal."

Ivan kept tracking and heard sighs behind him, an occasional catch in his friend's voice, and another weird hacking sound. Ivan turned to the narrows and thick tag alders below, crept twenty feet forward, and stopped. "C'mon," he whispered. "You've got to keep up with me, Marcel."

"Maybe I can't."

"You can, you will."

As Ivan talked, he kept his eyes on the trail ahead through the tag alders. He saw the bear moving slowly, its snout straight up trying to catch something off the wind telegraph. He thumbed the safety off, took aim, saw the bear looking directly at him. Okay, then. You've got my scent. What will you do about it?

Ivan took a deep breath, the way his father had taught all his boys, and let it out slowly and steadily. He started to squeeze the trigger.

"Arg, ahh, ulg," Marcel mumbled behind him, and Ivan knew what it was. Not now, God, please not *that*. *Not* here, not *now*. Ivan looked over his shoulder, saw Marcel on his back, his eyes rolled back, drool cascading, shoulders twitching, knew a fit was on him, his friend an epileptic since birth. Can't let this bear come up on us while Marcel is like this. He put the peep on the bear, squeezed, saw the bear collapse, ejected the cartridge, and fired a second time. The bear struggled to get up but fell heavily sideways as Ivan discharged a third round, and turned immediately. His friend's father had created a leather strap which Marcel wore, looped around his belt. Ivan unsnapped it and jammed it into his friend's mouth to keep him from biting off his tongue. There was already some blood on his lips. Damn. Pad's in, nothing more to be done now. The fits passed, eventually.

Ivan turned back to watch the bear, which remarkably was now standing and trying to sniff and see them. The boy knelt and put the kill-shot into the animal's chest. This time it dropped straight down, and did not move. Marcel was still twitching and shaking. Ivan took Marcel's ruck, went cautiously down to the bear, and used his hatchet to chop off the four paws for his friend Harvey Wang, the grocer's son. Harvey's grandmother lived with the Wangs, and she was like a million years old in Chinese years, and she was smelly too, all wrinkles and always smoking, a screamer and finger-wagger, but okay once you got used to her ugliness and shrieking. The Wangs used crazy remedies like powdered snake and made soups of bear paws.

He dragged the carcass, but not far. Way too heavy, three hundred easy, maybe even four. They couldn't take it all home. The old man would not have approved. He hated wasting anything they got in the woods, but the old man could never know about this. They had no license for the animal and no permit for a problem bear.

Marcel was sitting up when he got back to him. "What about the bear, did I have . . .?"

"I took care of the bear, and yeah you did. Your mouth okay?"

"Bit my tongue a little. I've done worse."

Ivan opened his pack, took out a hunter sandwich and took a big bite. "There's blood on the bread," Marcel said.

"Bear paws," Ivan said with his mouth full.

"Paws for what, a necklace? Indians make nice necklaces from claws."

"They're for Harvey Wang's granny to make soup."

"Chinese eat the weirdest shit," Marcel said. "It's disgusting."

"Like eels in green vomit sauce? Maybe the Chinese think bear paws eat like eel."

"That's stupid," Marcel said with a grin.

"Let's go clean the camp."

"Can we have a real breakfast?"

"Sure," the makings were in Ivan's pack, which was still hanging in the spruce.

"Eggs first?" Marcel asked. They had brought a dozen, some potatoes, a can of beans, a half-pound of bacon.

Marcel, predictably, preferred supervision to labor, and watched while Ivan did most of the physical labor. "Maxine Wang ever let you feel her titties?" Marcel asked.

Maxine was Harvey's older sister by a couple of years and she was said to be "fast."

"All the time," Ivan lied.

"She *show* them to you?"

"Sure," Ivan said, holding up a thumb. "Got the nips like thimbles."

"Dear Jesus," Marcel said. "Nothing good happens to me."

"Jesus isn't part of this deal, my friend. Maxine is Buddhist, not Christian, and she don't eat no damn eels."

"But she eats bear feet soup."

"Bear *paw* soup."

"You ever eat it?"

"Once."

"Good?"

"Better than eel."